27 JAN 2023

To renew, find us online at:
https://prism.librarymanagementcloud.co.uk/bromley
Please note: Items from the adult library may also
accrue overdue charges when borrowed on
children's tickets.

In partnership with

CHISLEHURST
020 8467 1318

BETTER
the feal good place

The Prisoner

B.A. PARIS

The Prisoner

HODDER &
STOUGHTON

First published in Great Britain in 2022 by Hodder & Stoughton
An Hachette UK company

1

Copyright © B.A. Paris 2022

The right of Bernadette MacDougall to be identified as the
Author of the Work has been asserted by her in accordance
with the Copyright, Designs and Patents Act 1988.

A CIP catalogue record for this title is available from the British Library

Hardback ISBN 978 1 399 71021 3
Trade Paperback ISBN 978 1 399 71022 0
eBook ISBN 978 1 399 71023 7

Typeset in Plantin Light by Hewer Text UK Ltd, Edinburgh
Printed and bound in Great Britain by Clays Ltd, Elcograf S.p.A.

Hodder & Stoughton policy is to use papers that are natural, renewable
and recyclable products and made from wood grown in sustainable
forests. The logging and manufacturing processes are expected to
conform to the environmental regulations of the country of origin.

Hodder & Stoughton Ltd
Carmelite House
50 Victoria Embankment
London EC4Y 0DZ

www.hodder.co.uk

For the two men in my life,
Calum and Henry

PART ONE

The Kidnap

I

Present

I sense the shift of air beneath my nose a millisecond before something – thick, sticky tape – is clamped over my mouth, silencing the scream that would have ripped from me. My eyes snap open. A dark silhouette is bending over my bed.

Adrenaline surges. *Move! Grab the knife!* I twist my arm towards my pillow, but a hand slams onto my wrist, holding it still. Pulled from the bed, I kick out. But my feet flail uselessly, find only air. I try to focus but my mind is spinning. Why did I fall asleep? I should have been expecting this.

My arms are pulled behind my back, my wrists bound together. I try to twist away but something is pulled over my head, material, rough and tight, a hood of some kind. Panic spreads through me like wildfire. *Don't. Keep calm, Amelie. You know what this is.*

He pushes me from the room, my feet tangle, I stumble, he jerks me upright. Under the hood, my head is filled with the frantic pulse of my heartbeat. I fight back the fear. *I can outwit him; I've done it before.*

The soft carpet beneath my feet gives way to the cold polished floor of the landing. My toes bump the edge of the carpeted runner, in my mind I see its intricate green and red pattern of leaves and animals. I inhale the chemical smell of glue from the tape and a mix of a cough and a choke burns

3

my throat. I draw a breath, and the material from the hood sucks into my nostrils. *Where is he taking me?*

The grip on my shoulders tightens a little, there's a slight pulling back. Instinct tells me we are at the top of the stairs and I hesitate, afraid to fall. Pushed forwards, I find the first step, then move downwards until the soles of my feet touch the cold checkered tiles of the hall. We move down the hallway to the left, my ragged breathing amplified in the eerie silence. I know where we're going. He's taking me to the basement, where the garage is.

I turn, wrenching my body away from him, and for a precious moment, his grasp on me weakens. But it's not enough; I'm hauled back into place, and pain flashes up my arms. Angled to the right, more steps down, the space narrows, the air shifts, becomes cooler.

And then, an influx of sounds, stifled by the hood but recognisable still – scuffling feet, a muffled whine, a sense of others there waiting. I push back, then stop. The scuffling, the whine – they didn't come from me. My mind reels. *It can't be, it's not possible.*

But I know the voice behind the smothered protests – Ned.

This is not what I thought it was.

2

Present

Under my hood, my eyes dart, looking for a way out of this nightmare. *Think, Amelie, think!* But my mind is paralysed. *What is this? Who are they?*

I hear the clunk of a car boot opening. There's more scuffling, Ned's muted protests become louder. A grunt and a thud, have they put him in the boot? My body tenses; I can't be put in there with him. Then, without warning, I'm pushed into the interior of the car, facedown in the space between the seats, my knees forced up against the thin material of my pyjamas. Heavy shoes push against my back, holding me down when I try and get up.

At first, I attempt to keep track of where we're going. But I quickly become disoriented. I concentrate instead on drawing small sucks of air into my lungs. My stomach heaves, I'm breathing too fast. I close my eyes, imagine I'm outside in the cool night air, looking up at the sky, the stars, the infinite space. Gradually, my breathing calms.

Later, hours it seems, the car slows, the road becomes rougher. My mind has wandered. I force myself to focus, I know that for survival, every second counts. The car rocks, I picture a dirt track under the wheels, a forest around us. I should be more afraid. But I'm not scared of dying, not anymore. Not after everything.

There are sudden thuds from the boot and cries of pain from Ned. He must be terrified – but shouldn't he have been expecting this? Hunter, his security guard, brutally murdered three days ago, replaced by Carl, an unknown quantity. Where was Carl while we were being abducted? For this to have happened, there has to have been a massive breach of security. *All eyes on Carl.*

The car comes to a halt. Doors click open, the shoes are removed from my back. I'm pulled from the footwell, made to stand. The cool August night air wraps itself around my legs, goose bumps rise on my arms. There's the smell of dirt, foliage, tree sap.

I hear Ned being dragged from the boot. We're pushed forwards, Ned in front, I can hear him mumbling. The ground is sharp under my bare feet, stones digging into soft flesh, like shingle on a beach. I wait for the softer undergrowth of bracken, the crisp snapping of twigs. But the stones become smooth slabs, a path of some kind. *Not an execution then. At least, not in a forest.*

We stop. I hear the creak of a door pulled open, the scrape of wood along the ground, not a door to a house, an outbuilding perhaps. Propelled forwards into a blast of cold air, I tremble. It's not a shed, it's a dungeon or basement, its thick walls untouched by the warmth of the sun.

I'm shivering now despite the crush of bodies around me. A door opens somewhere in front, another scuffle, Ned frantic, my foot trampled as they move to contain him. I hold my breath, wait it out. A door slams, followed by thuds as Ned throws his body against it, raging from behind his gag. *Be quiet. It's not going to help.*

We move on, climb stone steps, I count them, twelve in all. Then, at the top, the worn stone under my feet becomes warm wood, softer against my skin. A door is opened, I'm moved forwards.

There's a movement behind me and I steel myself for a blow. Instead, the hood is pulled up and off my head. My hair crackling with static, I draw a deep breath in through my nose, then blink and blink again, waiting for my eyes to adjust to the darkness. But there's nothing. No flicker of light, no paler shade of black.

Without warning, there's a tug on my hand, strong fingers on my wrists. A cry of alarm builds, pushing against my throat. *Not this.* I kick back and my feet connect with flesh and muscle, but whoever is behind me holds me tighter. Then, a sawing sound and the rough scratch of a knife echo around the room until suddenly, there's an audible snap. The pressure on my wrists releases and the momentum trips me forwards. Before I can turn, there's the slam of a door, the click of a lock.

That's when I realise: from the moment the man came into my bedroom, our abductors haven't said a word.

3

Past

'When is your aunt arriving?' the doctor asked, straightening up from Papa's bed.

'Later today. She's on her way over from Paris.'

The doctor looked relieved. 'That's good.'

In his bed, Papa looked so small, his skin papery thin and yellow, his arms skinny as sticks. It was frightening how fast the cancer had spread through him. He had been diagnosed six months ago and until last week, he had been walking around, eating, drinking. Now he was unable to do anything for himself. I had to feed and wash him; he was like my child.

'What will you do?' the doctor asked. 'After?'

I knew he meant once Papa had died and a rush of tears built up inside me.

'I'm going to live in Paris, with my aunt,' I said, swallowing them down.

I didn't like lying but I was scared that if the doctor knew there was only me to look after Papa, he'd insist that Papa go into hospice. And Papa didn't want to go into hospice, he wanted to stay at home. But I didn't have an aunt, I didn't have anyone. I was sixteen years old and soon, I'd be alone in the world.

What I would have liked, once Papa was gone, was to stay on in the house. I was capable of looking after myself, I'd been doing the shopping, cooking and cleaning for years. I'd had to take over when Papa's drinking meant he couldn't do any of those things anymore. But we only rented the house, and with no relations to take me in, I'd be taken into care. And there was no way I wanted that to happen.

At first, I thought about asking my friend Shannon and her mum if I could live with them until Shannon and I finished school next year, and I'm sure they would have said yes. But in the summer, they were moving to Ireland, where Shannon's mum came from.

Shannon and her mum didn't know that I was looking after Papa on my own. When they'd asked, I'd invented my French aunt, because I hadn't wanted them to worry about me.

'I thought you said you didn't have any relations?' Shannon had said.

'Apparently, she and Papa fell out years ago,' I'd explained. 'But when he got sick, he phoned to tell her.' I paused. 'I'm going to live with her in Paris.'

And Shannon had hugged me. 'Is she nice, your aunt?'

'She's lovely.'

I hadn't been to school for two weeks now. It didn't matter, because it was nearly over anyway. My teachers knew that Papa was sick, and when they'd asked, I told them what I'd told Shannon, that I was going to live in Paris with my aunt, and wouldn't be back next year.

But I wasn't going to Paris, I was going to London. And once in London, I would look for a waitressing job and start saving to go to college.

4

Present

I raise shaking hands to my face, begin clawing at the tape still covering my mouth, then freeze. There's someone in the room with me, I can hear the raspy sound of their breathing.

My nostrils flare and I press my hands against my face, my fear so raw that I want to scream out. I hold my breath and when there's no sound, I realise it was my own breathing I could hear. There's no one else; I'm alone.

Desperate to breathe properly, I rip off the tape in one painful movement, and with the sting of fire on the skin around my mouth, I begin drawing in great gulps of air. The taste of glue makes me gag. I take a deep breath, calm myself. I need to think clearly.

In the darkness, I turn around and with my hands stretched out in front of me, I walk slowly back to where I think the door is. My fingers hit a wall; I stop. The surface is cold, painted, not wallpapered. I gradually push my palms across, the skin of my hands distinguishing every little bump and scratch, until they reach a doorframe and the rough face of a door. I move my hands downwards, find a handle, round and smooth. I wrap my fingers around it, turn it. It doesn't move.

I pat the wall next to the door, searching for a light switch. But I can't find one.

I thump on the door.

'Hello?' I shout.

No one comes.

'Hello!' I yell it this time.

There's no answer.

Dropping to my knees, I trace the outline of the keyhole with my fingers and put my eye to it. Only darkness. My fear escalates.

'Let me out! Please!'

Don't. Stay in control. You can't afford to let fear win.

Ned fills my mind. His voice last night, the things he said. Is the room in the basement where he's being held under this one, can he hear my panic? Tears rise from deep inside me. I rest my forehead against the wood of the door, put the palms of my hands flat against its surface. I can feel the rivets of panels and think of Carolyn. Of her apartment in London, with its wood-panelled doors. Of the home she made for me. I take another breath. I can't give up, I need to make everything right.

'Move, Amelie,' I whisper. 'Find the light switch. There has to be one.'

I turn to face the wall and begin shuffling sideways along it to the left, moving my palms up as high as I can reach, then down towards the floor. I had expected to find a switch close to the door, but I reach a corner without finding one. I move along the next wall and after a few steps, my fingers find a socket close to the floor. I straighten up, place my hands flat on the wall to continue my search, and my left hand bumps against something jutting out. I run my hands over it; it's a wooden board with a window behind it, I can feel its frame. I claw along the sides of the panel, trying to get enough purchase to pull it off, and feel the heads of small metal nails buried deep into the wood, too deep to get any traction under them. But the knowledge that there's a window gives me hope.

I move past the boarded-up window and immediately, my hands find something else, something material, hard. I feel along it; it's a mattress, propped in a corner. I sniff it tentatively; it smells new. I lay my head against it for a moment, the adrenaline draining away. But I can't rest, I need to find a light switch.

There's nothing on the wall behind the mattress so I move around it and along the next wall. After four small steps, I find a door. For a moment I think I must have lost my bearings in the darkness and have gone back the way I came. But no, this must be another door.

'Hello?' I call.

There's only silence.

I feel for the handle, turn it. And without any resistance, the door pulls open.

My heart jumps, I take a quick step back. There's no sound. No movement. I edge inside, both arms outstretched and almost immediately my knee whacks against something. Pitched forwards, my hands slam into a wall, and with a cry, I crumple onto the floor. What did I hit? I twist around and my hands find it, cold enamel, a toilet.

I push myself up from the floor, turn, find the door, then feel for a light switch. There doesn't seem to be one, it must be on the outside wall. I move carefully back to the main room, close the door, search the wall. Nothing. I shiver at the thought of being in such a confined space without light. If I want to use the toilet, I'll have to leave the door open.

My whole body is trembling now, my teeth tapping against each other as I move past the bathroom door and continue moving along the wall. I reach a corner, turn left along the next wall; in my mind it's parallel to the wall with the boarded-up window. Still no light switch, only a socket near the floor. Then another left turn until I'm back at the main door.

I pause a moment to regroup; this wall has the main door, the next wall has a boarded-up window. The third wall, parallel to this one, has the toilet. The fourth wall is blank. There are two sockets but no light switch. I'm going to be kept in the dark.

A new terror fills me. Fighting for breath, I drop to my knees, close my eyes, remind myself of all I have already been through. I can get through this, I have to.

I push to my feet, put my back to the door and walk carefully across the wooden floor in a straight line, my hands outstretched, counting as I go. After seven small steps, my fingers touch something wooden. Another three small steps, I'm flush against it. I reach down, find a handle. It's as I thought: the bathroom door is directly opposite the main door. Satisfied, I drop to my knees and begin a painstaking crawl back and forth along the floor, checking that there isn't anything else in the room. Apart from the mattress, there isn't.

My energy drains from me. I crawl to the mattress, pull it to the floor, sit down. After a moment, I look towards the door; I can't see it, but I know where it is. I think about the mattress, about where it's positioned, and then I think about the door. When I had stood facing it, the handle was on the left, which means that the door opens – from the outside – to the left. For the first time, something makes sense: they've placed the mattress on the right-hand side of the room so that when they open the door, I am there, like waiting prey.

Standing, I take hold of the mattress and drag it past the

door to the toilet, to the corner on the opposite side of the room, and lie it along the wall. Now, anyone coming in will have to walk around the open door and across the room to get to me.

I sit down, wrap my arms around my knees, and do the only thing I can do. Wait.

5

Past

I slowly sipped my coffee, hoping it would take the hunger pains away. I'd been in the café for an hour already and it was so cold outside that I couldn't face leaving. But there were only so many free refills I could have before they'd ask me to buy a new drink, or leave. So far, nobody had come to disturb me.

I'd been in London for seven months now, and everything had been going well until a few weeks ago. I'd found a job in a restaurant and at first, I'd stayed in youth hostels. But because of the two-week stay limit, I'd had to move to a new one every couple of weeks, and moving from hostel to hostel had also meant moving farther and farther away from where I worked. My transport costs had become so expensive that one of the waitresses at the restaurant, who'd been struggling to pay her rent, said I could sleep on her floor for ten pounds a night. It meant that I'd finally been able to start saving money for my college fund.

Three weeks ago, I'd been called by my manager at L'Escargot. The Christmas season was over, he explained, and so few people were coming into the restaurant that he could no longer justify my salary. 'You only pay me five pounds an hour!' I'd wanted to shout. But I hadn't, in case I needed him to employ me again. I'd tried to find another job but no one was hiring until the spring, another three months away.

The money I'd saved was almost gone. Last week, I'd had to move out of the apartment because I couldn't even afford the mattress on the floor, and I'd been sleeping rough since. The first night, I'd sat near a group of young people and it had been fine; they'd ended up inviting me to join them, explaining they'd come to London for a rock concert and had missed the last train home. But since that night, my experiences hadn't been great. The previous night, as I'd lain on a bench, my belongings tucked under me, I'd been bothered several times, and I'd had to fight off another homeless person who tried to pull me off the bench for my place or possessions, I didn't know which. And the cold night meant that I'd spent most of it shivering.

I was scared to sleep rough again – and if I did, I would need to buy a sleeping bag, which would mean dipping into the little money I had left. There were hostels for the homeless but my conscience wouldn't let me go there, not when I had a hundred pounds tucked into my money belt. But maybe I would have to.

I took another small sip of coffee. It was warm and cosy in the café and for a moment, my eyes closed.

The door opened, waking me, and I blinked my eyes as two women entered. One was tall and beautiful, with long limbs, flawless skin, and short peroxide-blond hair. Her coat, black, belted at the waist, her red ankle boots and matching bag all looked expensive. The other woman, shorter, pretty, dark-haired, was wearing a beige raincoat and as they made their way to the table next to mine and draped their coats over an empty chair, I saw that the raincoat had a faux-fur lining, and wished it were mine. She was wearing a navy business suit underneath and a white silk shirt, and in my jeans and sweater, I felt horribly shabby.

18

I watched, fascinated, as the waitress took their order and came back with coffee and cakes. My eyes were instantly drawn to the blueberry muffins. The blond woman tucked into hers, breaking off small pieces with delicate fingers and popping them into her mouth. Her friend pushed hers out of the way and left it untouched.

I couldn't hear what they were saying but suddenly the dark-haired woman's eyes filled with tears. As she nodded at what her friend was telling her, I could see she was trying to fight them back. After a few more minutes and a quick check of the time on the huge gold watch that seemed too large for her delicate wrist, the blond woman reached across the table, placed a manicured hand over her friend's, then stood to leave.

'It will be okay, Carolyn, I promise,' she said, and I noticed a slight accent as she spoke.

She walked out of the café, her red bag slung casually over her shoulder, drawing admiring glances from other customers as she went. Left alone, the dark-haired woman took her phone from her bag and began scrolling the screen. Her tears spilled over and she hurriedly wiped them on the corner of a napkin, then pushed her chair back and got to her feet. As she moved away from the table, I waited for her to take her uneaten muffin, but she didn't.

'Excuse me,' I said before I could stop myself. 'If you're not going to eat your cake, would you mind if I have it?'

The woman turned. 'Yes, of course,' she replied hurriedly. 'Help yourself.' Then ducking her head, embarrassed maybe that I'd seen her tears, she left the café.

Before the waitress could clear the table, I bundled the muffin into a napkin and followed the woman outside. I didn't know why I was following her, but it felt important to make sure she was all right. I expected her to go to an underground station, or wait at a bus stop, but she kept on walking until she stopped in front of a modern block of apartments off Warren Street. Pressing a key to the intercom, she disappeared through the door, and I watched her reflection in the mirrored entrance hall as she waited for the lift. Maybe she saw my outline reflected in the shiny lift doors because, as it arrived and she stepped inside, she turned and looked at me through the window. For a moment, our eyes met. And then the lift doors slid shut.

6

Present

I must have dozed off because the sound of the key rattling in the lock jolts me awake. There's a moment's disorientation before I remember where I am: sitting on a mattress in a pitch-black room. I hear the whoosh of the door opening and strain my eyes, hoping to see a glimmer of light from the hallway outside. But there's nothing, except the sense of someone there. My breathing quickens. *Is this it? Is this where it ends?*

They move towards me, and I shrink farther into the corner. It's terrifying – if I can't see, how can I know what to expect? I hear them breathing; I think it's a man, one of the men who brought me and Ned here, or someone else, I don't know. For him to have pinpointed my position in the far corner of the room, I realise that he must be able to see me, that he must be wearing night-vision goggles. There's a scrape of something being put down on the floor.

'Please – I shouldn't be here.' My voice croaks.

I sense him move away and think of how I can distract him, make him realise that I'm not a threat. 'Could I have some water, please?'

There's a shift in the darkness, then hands on my shoulders lift me to my feet. Is it the man who took me from my bedroom? He pushes me forwards, along the wall towards the toilet. A stab of fear – sharp, instant – knives my body.

He's going to lock me in! He opens the door, and my panic careers out of control.

'No,' I beg, twisting towards him. 'Please don't put me in there.' I try to pull away from him, but he pushes me in backwards.

Adrenaline floods my body. I fight to get back through the door, but the man holds me at arm's length with a hand on my shoulder. My arms flail uselessly, I kick out with my feet, but find only a void. Suddenly, without warning, he removes his hand from my shoulder. Before I can react, the door slams shut.

'Let me out!' I yell.

My terror mounts as I wait for the click that will tell me he's locked me in. But it doesn't come, and hope surges – maybe there's no lock, I don't remember finding a keyhole, maybe I can get out. I fumble for the handle; it turns easily but I can't push the door open. I try again, using my shoulder, putting every ounce of my strength into giving it an almighty shove. The door gives slightly before snapping back. And I realise – the man is leaning against it to prevent me from getting out.

Bewildered, I stop pushing. Why has he put me in here if he can't lock me in? I slam my hands against the door and the edge of my palm catches something, a latch of some kind. My fingers find a bolt and without thinking, I slide it into place. And as the lock connects, a light comes on, faint, but there.

I blink, then turn slowly and see the toilet that I'd crashed into. Next to it, there's a small enamel sink with hot and cold water taps and a cupboard underneath. He pushed me in here for the water. My hands are dirty from crawling along the floor so I turn on the hot water tap and wash them as best

I can. I run the cold tap, scoop some water into my hands, and drink.

I look around. The walls are painted cream, the woodwork white. Apart from the sink and the toilet, the room is bare. I lift the toilet lid and peer inside. It's clean and smells of disinfectant. I use it quickly and find a toilet roll on the floor, wedged into the space between the bowl and the wall.

I flush the toilet, wash my hands again, wipe them on my pyjamas and tug open the cupboard door, not expecting to find anything inside except perhaps a second toilet roll. To my surprise, as well as another toilet roll, there's a folded towel and a washcloth, and beside them, a cloth bag with a zip along the top.

Taking it out, I place it in the sink and examine the contents. A small tube of toothpaste, a toothbrush, and a bar of soap wrapped in soft white paper. I stare at these treasures, then check the cupboard again and find on the lower shelf, a box of tampons. My heart sinks. How many weeks am I going to be here? This can't be a revenge killing, as I first thought.

Suddenly claustrophobic in the small space, I turn to the door. Will the man still be there, on the other side of it? I slide the bolt to the right – and the room is immediately plunged into darkness. Panicked, I slide the bolt back to the left, hoping the light will come on again. It does. I take a steadying breath; it must have been designed so that I could only have light in the bathroom, not the main room. I quickly unlock the door and push against it. There's no resistance; it swings open easily. The same blackness greets me. I wait, listening. Nothing. The man has gone.

I move a few steps into the outer room, close the bathroom door behind me. With my hand on the wall to guide me, I feel my way to the corner where I was sitting. My foot knocks against something rigid. I crouch down, grope around it – it's a tray with a bowl and a spoon, both made of plastic, and a plastic cup. I lift the cup; it's empty. If I want to drink, I'll have to fill it with water from the bathroom. But there's something in the bowl, I can smell it.

Shifting onto my mattress, I take the spoon and guide it to where my other hand is holding the bowl, such simple movements but reliant now on feel and touch. I dip the spoon in and raise it tentatively to my mouth, bending my head to meet it. My lips find a gluey consistency – porridge, unadorned but edible. I begin to eat, slowly, carefully, in case there's a hidden surprise. And as I eat, I think of Ned.

He hates porridge.

7

Past

I was so lost in thought that I didn't notice anyone standing by my table until a plate was placed in front of me. I looked at the blueberry muffin, then raised my eyes to tell the waitress it wasn't for me. But it wasn't the waitress, it was the woman I'd followed home the week before, after I'd seen her crying.

'Can I sit here?' she asked, indicating the empty chair opposite me.

I nodded, still confused about the muffin, about why she'd bought it for me.

'I thought you might be hungry,' she said, seeing the question in my eyes.

'Thank you.' I didn't see the point in pretending that I wasn't.

'Then go ahead, eat.'

I tried not to cram it in my mouth.

'Do you live around here?' she asked, as I ate.

I nodded.

'In an apartment?'

'A youth hostel,' I lied.

She studied me for a moment. 'How old are you?'

'Eighteen,' I said, adding a year to my age.

'And where is your family?'

'Dead.' Then seeing her expression, I hurried to explain. 'My father died from cancer earlier this year, my mother when I was a child.'

'That's very sad, I'm sorry,' she said, and briefly touched my arm.

'Thanks.'

'What do you do?' she asked, taking a sip of her coffee.

'Mainly kitchen work. But I've just been let go.' I gave a little shrug. 'Not enough customers.'

'What kind of work are you looking for?'

'Anything. I'm saving to go to college.'

She nodded. 'How are you with housework?'

'Good,' I told her. 'When my father was ill, I did everything.'

The woman looked at me for a moment, then raised her eyebrows. 'You followed me home last week.'

'Not to see where you lived, or anything,' I replied hastily, in case she thought I'd intended to rob her. 'I saw that you were upset and I wanted to make sure you were all right.'

She gave a sad smile. 'That was very kind of you. Perhaps we should introduce ourselves. I'm Carolyn Blakely and my husband has just left me for someone younger, which is ironic really, because I'm only thirty-three and I never felt old until he told me she was twenty-five.' She reached for her bag and pulled out a silver lipstick, rubbing it on her lips until they were as red as her nails. 'I work long hours in PR, I have my own business, and my husband used to do most of the cooking, which was great. And most of the shopping. And some of the cleaning. So, basically, I'm looking for someone to do all the things he used to do, but with none of the moaning.'

'I won't moan, I promise,' I said, and she laughed.

'You might have to work late in the evenings because what-ever time I get home, I'd like dinner ready, and that might mean ten o'clock. But once you've done the shopping and cleaning and prepared the meal, the rest of the day is yours.'

'Really?' I couldn't believe my luck. 'And that's all?'

Carolyn smiled. 'Yes, I think so. What's your name?'

'It's Amelie, Amelie Lamont.'

'Pretty. Is it French?'

I nodded. 'My father was French.'

'Shall we talk about salary before either of us go ahead?' I folded the blueberry muffin wrapper into a tiny triangle and nodded. 'I'm offering a hundred and fifty pounds a week. Would that be all right?'

I'd known it was too good to be true. I did the maths, but I couldn't stay in a youth hostel forever and with a room in a house costing around a hundred and twenty pounds a week, it would only leave me thirty pounds for food, transport, and any essentials I needed. But I didn't want to turn it down. Maybe I could work other jobs in around this one. Or make her apartment so clean, and make her such lovely meals, that she'd give me a raise.

'Yes, that would be fine,' I said. 'Thank you. You won't regret it, I promise.'

'Great! Then perhaps you can come back with me now and I'll show you your room. I'd rather you saw it before you move in, in case you don't like it.'

I stared at her, not sure I'd understood correctly. 'It's a live-in job?'

'Yes. I hope that's not a problem?'

'No, no, it's not a problem at all.'

'Shall we say a month's trial period? When can you start?'

Tears flooded my eyes. 'Now,' I said, blinking them away. 'I could start now.'

8

Present

How long have I been here? I've lost any sense of time, I don't know whether it's night or day. I hold my breath, listening for the slightest sound. There's only silence, and the thought that I've been abandoned here makes my heart race.

I force myself to remain calm. They brought me food, they've given me a bathroom, they wouldn't have gone to the trouble if they intended to leave me to die. The thought of food brings back the taste of the porridge I'd eaten. Was that breakfast?

In the silence, a mosaic of images flit through my mind. I see myself as a seven-year-old, in the cemetery in Paris, watching my mother's coffin, stripped of its garnish of lilies and roses, being lowered slowly into the ground, then as a nine-year-old, arriving in England with my father, moving into the house with the brown door, two streets away from where my English grandmother lived. I see myself two years later, at her funeral, and three years ago, at Papa's. There are more memories clamouring for attention, of others loved and lost, but I push them away before the tears can come. They are too recent, and my grief still too raw. If I think of them, I'll break. And I can't break, not here, not now.

I turn restlessly on my mattress, lie with my face to the wall. Has anyone noticed yet that Ned is missing? Carl will have, if he isn't involved in our abduction. He reports to Ned at eight each morning; if he can't find him, he'll know something is wrong. But if he is involved in our abduction, if he's one of the men holding us here, no one will notice that we're missing for hours, maybe longer.

My sigh fills the darkness. This isn't even about me, it's about Ned, about who he is. Ned Hawthorpe, the son of billionaire philanthropist Jethro Hawthorpe, founder of the Hawthorpe Foundation. I am nobody. I don't know why they didn't kill me straight off. If they had, it would have served as a warning that they were serious – me dead, Ned taken. But if this is a kidnapping, not a revenge killing, maybe they think they can demand a higher ransom for the two of us. They can't know that Jethro Hawthorpe won't pay a penny to get me back. And there's no one else who would.

For the first time, I'm glad my parents aren't alive. I'd hate for them to be worried about me, to not know where I am. My throat swells at the thought of Papa seeing what I've become, a prisoner in a pitch-black room. Three weeks ago, my life was perfect. I had an apartment, a job, friends. Friends. A rush of tears makes me almost choke. I fight against it, taking deep, shaky breaths. If I'm to survive here, I have to block out the last few days. I try to find a positive, something to make me not give up, not lie here and weep. Carolyn. I still have Carolyn.

I raise a hand, trace the wall with my fingers. I'm still confused about why she didn't come to Ned's house after the press interview, demanding to see me. I'd been so sure she would, so sure she'd understood the position I was in. *I don't believe you!* she'd shouted, pointing at her phone. But maybe she had changed her mind, believed the narrative spun by Ned.

It's another reason why I need to get out of here, and I will escape. I need to explain to Carolyn why I did what I did. That I only had a moment to decide. That if I could turn the clock back, I would. Because then none of this would have happened.

I hear the key turn in the lock and my heart starts racing again. I lie very still as he crosses the room towards me. He puts something on the floor, there's a scrape of something else, and then he leaves without a word.

I sit up, feel around with my hand, find a tray, feel a little bit more, and find what feels like a long bread roll and an apple. This is a new tray – I tap around the floor with my hand – the old one with the porridge bowl is gone. That must have been the scrape that I heard, him picking it up. I smell tomato and pause. I like tomato but I don't really want to eat the sandwich without knowing what's inside. I'm about to start deconstructing it to try and work out its contents when I realise that if I take my tray to the bathroom, I'll be able to see what's on it.

I move from my mattress and crawl along the floor, pushing the tray in front of me. I open the bathroom door, manoeuvre the tray around it, push it inside. Standing, I step into the bathroom and shuffle around to face the door; on the tiny floor space, there's barely enough room for both the tray and my feet. I pull the door closed, slide the bolt into place, and the light comes on. I crouch down clumsily and pick up the bread roll, which is sitting on a sheet of white kitchen paper. The bread is brown, the filling cheese and tomato, and it looks freshly made.

The apple is green and there's also a white plastic cup. And, set along the edge of the tray, a small bar of chocolate.

My spirits lift at the sight of the chocolate. It seems a kind gesture, an effort to give me something nice. But it could be a trap, a ploy to win me over. I harden my resolve. They have abducted me, and I am their prisoner. The chocolate doesn't change anything.

9

Present

Another meal is brought, by the same man or a different one, it's hard to tell when I can only sense him, not see him.

'Thank you,' I say. But he doesn't answer.

I'm not sure if my last meal – the cheese and tomato sandwich – was lunch or dinner. I ended up pushing the tray back to my corner and ate sitting on my mattress, because I'd rather eat in the dark than sitting on a toilet. I fell asleep soon after and when I woke, it seemed like a long time had passed. So maybe I've slept through the night.

I pull the tray towards me, feel with my right hand. There's a bowl. I lift it to my nose; it smells like porridge. I dip my finger in to taste; it is porridge. So, unless they intend to feed us porridge in the evening as well as in the morning, this is probably day two. I'll need to keep track of the days; Ned and I were taken in the early hours of Saturday, the seventeenth of August, so today is Sunday the eighteenth.

I pause, wondering if I should push the tray to the bathroom to check what they've brought me. But porridge is porridge. I feel around the tray and find a banana; did I miss one yesterday? I search some more and find a wrap of paper, about two inches long. I pick it up, press it with my fingers, and feel tiny crystals. Sugar? I tear the top off, shake the contents into the palm of my hand, dip a finger in, raise it to my mouth. It's sugar, and the taste and slightly larger crystals tell me that it's brown. Did I miss this too yesterday? I find the bowl, tip in the sugar, find the spoon, stir it in.

I eat the porridge, carry my cup to the bathroom and drink some water, grateful for the small change of scene, the chance to be somewhere other than the suffocating darkness of the main room. Stripping off my pyjamas, I lather soap into my hands, wash my body, wet a corner of the towel to rinse the suds from my skin, then dry myself with the rest of it. Feeling clean and refreshed, I put my pyjamas back on, wishing I could wash them too; they're dirty from when I crawled around the floor. But I have nothing to change into. I comb my fingers through my hair, glad that it's shorter now, just to my shoulders, brush my teeth, then pull down the toilet seat and sit.

My mind wants to go to the past again, but I distract myself by watching my hands, studying my fingers as they bend and stretch. Suddenly, the room is plunged into darkness. I jump to my feet, my heart racing, waiting for the next threat. But nothing happens. There's no sound of the other door opening. Of thumps on this one.

With shaking hands, I feel for the lock and pull it back. Nothing happens. I slowly push it across again, and after a brief pause the light comes on.

I lean my forehead against the door, gulping in air. The light must be on a timer. Another way for them to snatch away any control I might think I have.

I unbolt the door again, push it open and step quickly into the other room. The darkness might be the same, but the space is not.

I stand for a moment, waiting for my heartbeat to settle. So far, I've managed to stay relatively calm. They haven't hurt me – but they might. The thought cramps my stomach.

I need to escape. But I'll have to be patient, watch for the moment when they make a mistake. Because it will come, and I will be ready. I'm not being trapped again.

I move to the corner where my mattress is, then start walking, my hand on the wall to guide me, counting as I go. I expect to reach the corner at ten steps. But now that I'm more comfortable in the darkness, my strides are longer, and I crash into the wall after seven. Regrouping, I continue along the next wall, past the main door. Seven steps take me to the corner. I turn and walk along the next wall, my fingers bumping over the board covering the window. At seven steps I reach the corner. I turn, move past the bathroom door back to my corner. Seven steps. The room is a perfect square. I begin to walk around the room in circles, my hand trailing the wall, counting my steps. At five hundred, I stop, so dizzy that I have to crouch down and crawl the rest of the way to my mattress.

I'm halfway there when I hear it, the minutest of sounds. A voice. I hold my breath, waiting for it to come again. It doesn't, so I rotate quickly and crawl across the room towards the main door. I kneel against it, press my ear to the painted wood. But there's nothing, no sound from the hallway outside. Whoever was speaking must have gone.

I'm crawling back to my corner when I hear it again. It seems to be coming from below. I lie flat on my stomach and press my ear to the floorboards, chasing the sound. An indistinct voice reaches me. I close my eyes in concentration, wriggle forwards, listen, move again, searching for the optimum place. It seems to be coming from the left-hand side of the room, near the corner where I sit. Still moving on my stomach, I reach my mattress and push it out of the way. The voice is louder now, coming from the corner. Feeling around, my fingers find a small circular hole where the two walls meet. I place my ear as close to it as possible and hear Ned's voice, belligerent, arguing.

At first, I can't make out his words. I don't know if he's speaking to himself or if there's someone with him. And then, a crack – a slap maybe? – and Ned begins speaking, a seeming monologue. I pick out words – *name, Ned Hawthorpe, prisoner, negotiate, police, killed*. I imagine him holding a copy of today's newspaper as he stares at a camera, his eyes wide with fear. Ned isn't the bravest of men.

A door slams below.

'Hey, wait!' I hear Ned shout. But there is only silence.

A wave of sadness flows through me. If we were another couple, I might have put my mouth against the hole and called quietly to him, let him know I was nearby, tell him we would find a way to escape together. But we are not that couple, and when I escape, it will be to get away from him, not just our abductors.

10

Past

'Amelie, I have a surprise for you!'

I smiled, happy that Carolyn was back from work. I'd been working for her for five months now and she'd never once made me feel like a housekeeper, more like a pampered guest. I had a beautiful bedroom, my own bathroom, and if I kept the apartment clean and tidy, and had an evening meal ready for Carolyn when she arrived home from work, my time was my own.

I'd finally admitted to Carolyn that I wasn't eighteen when we met, but seventeen. By then, my birthday had come and gone, so I was officially an adult. When I also admitted that I'd been sleeping rough and was down to my last ten pounds, she'd been appalled.

'I don't know what would have become of me if you hadn't offered me this job,' I'd told her. 'You saved my life.'

'I'm glad I did,' she'd said, hugging me. 'And actually, you saved my life. I was so depressed after my ex left me that there were days when I couldn't get out of bed. I couldn't focus on anything; my work was suffering and I was so close to giving up. But that day I saw you in the café – I couldn't get you out of my mind. You were so young, and so hungry, and I couldn't stop wondering what your story was, why you'd followed me home. You're amazing, Amelie, so resilient. When I think of all that you've been through – well, I'm in awe.'

Since then, we'd become really good friends. She was like the sister I'd never had and I would do anything for her.

I dusted the flour from my hands and went into the hall. 'Dinner's nearly ready,' I said, then stopped because she wasn't alone. Lina Mielkuté, the beautiful Lithuanian woman I'd seen in the café that day with Carolyn and whom I'd met several times since – was with her, and another woman, standing with her back to me. They turned at the sound of my voice and Lina came over, kissing me on both cheeks.

'Amelie, this is Justine Elland. She works with me at *Exclusives*.'

Justine smiled and I felt an immediate sense of connection.

'Lina told me about you,' I exclaimed, moving towards her. 'You're half-French, like me!'

'Yes, my mother is French,' Justine said, embracing me. *'Et maintenant, nous allons pouvoir parler français ensemble.'*

'Ça me manque de ne plus parler français,' I admitted, because I hadn't spoken a word of French since Papa died.

'Yes, Lina told me,' Justine replied in English. 'Don't worry. If you like we can meet each week and speak it together.'

'And then you'll be able to say things to each other that Carolyn and I can't understand,' Lina said, poking me in the ribs and laughing.

'I've invited Justine and Lina to stay for dinner, I thought we could order in if there's not enough,' Carolyn said, trying to catch my eye as she hung their coats on the hooks by the front door.

'There's plenty, I made a boeuf bourguignon.'

Justine clapped her hands. 'Perfect!' She took a bottle from her bag. 'I've brought some wine, will you have some, Amelie? It's a Bordeaux, the region where I'm from.'

'I'm afraid I don't drink,' I said. I felt horribly unsophisticated but Papa's dependency on whisky had made me wary of alcohol.

'I'll get you a soft drink,' Carolyn said, disappearing into the kitchen. 'And check on the dinner. It smells delicious!' she called over her shoulder.

'I'll get a corkscrew and glasses,' Lina offered.

I followed Justine into the sitting room and folded myself into an armchair, touched that Lina had thought to introduce me to Justine after I'd mentioned that I missed speaking French. I studied Justine a moment; with her long dark hair, dark eyes and matt skin, she reminded me a little of myself.

'So, Amelie, tell me about yourself,' she said, sitting down opposite me. 'I know from Lina and Carolyn that you came to London after your father died, and I know that you're working for Carolyn. What else?'

'I'm studying,' I said. 'I want to go to college, to study law.'

'And you came to London to do this? You couldn't study at home?'

'No, once my father died, I had to leave. We only rented our house. I couldn't stay, so I decided to come to London.'

'Couldn't you have gone straight to college?' Lina asked, walking into the sitting room with four glasses and a corkscrew in her hands. She put them down on the table and came over to sit on the large corner sofa.

I blushed. 'I didn't have the money. My dad was ill . . .' I glanced away. For a moment I could smell our old house, the mix of tobacco and whisky. 'It was hard for him.'

'For you too,' Justine said softly.

I nodded, and she reached over and squeezed my hand. 'Let's talk about something else. Your turn to ask.'

'Why did you leave France?'

'Because Britain is part of my heritage and I wanted to experience living here, for a year, at least. But then I found the job at *Exclusives* magazine and I enjoy it so much I can't see myself ever going back to France.' She waved a hand in the air dramatically. 'London has seduced me!'

I laughed. 'And are you an accountant, like Lina?'

Justine and Lina looked at each other, then burst out laughing.

'Sorry,' Justine said, smiling. 'We're not laughing at the question, it's just that I am terrible at maths. Lina and I lived together last year, and I couldn't even work out splitting the bills! I'm the features editor, which means I get to interview famous people. Part of the fun is persuading them to actually agree to an interview.'

'It must be interesting.'

'It is, I love it.'

'It's definitely *interesting* working for Ned Hawthorpe, that's for sure,' Lina said.

We were interrupted by Carolyn coming into the room carrying plates and cutlery.

'Let me do that,' I said, jumping up. 'It's my job.'

'No, sit down. Tonight, I'm serving you.'

We moved to the table and Carolyn insisted on going back to the kitchen to get the food I'd prepared.

'Hey, Carolyn,' Justine said, when she came back. 'I have suggested to Amelie that we meet once a week, she and I, to speak French. We thought every Thursday, when I finish work.'

'Would that be all right?' I asked.

'Of course!' Carolyn pushed her dark hair from her face. 'That's a great idea.'

And as Justine leaned over and hugged me, I thought that my life couldn't be any more perfect.

11

Present

I open my eyes, blink rapidly a few times, still unused to there being no difference in my vision whether my eyes are open or closed. Then I hear it, the turn of the key in the lock.

A man comes in and I turn my head towards the sound. Behind him is a shift of darkness; black but not quite, more a thick grey. My eyes search for any light, but there is nothing.

From the way he moves into the room, and the smell of him – almost like grass but something else, citrus maybe – I think it's the same man as yesterday. I hear him place a tray on the floor next to me and raise myself onto my elbows.

'Could I have a blanket, please?'

He doesn't reply. All I hear is a scrape as he picks up the tray from my last meal.

'Please,' I say. 'I'm cold.'

But there's no other sound until the door closes, and the lock clicks shut.

I slam my head back down. He's not going to understand why I asked for a blanket because it isn't cold in this room. But I'm cold inside; I crave the comfort of something warm to wrap around me. Why doesn't he speak, why do they keep me in total silence and darkness? My frustration builds, I want to scream and shout.

'Stay calm,' I whisper.

I stretch my left arm out, reach around for the tray. I find the bowl, dip my fingers in, bring them to my mouth. Porridge. Day three has begun. Monday, the nineteenth of August.

There's noise from below. I push the tray out of the way, move the mattress from the wall and put my head in the corner to listen. Ned is shouting, something about a toilet. There's an angry retort, followed by a cry from Ned. Maybe he doesn't have a bathroom like me, only a bucket.

He starts mumbling; I don't want to hear it, I push my mattress back into the corner to block out the sounds. I start eating, automatically spooning the porridge into my mouth, then remember the packet of sugar I found yesterday. My fingers move around the tray, I find it, add it to the porridge. There's also a banana.

I go back to my porridge, thinking of Ned's parents. How must it be for them, knowing he is missing, that he has been kidnapped? Will his disappearance be headline news; will his handsome, arrogant face be plastered on television screens around the world? Or has Jethro Hawthorpe kept the police out of it, for the moment, at least?

I finish eating, move to the bathroom. There's always a tiny panicky moment between pushing the bolt into place and the light coming on, that subconscious fear that it won't come on and the door won't open, and I'll be stuck in the small dark space. But the light flickers, then stays, and I feel myself relax.

I use the toilet, then strip off my pyjamas, wash, get dressed. As I squeeze toothpaste onto the toothbrush, I'm struck by a thought – what will come first, the end of the tube or the end of my life?

Leaving the bathroom, I start walking around the room. I try to sing, a nursery rhyme from my childhood, but the French words remind me of all that I've lost, so I begin counting instead. I'm on step three hundred and seven when I hear the rattle of the key in the lock.

I drop to my knees, crawl to my mattress, my heart thumping. It's the first time they've come during the day, between the two meals. There's an urgency to the sound of the door being pushed open, to the movement of air as the man crosses the room towards me. I'm sure it's the same man, there's the same clean smell, but there's something different about him; what is it? I sense him looming over me and instinctively press myself as far into the corner as I can.

It makes no difference; hands on my shoulders lift me to my feet, I'm turned to face the wall, my arms brought behind my back, my wrists held together, then bound with something elastic. A hood comes over my head, bringing a different darkness, airless, suffocating.

Everything is happening fast, too fast. My panic intensifies but I fight it down. Pushed from the room, I try to focus on where we're going. From the left-hand turn we make into the hallway, I know we're going towards the stairs that lead to the basement.

Without warning, I'm pulled to a stop, my body angled slightly to the side before I'm jerked forwards again. Instinctively reading the nonverbal signs, I extend my leg, feel the void, reach down with my foot, find the first step.

Twelve, I remember there were twelve stone steps, half the number of the stairs in Ned's house. I count them as we descend, and when the floor levels out at twelve, I feel a flicker of achievement. The sensation of cooler, fresher air on the bare skin of my arms makes me want to rip off my hood and take great gulps of it. A turn to the right, a few more steps, I don't know how many, I've lost concentration.

We stop. I hear a door being unlocked. Is this the room where Ned is being held? Panic flares in my chest, I try to push back, but it doesn't work. I'm pushed forwards, and the door slams shut behind me. I'm grabbed by someone else, forced downwards. My legs hit against a seat beneath me, I sit, feel hard wood against my back. Something is tied around my chest, binding my body to the chair. My heart races. *Is this it, is this the end?*

The hood is pulled off and for a moment, bright light sears my eyes before they're quickly covered by a blindfold. A hand grasps the back of my neck, holding it firm so that I'm facing straight ahead.

'State your name,' a man's voice says from behind me. 'State that you are being held prisoner with your husband, Ned Hawthorpe, and that they will be contacted again soon. If they do as we say, you'll be released unharmed. The police are not to be involved. If they don't comply with our demands, you'll both be killed.' The grip tightens. 'Speak.'

I take a breath. 'My name is Amelie Lamont,' I begin.

'No,' the voice says. 'Your married name.'

'My name is Amelie Hawthorpe,' I say, my voice shaking now. 'I am being held prisoner with my husband, Ned Hawthorpe. You will be contacted again soon. Do as they say, and we will be released unharmed. Do not involve the police. If you do not comply with their demands, we will be killed.'

The blindfold is whipped off and a sour smell has just the time to reach me before the hood comes down over my head,

46

blocking it out. My mind spins. If this is the room where Ned is being held, where is he? And then, from somewhere behind me, I hear it, muffled but full of hate.

'Bitch.'

12

Present

I open my eyes, darkness. For a moment, I wonder if it's morning, or the middle of the night but then realise that it doesn't actually matter.

I lie for a while, thinking about the recording I'd had to make. Did our abductors make me do it because Jethro Hawthorpe has refused to cooperate? Ned had been in the room; was he tied to a chair too, a knife at his throat? The thought almost makes me smile. He deserves this. For everything that he's done, he deserves this.

The lock turns. I don't bother to sit up or say anything when the man puts the tray down. There's a slight pause before he moves away; was he checking that I was all right? He leaves, but I stay as I am, realising for the first time how silent he is, not just verbally, but in the way that he moves. He must walk barefoot, or in his socks.

I sit up – that's it, that's the difference I noticed yesterday when he walked across the room to take me to the basement. He'd been wearing shoes. I smile, pleased to have learned something about my abductor. If he brings me food, he comes barefoot, if he's wearing shoes, it's to take me to the basement.

I feel for my tray, suddenly hungry, and my arm brushes against something furry. I yelp, scramble to my feet, stand on tiptoes, my heart pounding. I keep very still, listening. But there's no sound, no nibbling or scrabbling of paws.

49

Steeling myself, I stretch out my leg and push the tray with my foot, hoping to dislodge whatever it is. My toes sink into something soft, and a laugh bursts out of me. It's not a rat or some other creature, it's a blanket.

I gather it up and bury my face in its softness. I imagine an elaborate tiger print, with hues of brown, orange, and black. It smells new – did our abductors buy it especially for me? The smile falls from my face.

Dropping the blanket, I feel my way along the walls to the window and lay my hands flat against the board. It's warm beneath my skin, does that mean it's sunny outside? I close my eyes, imagine a beautiful garden with wide lawns, beds of roses, benches placed under blossom-laden trees. Reality hits; if this is an abandoned house, the garden is unlikely to be beautiful. I adjust my expectations, imagine instead a tangle of overgrown hedges, brambles coiled like barbed wire, grass high with nettles and other dangers. My eyes snap open. If I manage to get through the window, that is what I'll be faced with.

I run my hands down the sides of the board, searching blindly for a gap between it and the window frame, somewhere I could jam my fingers in and pull the board away. A sudden stab of pain has me pulling my hand back; one of the nailheads must have cut my skin. I put my finger in my mouth and taste the metallic tang of blood.

I don't want to give up on the window, but I know I'm not going to be able to pry the board off without some sort of tool. I'm only brought plastic spoons with my porridge. A thought comes to me. The man brought me a blanket, will he bring me anything I ask for? It would need to be something seemingly innocent, but something I could use as a tool. But what?

I'm about to go to the bathroom when I remember the tray I was brought. I grope my way to my mattress. The porridge is almost cold, I don't want to eat it. But if I'm to escape, I need to keep my strength up.

I find the banana, peel it, break it into pieces with my fingers, add them to the porridge, then chop randomly with my spoon in the darkness to make them smaller.

I add the sugar; it tastes better now.

In the bathroom, now that I have a blanket to wrap around me, I decide to wash my pyjamas. I fetch my blanket and in the light, discover that it is not tiger print, but a soft grey. I lather soap onto my pyjamas; the fabric is navy cotton, and in the dim light, I watch the water turn grey as the dirt is washed away.

I squeeze as much water as I can from them and drape the bottoms over the sink, the legs hanging down. Water drips onto the floor; I'll have to mop it later with toilet paper. I drape my top over the taps, spread it around the enamel bowl.

Back in the room, wrapped in my blanket, I begin walking, my hand trailing on the wall. When all this is over, will they be able to see marks on the floor from where I walked in never-ending circuits? I'd like to think that they will. It's the only legacy I'll be able to leave, the only proof that I was once here.

Suddenly, the thought that no one might ever know that I was kept in this room makes me breathless. I stop walking, find the wound on my finger, press it with my nail, touch it to my lip, feel the stickiness of blood. I squeeze again, forcing more blood out. Then, reaching as high as I can, I smear my DNA along the wall.

13

Past

I held the key card against the control pad, waited for the click, then pushed the door open and walked into the marble entrance hall. I didn't think I'd ever get used to living here. I felt the same rush when I tapped the code for the lift, pressed the button for the fifth floor and used my keys to get into the apartment.

I carried the bags of shopping into the kitchen, put them down on the floor and asked Alexa to play Radio London. While I cooked, I hummed along to the music.

I set the table, lit the candle I'd bought and placed it in the middle. The door opened and I smiled to hear Carolyn and Lina laughing together as they took off their coats in the hallway.

'Amelie, we're here!' Lina called.

'Hello! Dinner's ready!' I called back.

'It had better be,' Carolyn joked. 'I'm so hungry I could eat a horse.'

'It's fish,' I told her, going into the hall. 'I hope that's all right.'

'Perfect.'

'Where's Justine?' I asked, noticing she wasn't with them. The four of us had dinner together every two weeks, on a Friday night, sometimes at Lina's apartment, sometimes at Justine's, but usually at Carolyn's.

Lina pulled a face. 'Ned needed her to do something for him. I think it's just an excuse. But she said to start without her.'

'Is he still pestering her to go out with him?' Carolyn asked, moving to the kitchen and drawing a deep breath in through her nose. 'That smells so good.'

'Yes.' Lina dragged Carolyn from the kitchen into the sitting room, and I followed them in. 'And she tells him what she always tells him, that she doesn't mix business with pleasure.' She folded her long legs onto an armchair and sat cross-legged. 'That's one piece of advice I can give you, Amelie. No office romances.'

Carolyn nodded. 'She's right, look where it got me.' She walked to the table, drawn by the candle. 'What a beautiful scent! Amelie, you're too kind.'

'At least you're your own boss now,' Lina said.

'I know I'm better off without my ex, but it was hard at the time,' Carolyn replied, coming to sit next to me. 'If Amelie hadn't come along, I'm not sure where I'd be.' She turned to me and smiled. 'You saved my life.'

'No, you saved mine,' I told her. 'I could have ended up on the streets if it hadn't been for you.'

Lina rolled her eyes in mock exasperation. 'Always this same argument. How about you agree that you saved each other?'

'No,' Carolyn said. 'Because Amelie saved me.'

'No,' I said. 'Because Carolyn saved me.'

We ducked as Lina threw a cushion across the room towards us.

Justine arrived as we were having dessert.

'That took a long time,' Lina said, raising her eyebrows. 'What did Ned want?'

'A party.' Justine reached for her wineglass. 'And to invite all the people that we've featured in the magazine, as well as those we'd like to feature. He wants me to help him organise it.'

Lina nodded. 'Sounds good. Will we be allowed to go, do you think?'

'Yes, the staff will be invited, and we can bring a plus-one.' Her eyes danced as she looked across the table at me. 'I don't have a boyfriend so I can take Amelie. But I don't know about you, Lina. It would be a shame if Carolyn couldn't come.'

Lina sighed. 'You know I don't have a boyfriend, Justine. So yes, Carolyn can be my plus-one.' But I saw that her cheeks had flushed. Maybe Justine was right, maybe Lina did have a boyfriend.

'When will the party be?' I asked, feeling a buzz of excitement. I'd never been to a glamorous party.

Justine pulled her panna cotta towards her. 'Not until late September. We need time to arrange it and for everyone to be back from their summer breaks. Ned wants to make it a fundraiser, with the proceeds going to the Hawthorpe Foundation. I wanted to tell him that his father will never accept it. But I want to keep my job, so I didn't say anything.'

'Why won't his father accept it?' I asked.

'Because Jethro Hawthorpe doesn't approve of the way Ned lives his life.' Justine glanced across at Lina and they exchanged a look I couldn't quite read. 'I'm not telling Amelie anything she can't find out from the internet. Everyone knows that he didn't intend for Ned to inherit vast amounts of money, which is why he invested it in the foundation instead.'

Lina leaned towards me. 'Jethro had another son, but he died from a drug overdose.'

'She doesn't need to know about that,' Carolyn reproached, and I loved that she was so protective of me. But I was intrigued.

Later, when Lina and Justine had left, and Carolyn was in bed, I googled Jethro Hawthorpe and discovered that after the death of his eldest son, he created the Hawthorpe Foundation to help fight drug addiction, and donated almost all of his money to it. If some of the more salacious articles were to be believed, Ned resented what his father had done and appealed to his doting grandfather, who changed his will in Ned's favour, bypassing his own son Jethro. He then conveniently died when Ned was twenty-one, making him one of the wealthiest young men in the whole of the UK.

14

Present

I'm standing at the boarded-up window, my fingers working their way over the wood, feeling again for any weakness in its barricade.

There are twenty-four nails along the top and bottom of the board, and eighteen down each side, spaced about two inches apart. Whoever hammered them in was meticulous about conformity. I push my hair from my face and continue my search.

I find it halfway down the left-hand side – the nail that cut me, its head slightly raised. With a rush of adrenaline, I grip the tiny nailhead between my index finger and thumb, and try to pull it out. But I can't get enough leverage.

I think for a moment, then reach down and take hold of my pyjama top. It was still a bit damp when I put it on earlier although the bottoms were dry. With the material between my fingertips, I grip the nailhead again, using the traction to wiggle it. I can feel it giving, becoming looser.

'Come on,' I hiss, placing my left hand flat against the board and giving the nail a massive tug.

It pops out.

I hold it between my fingers, a tremor of excitement running through me. Such a small thing, but it means so much. I make my way to the bathroom, five steps forward, four steps to the left. With the door locked, I examine the nail in the dim light. It's small, about an inch long, its metal not yet rusted with age. If I can pry another one out, and another . . . in my mind, I'm already escaping through the window. I rein myself back. One step at a time.

The nail is also the answer to something that has been worrying me, which is how to keep track of the days. So far, I've been given porridge five times. If I'm working on the theory that the bowl of porridge is breakfast, today is Wednesday, the twenty-first of August – day five of our kidnapping.

I look around the bathroom, searching for the best place to start my calendar, and choose the thin strip of wall behind the door, between the doorframe and the corner. Scratching back and forth with the nail, I gouge a line, level with the top of the door, then another half an inch below it, then another three, spaced at roughly half-inch intervals. I stand back. The fifth line isn't as clear as the others, so I gouge a little deeper. But my calendar isn't complete, I need a start date. Reaching up, I scratch, above the first line, a shaky *1* and *7* and then a dash, then a *8* – the date Ned and I were taken.

I hold the nail delicately in the palm of my hand. Where should I keep it? I raise my eyes to the ridge above the doorframe, but the movement of the door opening might cause it to fall, and I might not be able to find it. In the cupboard, then. Taking out the little toiletry bag, I drop the nail inside.

I return to the window, think about the weak spot where the nail used to be. Turning, I walk carefully across the room, find the tray, find the plastic spoon I used for my porridge, then walk back to the window. I search for the tiny space between the edge of the board and the window frame, and wedge the end of the spoon in. But it's too thick and bends uselessly. Frustrated, I throw it across the room and go to the bathroom to sit in the dim light for a while. It helps to be able to see my hands, my feet, my body, to know that I still exist.

When the light goes off, I return to the outer room, walk to my corner, feel for my tray, lift it out of the way onto my mattress and begin walking my daily circuits. I no longer place my hand along the wall to guide me; I want to get used to walking in the darkness, to feel as comfortable as possible in my space, so I walk with my arms by my side, counting seven steps before turning and walking along the next wall, remembering to move around my mattress each time. At some point I decide to turn after only six steps, and then five, then four, so that I'm walking in ever-decreasing circles.

The dizziness is just beginning to make it hard to continue when my foot steps on something, the plastic spoon I threw across the room earlier. I stoop, pick it up, wait for my head to stop spinning. The spoon is sticky with porridge but when I stand, I've lost my bearings and I don't know which way I'm facing. I stretch out my arms and walk with tiny steps until I find a wall, then grope my way around the room until I get to the bathroom. I wash the spoon, dry it on the towel. I'm about to take it over to the tray, when I find myself pausing. If the abductor sees that it's missing, will he ask for it? Or will he just replace it?

The thought that I might be able to provoke him into speaking is exciting. And if he doesn't, if he replaces it without saying anything, I'll hide the new one, and the one after that, until he won't be able to stop himself from asking where they are. But where can I hide it? Under the mattress is too obvious; if he searches the room, it will be the first place he'll look. If I hide it in the bathroom, he might take that privilege away and padlock the door. I want to provoke him into speaking, not anger him.

I think for a moment, then walk to the main door and place the spoon on the floor directly behind it.

15

Present

I wait for the man to come. *The man.* He's never threatening, just silent and calm. I pull my blanket around my shoulders and lean against the wall. Perhaps his kindness will be his weakness.

I close my eyes and think of Papa. Of how the sun used to push through the window of our small kitchen and land on the skin of his hands and arms as I ate breakfast. I can smell his coffee, see the old metal spoon I used for my cereal, hear the gentle *tick tock* of the old clock that hung on the wall by the back door. 'You're a clever girl, Amelie,' my father says. I try to look up at his face, but there's only shadow there.

The sound of the key turning in the lock drags me back to the present. The man is here. Will he mention the spoon, did he notice it was missing from the tray he collected last night? I let the blanket fall and sit up.

'What time is it?' I ask, trying to keep my voice low, friendly.

He doesn't answer and instead I sense the air shift, then hear a *clunk* as a tray is put down, a scrape as the old one is collected.

'Why won't you speak to me? Has Carl told you not to?'

There's a pause and I hold my breath. Did he react to the name Carl? I get to my feet, swaying a little as my body adjusts to the darkness, and sense him step back. A moment later, the key turns in the lock. He's gone.

I bend and reach along the floorboards for the tray. I find the bowl and next to it, a spoon. He didn't notice that the old one was missing. I smile; he doesn't know yet that he's playing my game. That finally, I have control over something.

16

Past

Justine tipped her head back and closed her eyes.

'Isn't this weather glorious?' she murmured.

'It's perfect,' I said. 'Everything's perfect. So perfect that I don't want it to come to an end.'

Justine opened an eye and squinted at me. 'Why should it?'

It was a Thursday evening in late August, and we had moved from the café where we usually met to speak French, to a bench in Hyde Park.

'Because I can't stay at Carolyn's forever. I've been there for over a year and a half now. And at some point, she and Daniel might want to move in together.'

'It's lovely that she's met someone,' Justine said. 'But it's still early days. And if they do move in together, and you need to find another job; you can come and work at *Exclusives* with me and Lina.'

I shook my head. 'I'm going to be a lawyer, don't forget.'

She turned curious eyes on me. 'Was it your father who influenced you to study law?'

'Not as such.' I rarely spoke about Papa, maybe because the memory of his death was still too painful. 'When my mother died in childbirth, he sued the hospital in France for negligence. But he was passed from lawyer to lawyer and never managed to get very far. I don't think that living in

63

England helped.' I paused. 'Nor did the whisky. His illness made him rely on it to relieve the pain. He was never a horrible drunk,' I added hastily. 'It just made him retreat into himself.'

She reached out and gave my hand a squeeze. 'You don't have to talk about it if you don't want to.'

'No, it's fine,' I said, realising that it was. 'I just wish he'd managed to get justice for my mother and baby brother before he died. It was all he wanted, an acknowledgment from the hospital that they'd been negligent. It consumed him as much as the cancer did. It's why I want to be a lawyer, to help people like him.'

Her phone beeped, a message coming in. She dug in her bag, took out her phone, glanced at the screen.

'Ned,' she said with a grimace. 'You'd think he'd take no for an answer.'

'What do you mean?'

She put her phone away without answering it. 'He is always asking me to have dinner with him and I tell him no, that I don't date men I work with. And you know what he says?'

'What?'

'That I don't work *with* him, I work *for* him. He thinks it's funny.'

I frowned. 'He shouldn't be putting you in that position.'

She sat up. 'You're right, he shouldn't,' she said indignantly. 'Do you know what he said when he heard I was looking for somewhere to live, because I was moving out of Lina's? He said I should go and live with him. He was joking, but it made me uncomfortable.'

'It must have been fun living with Lina.'

'Yes, it was, we had some great times. It was only meant to be temporary, while I looked for an apartment, because I'd just arrived from France. But we got along so well that she said I could stay as long as I liked.'

'So why did you move out?'

'Because, after about a year, she began going out a lot, and once or twice she didn't come back until the next morning. That's when I first suspected she had a boyfriend. I teased her and asked her if she was going to introduce me to him, but she told me that she'd been out with one of her girlfriends. I didn't really believe her, and I was worried that maybe I was cramping her style, so I began looking for my own apartment.'

'Do you still think she has a boyfriend?'

Justine nodded. 'You must have noticed the way she blushes when I tease her about it.'

'I wonder why she doesn't want to introduce him to you or Carolyn?'

'I think she will, in time. It's a big thing, introducing a new man to your friends.'

'I suppose,' I said distractedly. 'When I move out of Carolyn's, I want to stay in the area. You, Carolyn, and Lina are like my family now. I feel so lucky to have met you.'

Justine laughed. 'We are the privileged ones. You keep us young – and yet you are very wise for someone who is just nineteen. When I was your age, I knew nothing. When I think of you coming to London without knowing anyone, of being alone in the world at sixteen, well, you're quite amazing, Amelie Lamont.'

'Lina was even younger than me when she was orphaned,' I said, remembering what Lina had told me. 'She has no family either.' I paused. 'I am an orphan like Lina and half-French like you, and Carolyn is like my big sister. It makes me feel as if I belong, as if I have a family.' I gave a contented smile. 'What more could I want?'

'I don't know – a man, maybe?'

I shook my head. 'It would be too much of a distraction. Maybe once I'm a lawyer, but not before.'

We were interrupted by her phone ringing. She peered into her bag. 'Ned. Oh God, I hope he's not going to start phoning me now.'

'Maybe it's to do with the party? It's only a few weeks away, isn't it?'

'Even if it is, it can wait until tomorrow. He might be the boss, but I don't want him to think that he can contact me out of hours. It's one of those slippery-slope things.' She stood up, stretched her arms above her head. 'How about we go and get pizza?'

'Good idea. As long as we don't bump into Ned,' I teased, because their offices were just around the corner.

'I can't imagine him eating pizza, so I think I'm safe on that score. Shall we invite Carolyn and Lina? Have an impromptu "family" dinner?'

'Carolyn is out with Daniel tonight.'

'Then I shall phone Lina.'

But Lina was also going out.

'Although she didn't say who with,' Justine said, raising her eyebrows comically. She linked her arm through mine. 'So, it looks as if it's just you and me.'

17

Present

I've been dreaming of Papa. I don't know where I was, in this room, or somewhere else, but he was standing next to me.

Well, Amelie, he asked. *Which would you choose?*

And I'd shaken my head and told him that I hadn't decided yet.

I haven't dreamt of Papa for a while, so I want to believe that the dream means something. And a memory comes flooding back, of me standing by his chair, and him asking me the same question.

'Well, Amelie, which would you choose?'

'Could you repeat it, please?' I asked.

'If I offered you a million pounds today, or I promised to give you a pound now, and double it to two pounds tomorrow and four pounds the next day, and eight pounds the day after, and carry on doubling each day's total for a month, which would you choose?'

My heart leapt. 'Has the money from the hospital come through?'

My father shook his head and my shoulders sagged.

'It's just a hypothetical question,' he said.

I thought for a minute. 'Would it be a month of thirty days or thirty-one days?'

'Would that make a difference to your answer?'

67

'It might, because if the doubling thing got to over five hundred thousand on day thirty, then it would come to more than a million the next day.'

He smiled. 'In that case, let's make it a month of thirty-one days.'

'Then I choose the doubling thing – as long as you promise not to die before the thirty-one days are up,' I added.

He laughed. 'You're a very clever girl, Amelie,' he said, patting my hand. 'You're going to be fine.'

Maybe the dream was an omen, maybe Papa was telling me that I'm going to get out of here.

I go to the bathroom, scratch an eighth mark into the bathroom wall. Today is Saturday, the twenty-fourth of August. My heart sinks; we've been here for a week. No one is coming for us.

I rinse the spoon I used for my porridge, walk six steps towards the main door, stop, crouch down to place the spoon alongside the other three. But I can't find them. I shift on my haunches; maybe I'm not as close to the door as I thought. I stretch out my hand, find the doorframe, move my fingers downwards to the floor. Nothing. But they have to be there, they always are. I sweep my fingers farther to the right. Nothing. I put my hand flat on the floor and move it around, searching frantically for my spoons. They aren't there.

Shock rocks me backwards onto the floor. The spoons were there yesterday, now they have gone – but when did they go? The man didn't remove them when he brought my porridge; I'm certain of it. I heard him pick up the tray from last night and go straight out of the room. I would have known if he'd stopped, I would have heard the rattle of plastic as he put the spoons on the tray. But I hadn't heard anything, which can only mean one thing. He removed them at some other time.

Frightened of what it means, I move unsteadily to my mattress, clutching the spoon to my chest, and sit down. I thought that this room was my room, my universe. But it isn't. The abductors can come in whenever they want, they can come in while I'm in the bathroom, or during the night, they can remove spoons, watch me while I sleep, listen on the other side of the bathroom door. The knowledge is devastating.

The need to escape presses down on me. I push up from the floor, steady myself against the wall, walk to the window. My fingers find the board, I move my hands across it until I reach the left-hand edge, searching for the gap from the missing nail. I find it, feel for the next nailhead up. I try to grip it between my index finger and thumb, but it's too firmly nailed in to be pulled out, even with my pyjama top padding my fingers. Sliding a fingernail under the nailhead itself, I try to wiggle it. But I can't pull it out. I try the other nails and by the time I've made my way around the whole of the board, I'm panting, and my fingernails are sore and broken. I blow air up my face. I'll never be able to pry the board off, not without a tool of some kind. Which means that when I escape, it will have to be through the door.

But then what? The hall outside is kept in darkness, I know that because there is never the slightest glimmer of light when the man comes into the room. How will I be able to negotiate an unknown space in the dark? How would I get out of the house? If I turn left in the hallway, I'd be able to find my way to the door that leads to the basement. But what if it's kept locked? If I were to find it open, and I went down the twelve stone steps and along the corridor to the door we came through eight days ago, it would probably be locked too.

There must be a main door to the house, somewhere on the ground level where I'm being kept, possibly to the right. It will probably be locked but there might be a key nearby, or a window I can break. I would just need to find my way in the dark.

But the whole house can't be in darkness, just as the door to my room can't be the only door in the hallway. There must be other doors that lead to rooms with windows that aren't boarded up, windows that I could open, or break. And once outside, I would run, find help.

I think it through. If I could immobilise the man when he comes with my tray, I could take his night-vision goggles and use them to navigate my way along the hallway. But I have nothing to use as a weapon, only my strength and I know I'm not strong enough to overpower him.

How does it happen when he brings me food? I close my eyes, replay his movements in my head – he unlocks the door, comes in, walks over to where I'm sitting, puts the tray on the floor, picks up the previous tray, goes back to the door, leaves, locks it behind him.

My eyes snap open. I've never sensed him pause on his way out, I've never sensed him adjusting his grip on the tray so that he can hold it with one hand and open the door with the other. Which means that when he comes into the room, he doesn't close the door behind him, he leaves it open.

My heart thumps with excitement. If what I think is true, I can get out of the room.

18

Past

'So, Amelie, what do you think?' Justine asked.

We'd arrived at the party and were standing in the vast entrance hall of the *Exclusives* offices. I stared up at the atrium ceiling, hung with thousands of tiny lights.

'It's stunning,' I said. 'Does all this really belong to *Exclusives*? The whole building?'

'Yes – well, to Ned. Impressive, isn't it?'

She took my arm and led me towards the main hall, where people wearing beautiful dresses and designer suits were standing in small groups, while live music played in the background. 'Don't get me wrong, it's a great place to work. But having a few men around might dilute the cutthroat atmosphere a bit.'

'What do you mean?'

'Just that it's hard to stand up to Ned. He can fire you for no discernible reason. It happened to Sam the other day, he made her leave, just like that.' She snapped her fingers. 'She didn't say a word, just packed her things and left.'

'Can he do that?'

She shrugged. 'Ned Hawthorpe can do anything he likes.'

It was hard to know where to look. To the right, emerging periodically from a side door, elegant waiting staff circled with trays of champagne and canapés. Along the back wall, cooking stations had been set up.

'This is amazing,' I said. 'Did you really organise it all?'

'With a lot of help.'

We passed a stand with dishes piled high with caviar.

'So much food!' I said.

'There's every cuisine you can possibly think of,' Justine explained. 'Italian, French, Thai, Malaysian, American; you name it, it's probably here.'

'Where's Lina? And Carolyn? Didn't they say they were going to get something to eat?'

'Over there, I think.' She leaned closer to me, and I smelled her distinct rose-based perfume. 'Look, there's the boss.'

I looked to where she was pointing and saw a dark-haired man weaving his way through the crowd, accompanied by two other men, one of whom was dressed in a black suit. A head shorter than his friends, Ned Hawthorpe moved with the ease of someone comfortable in his skin. I watched as they headed towards a table at the side of the room. Ned and one of the men sat down, while the other stood to one side.

'Who's the man with Ned?' I asked.

'His best friend, Matt Algerson, heir – along with his sister – to the Algerson fortune,' Justine said. 'I love his shirt; it matches my dress.'

'No, I meant the other man, the one dressed in black.'

'Oh, that's Hunter, Ned's bodyguard.'

'Bodyguard? He has a bodyguard?'

Justine laughed. 'That's what we call him. He's Ned's security guard and driver.'

I studied him a moment. He wasn't good-looking in the way that Matt Algerson was, or even Ned Hawthorpe, but there was something about him that I found incredibly attractive.

'He looks nice,' I said.

'He is.' She grabbed my hand. 'Come on, I'll introduce you to Ned.'

'No,' I said, horrified. 'We can't disturb him.'

'Yes, we can.'

She pulled me across the room to Ned's table, and Lina and Carolyn came to join us. Justine introduced Carolyn and me to Ned and Matt Algerson and after ordering champagne for everyone, Ned started a conversation with Lina and Justine about something work-related, so Carolyn and I sat down a little farther away. The champagne arrived and as I politely waved away a glass, my eyes met those of Ned's security guard.

Justine stood up. 'Let's go and find some food!'

She looked so happy in that moment, in her silver-sequinned dress, strands of dark hair already escaping from her updo, her head thrown back as she laughed.

'Come on, Amelie!' she called when I remained sitting. But I smiled and shook my head, content to sit and watch everyone enjoying themselves. What must it be like to be able to afford to pay hundreds of pounds, more even, for the privilege of coming to such a glamorous event?

Aware of Ned's security guard standing somewhere behind me, I turned to him.

'Don't you want something to eat?' I asked.

He gave me an amused smile. 'Not when I'm working, no.'

I flushed. 'Oh, of course. Sorry.'

His eyes met mine and for a moment, the world stopped. There were bottles of sparkling water in the middle of the table, so I reached for one to hide my confusion. As I poured myself a glass, I stole a quick glance and found he was still looking at me. Even more flustered, I turned my eyes to where Justine was standing with Matt Algerson, small plates of food in their hands. As I watched, Ned joined them, interrupting their conversation, and positioned himself directly in front of Justine. A flash of annoyance cast a shadow over her pretty face, and I smiled as she pointedly angled her body away from him and towards Matt. I couldn't work out if she was doing it because she liked Matt Algerson, or if she was trying to annoy Ned.

Whichever it was, Ned soon gave up and came back to the table.

'You don't work for me, do you?' he asked, sitting down next to me.

I smiled and shook my head. 'No, I work for Carolyn, Justine and Lina's friend.'

'And what line of work is that?'

'Oh, just a kind of a live-in housekeeper. But I'm studying too.'

'What do you want to do in the future?'

'Law.'

He nodded. 'Everyone needs a lawyer,' he said approvingly, then looked curiously at me. 'Do you enjoy being a housekeeper?'

'I love it. It's a dream working for Carolyn, she's so kind to me. But her partner is moving in after Christmas, so I'll be looking for a new job.'

He smiled. 'Why, don't you like him?'

I laughed. 'It's not that, he's one of the nicest people I've met. They've said I can stay, but they don't need me in their way.'

He reached into his pocket and pulled out a business card. 'We're going to be looking for another assistant at the magazine in the New Year. The job is basically answering calls and emails, and arranging my diary. If you think it's something you might like to do, give me a call and I'll arrange an interview with HR. I'll also arrange for you to meet Vicky, my PA, as you would be working for her.' He paused. 'What do you think? Would you like to come and work at *Exclusives*?'

I thought of Lina and Justine, and his security guard, who I was sure could hear every word.

'Yes, I think I'd like it very much.'

A woman, dressed more casually than most of the other women I'd seen that evening, approached the table.

'Mr Hawthorpe?'

Ned looked up. 'Yes?'

'I'm Sally Webster, from the *Mail*.'

Ned's face hardened. 'This is a private evening.'

The young woman took no notice. 'Can I ask you about the Hawthorpe Foundation? Is it true that your father doesn't want you to have anything to do with it? Can you confirm that you're barely on speaking terms?'

But before she'd finished speaking, Ned's security guard was propelling the journalist towards the door.

19

Present

Last night, when the man came with my evening tray, I wanted to ask him when he had removed my spoons. But acknowledging their disappearance would have given away something about me; it would have told him how much it had destabilised me to find them gone, and I preferred to let him think that it hadn't bothered me at all. But it had bothered me so much that I forgot to listen to whether or not he'd left the key in the door. I need to listen carefully this morning.

At last, he comes. Pulling the blanket around me, I lay my head against the wall and close my eyes, wanting him to think I'm not quite awake when in reality, all my senses are on alert. I hold my breath, my ears desperate for any sound. But it's difficult to hear if he pulled the key out of the lock before entering the room, or if he left it in.

He puts the new tray down, picks up the old one.

'Thank you,' I say. 'Have a nice day.'

Why am I talking? I curse my nervousness. I need to stop; he's moving towards the door – I'm right, he goes straight through it without pausing. The door closes and is swiftly followed by the sound of the key turning in the lock. I fist-punch the air; it's what I hoped. When he comes into the room, he leaves the key in the lock.

Today, it's harder to eat the porridge because of the sameness. But I know what they're doing. If they brought different food each day, it would give me something to look forward to. A certain kind of hopefulness. And hope is not something kidnappers want to instil in their prisoners.

I'm not sure if my ears are becoming more attuned to picking up sounds, or if Ned is speaking more loudly than he usually does, because I can hear him from where I'm sitting, not the actual words but the rise and fall of his voice. I push my tray out of the way, move my mattress away from the corner, lie on my stomach and hang my head over the end of it.

'. . . not going to eat this crap every day!'

'Then starve,' a voice snaps back.

I wriggle farther forward.

'Or better still, pray that your father pays up, otherwise you'll be here for a very long time.'

I close my eyes. Jethro Hawthorpe still hasn't paid the ransom.

'And you really should stop moaning,' the man goes on.

'What do you expect?' Ned's voice is plaintive. 'You keep me here like an animal, bring me the same food day in, day out.'

'What were you expecting, a five-star hotel?'

'I wasn't expecting anything, least of all to be kidnapped,' Ned says. 'You're not going to get away with it, you know. You have no real idea of who I am, the connections I have.'

'Oh, don't worry, we know exactly who you are.' The man's voice drops. A sharp crack makes me flinch.

Ned cries out, I curl into a ball, rest my head against my knees. I don't want to listen anymore, but I have to; it might have an impact on my plan to escape.

'Who the fuck are you, anyway?' Ned is shouting now, trying to sound tough. But for all his bravado, I know he's scared.

'Shut up and listen. It's over a week since we first contacted your father and we're beginning to lose our patience. So, we're going to call him again and you better make him understand that this is his last chance. Tell him that if he refuses to cooperate, he'll be getting something in the post. Something of yours.' There's a pause. 'Or hers.'

'You can do what you like to her, I don't care. Kill her and send her body to him if you want.'

My head jerks as if I've been slapped. Without warning, my mind goes to Justine and Lina. I push them away; I can't think of them now, I need to focus on getting out of here.

Ned is speaking.

'Please, Dad, just do as they ask, otherwise there'll be terrible consequences for me. It's serious, Dad, they mean business. They keep me like an animal, I'm hooded most of the time. I have no toilet, almost nothing to eat . . .'

His voice stops abruptly. There's a dry laugh that isn't Ned's.

'Better not say too much, your daddy might think it's good for you to endure a bit of hardship for a while and decide to keep you here longer. Let's face it, he's hardly in a hurry to get you back.'

'Shut up!' Ned's voice rises to a crescendo.

Another crack, another cry, followed by muffled sounds; the scrape of a chair dragged across the floor, then the slam of a door.

I stay still, my face against the wooden floor. It isn't Carl, then, who is with Ned. Ned would have recognised his voice, he wouldn't have asked who he was. My heart sinks. It makes it somehow worse that our abductor is a stranger, worse for me. He will have seen what everyone else saw, and assumed that Ned and I were in love. That's why they took me, because they thought I had worth. Now, after what Ned said about killing me, they'll know the truth.

The sooner I escape the better.

20

Past

I left the *Exclusives* building, trying not to make it obvious that I was looking for Ned's car on the road outside, as I did every evening. When it was there, I'd wave to Hunter, sitting behind the wheel, and he would always smile back. But he never made any move to get out of the car and talk to me. Sometimes, I thought I should stop waving. But I was worried he would think badly of me if I did.

There were a few paparazzi outside, waiting for Daphne Danaher, who had come in earlier for an interview. Or maybe they were waiting for Ned. He was often targeted in the media; people were fascinated by the Hawthorpe family, and the press loved to compare Ned and his father. Ned never came out well. Jethro was portrayed as an honourable man who worked tirelessly for his foundation, and Ned as a playboy who spent his time courting soccer players and rock stars, trying to persuade them to appear in his glossy magazine. I felt sorry for Ned. I liked him, he was funny and generous.

Ned's car wasn't parked outside the building where it usually was, so I stopped and pretended to search in my bag for my phone, trying to see if it was parked farther down the road, acknowledging that my need to see Hunter each day was getting ridiculous. Then, out of the corner of my eye, I saw something hurtling along the pavement. I looked up, but before I could move out of the way, a scooter smashed into me, and I was knocked to the ground.

A crowd gathered.

'Are you all right?'

'Bloody scooters, they shouldn't be allowed. I almost got knocked down by one myself.'

'Can you stand? Do you want me to help you up?'

'It's all right, I've got this. Do you think you can stand, Amelie?'

I looked up and saw Hunter bending towards me.

'Yes, I think so.'

'Here, let me help.' He took hold of my forearms, lifted me to my feet. I winced as my right foot touched the ground.

'How bad is it?' he asked.

'Just a bit bruised, I think.'

He picked up my bag from where it had fallen. 'Why don't you come and sit in the car while you get your breath back?'

'Yes, good idea.'

'You'd better check that ankle,' he said, opening the door and helping me onto the passenger seat. 'You might need to see a doctor.'

'I'm sure it will be all right. If I can just get my shoe off.'

I bent to unlace it, trying not to flinch at the pain.

'Here, let me do that.'

He crouched down and I watched as his fingers slowly untied the lace, then eased my trainers from my foot. I looked away, trying not to blush at the feel of his fingers on my skin as he took off my sock.

'Does this hurt?' he asked, pressing around my ankle.

'Not much,' I lied.

'It's not broken but it's had a bad knock. It needs ice. Where do you live?'

'Camden.'

He took out his phone. 'Give me a moment, then I'll drive you home.'

'You don't—' I began. But he was already speaking to Ned.

I wanted to talk to him on the way to Camden, find out more about him. But he was focused on the traffic and anyway, I wasn't sure what to say. I knew from Justine that he was in his early thirties, but that was it. The only other thing I'd managed to find out was that he'd been working for Ned for five months. According to Justine, Ned had hired Hunter to protect him from the press, which was why everyone at *Exclusives* secretly called him the Bodyguard.

I turned my head to look at him, and for the briefest of seconds he met my eyes before concentrating again on the road ahead.

'Have you been working for Ned long?' I asked, even though I already knew the answer.

'Around five months.'

'Did you always want to be a security guard?'

'Yes, I always wanted to be at someone's beck and call,' he said, his voice grave.

I smiled. 'So how did you end up being one?'

'Circumstances.'

'What were you before?'

He turned his eyes on me again and I saw how dark they were, almost black. 'You sure ask a lot of questions.'

I flushed, worried that I'd overstepped some kind of mark. 'Sorry.'

'It's okay. But it's a long story.'

I wanted to tell him that I didn't mind hearing it, but he'd lapsed into silence, so I did the same.

We didn't talk again until he pulled up outside the building where I now lived.

'Thank you,' I said.

'Wait here a minute.' He got out of the car.

I watched as he strode into a nearby supermarket. Had he really gone to do his shopping? I sat back, thinking how lucky I'd been to find a studio apartment just down the road from Carolyn's apartment.

Hunter came back with a freezer bag. 'Ice,' he said, opening my door.

'Thank you,' I said gratefully. I fumbled in my bag for my purse. 'Can I—'

'Absolutely not.'

He helped me out of the car and insisted on coming up with me in the lift.

'Which floor?' he asked.

'Third.'

In the cramped space, I was so aware of him, of his height, of the musky smell of his aftershave. It was almost a relief when we arrived on the third floor.

He waited while I unlocked the door.

'Look after yourself,' he said, as I hobbled inside my apartment.

'I will, thank you.'

I closed the door, took a clean towel from the drawer in the little kitchen area. Then clutching the bag of ice, I moved to the sofa and lay down, thinking that it was worth being knocked over by a scooter, just to have that time with Hunter.

21

Present

It's time – at least, I think it is. The man should be here soon.

Today, I'm escaping. Last night, I pretended to be asleep when he came with my tray. I made sure I was huddled under my blanket, because if my plan is to work, I needed him to see me like that at least once.

Now, I grope for my blanket, lay it along the mattress, doing my best in the darkness to flesh it out. It's hard to know if I've managed to make a realistic body shape but he only needs to believe that I'm under it while he's crossing the room. If, or when, he realises that I'm not, I'll already be gone.

I cross to the door, take up my position behind it. I feel for where the hinges are. I'll need to distance myself from them; if I'm too close to the door, my body will bounce it back onto him as walks in. If I stand too far away, he'll be able to see me. I choose my position, flatten myself against the wall and think of the ninth line I scored on the wall in the bathroom yesterday. Hopefully, I won't have to score one today.

The waiting is unbearable. Even if I make it out of the room, everything depends on the man I thought was Carl not noticing that anything is wrong until I've had the chance to escape. If he's in the basement with Ned, he'll be able to hear my abductor if he starts shouting for help, and will be up the stairs before I've gone very far. But it's too late to worry about that now. The key is turning in the lock, he's here.

The air stirs around me, I hold my hand up, the door touches my palm, it's open. I sense the abductor come into the room, move past me. *Now!*

My fingers find the edge of the door, I slide my body around it, pull it after me, feel for the key – it's there. Relief weakens my body; shaking, I close the door, turn the key, hear the click, steel myself for a roar of anger. But it doesn't come and for a moment, the silence confuses me. Why isn't he objecting? He must know what I've done. I fight down the fear, force myself to move.

I inch my way down the pitch-black hallway, my breath coming in small panicky gasps, my fingers groping the wall. A sound reaches me, the handle being rattled. I tense, wait for shouting. But it doesn't come.

I quicken my pace and farther along the wall, my fingers find the ridge of a doorframe. I move to face it, explore the surface with my hands. Two doors, double doors, in my mind they lead to a vast room, a sitting room of some kind. I grope downwards, find two doorknobs side by side. I try them both, but the doors are locked, I don't waste time, I move on. Then, as I advance farther down the hallway, I see a thin sliver of light at floor level. My heart leaps: it must be coming from under a door and behind the door, there'll be a room, a room where there's light, where there'll be a window.

Using the light to guide me, I reach the door, find the handle. It turns, I push the door open. A light – bright, white, artificial – blinds me. I drop my head, screw my eyes shut, I'm wasting precious time. But I can't open them, the pain is too severe.

I bring my hands to my face, use them as shields, open my eyes, just a little, part my fingers, just a little, and see a table in front of me, behind it a fridge. I'm in a kitchen. I spread my fingers a little wider; to the right of the fridge, I see glass doors and quickly move towards them, my hands still shielding my eyes. I bump into a chair, move around it – *WHUMP!*

Something comes over my head, not a hood, a blanket, not my blanket, a different one, rough, not soft. An arm snakes around me, pinning the blanket down, muffling my protests. My hands are trapped in front of my eyes, I try to move them but there's no room to manoeuvre. My weight is shifted to one side, I'm lifted off my feet. Held tight against his body, I feel the rhythm of his stride as he begins to move forwards. I kick out and my feet whack against something hard. My mind scrabbles frantically, I try to work out where he's taking me, we're going back down the hallway, towards the room where I was kept, towards the door to the basement where Ned is being kept. *Please let him take me back to my room, please don't let him put me in with Ned!* Terror takes hold, I struggle under the blanket. But it makes no difference.

The man pauses, stoops, crushing my body within his. A door is unlocked, my feet, dangling uselessly, knock against something a second time. I feel myself being tilted forwards and unfurled from the blanket, I hit the floor hard.

Winded, I gasp for breath. Behind me, a door slams shut.

22

Past

My phone rang. I squinted, looked at the time, then frowned. It was 7.10 a.m. Who could be calling me so early on a Saturday morning?

There was no caller ID.

I answered the call. 'Hello?'

'Amelie, it's Ned. Sorry to disturb you so early.'

I sat up hurriedly, fully awake now. Questions flooded my brain. Was he phoning to fire me? On a weekend? How did he get my number?

'No, it's fine, really.'

'Have you ever been to Las Vegas?'

I grabbed my computer, thinking he wanted me to pull some information on the city.

'No, never. I've never been anywhere really. I've never even been on a plane.' Mentally, I told myself to shut up; Ned Hawthorpe hadn't called to listen to my life story.

'Seriously?'

'Seriously.'

'Well, I'm flying out this morning. Paul Martin has agreed to give us an interview. Well, almost agreed,' he added.

'Wow,' I said, flattered that he'd said *us*. 'That's amazing.'

'As I said, it's not a definite. But I'm going to try and persuade him.'

'Well, good luck.'

'Would you like to come with me?'

I felt my eyes widen. 'To Vegas?'

'Yes.'

'Seriously?'

He laughed. 'Seriously. I might need some help persuading Paul Martin. You can tell him what a great magazine *Exclusives* is.'

'But shouldn't Justine be going with you?'

'She can't, she's leaving for Paris today to interview Ophélie Tessier for the March issue.'

'Oh good, has she finally agreed?'

'Yes, her agent phoned last night. Now, about Vegas. I'm flying at ten, can you be ready by eight o'clock?'

'Um, yes, I think so.'

'Good. Hunter will pick you up. You have a passport, I hope?'

'Yes, I do. How long will we be going for?'

'Three, four days.'

I could hardly contain my excitement as I began to sort through my clothes. I just had time to shower, dress, and pack before Hunter rang on the intercom.

'I'm on my way down!' I called, already rolling my suitcase through the door.

Hunter and I had chatted a few times since the day I was knocked down by the scooter, a month ago now. Well, not really chatted, just exchanged a few pleasantries. He was definitely friendlier than before, but I was trying not to read too much into it.

'We should be at Farnborough in plenty of time,' he said as I climbed into the back of the car. 'We'll pick Mr Hawthorpe up on the way.'

'Farnborough?' I queried. 'What's at Farnborough?'

'The private jet waiting to take you and Mr Hawthorpe to Las Vegas.'

'Private jet?'

He gave me an amused smile via the rearview mirror. 'You don't expect Mr Hawthorpe to travel cattle-class, do you?'

I laughed, warmed by his smile. 'No, but I expected that I would. I thought he'd be going business-class or maybe even first-class. Do you ever go with him when he travels,' I asked hopefully, 'to drive him around when he gets there?'

'No, he usually hires a local driver.'

'You'll be having a couple of days off, then.'

'I will,' he agreed.

'Have you got anything nice planned?' I asked, then blushed. My questions were becoming personal.

'Not really. I might have planned something if I'd known in advance that Mr Hawthorpe would be going away. I guess I'll just hang out.'

I almost regretted it then, going to Vegas. And then berated myself for harbouring stupid fantasies. Even if I hadn't been going with Ned, the likelihood of Hunter suggesting we hang out together while our boss was away was less than zero.

'Well, if you want to hear all about Vegas when I get back, let me know,' I heard myself saying. Then steeled myself, waiting for the inevitable brush-off.

'I might just do that.' He turned to look at me. 'Maybe we could go for a drink.'

My heart somersaulted. 'Maybe we could.'

We picked Ned up at his home in Wentworth. The house was impressive, a huge white building with pillars and a balcony behind ornate black gates. He sat in the back next to me, and all conversation between Hunter and me ceased.

23

Present

I open my eyes and for a split second, I think I'm in my room in Carolyn's apartment. But when it remains dark, every-thing comes rushing back.

I'm cold, I've been cold since I was brought back to this black-as-night room. When was that? It's hard to tell when they haven't brought me anything to eat. I keep telling myself that they will eventually feed me. If they wanted me to die, they'd have killed me for trying to escape.

My blanket is gone. I searched everywhere for it but I couldn't find it. They must have taken it away as punishment.

How did they find me so quickly? The man hadn't shouted when I locked him in, but the other abductor, the one who grabbed me in the kitchen, hadn't stumbled on me by chance, he'd come prepared with the blanket. He must have known within seconds that I'd escaped, which meant that he must have been alerted – because of course, they must have mobile phones or walkie-talkies, something I'd stupidly failed to consider.

I push away the wave of depression that threatens to engulf me. I'm alive. I might not have succeeded completely, but I did manage to escape from this room. And I have knowledge about the house where I'm being kept – next to this room, there's a room with double doors, next to that, a kitchen.

The kitchen itself – a large room, a table down the centre, chairs. And at the far end, glass doors leading to the outside, the sliding sort. If only I'd been able to reach them. But blinded by the light, I'd lost precious time waiting for my eyes to adjust. Next time, I promise myself. Because there will be a next time.

I don't want to score another line on the wall, but I do it anyway. Day ten, Monday, the twenty-sixth of August, the day of my failed escape.

I leave the bathroom, return to my mattress. It hits me then, that I'm back here, back where I started, and I kick the wall in frustration.

24

Past

I strapped myself into my seat, my fingers fumbling on the buckle, nervous and excited at the same time, hardly able to believe that I was on my way to Las Vegas.

A hostess brought champagne.

'No, thank you,' I said, smiling at her.

Ned lifted the two glasses from the tray.

'Go on,' he said, handing me a glass. 'You need to celebrate your first-ever flight. But there are soft drinks, if you prefer.'

'No, this is great.'

He clinked his glass against mine. 'Here's to the first of many flights.'

'Thank you.' I took a sip. The sensation of bubbles bursting on my tongue added to my excitement. It seemed surreal to be sitting on a private jet, drinking champagne. I wished Carolyn could see me. She didn't even know I was on my way to Vegas; I had wanted to call her, but in the rush to get ready, I hadn't had time.

I took my phone from my bag and turned to Ned.

'Would you mind taking a photo for me to send to Carolyn?'

'Of course.' He put his phone down on the table in front of him. 'Do I know Carolyn?'

I raised my glass and smiled for the camera. 'You met her at the *Exclusives* party. She's a friend of Justine and Lina's.'

'Ah yes, I remember now.'

I sent the photo to Carolyn, with the caption *Guess where I am – on my way to Las Vegas! In a private jet, no less!*

A message flashed on the screen of Ned's phone. Out of the corner of my eye I saw a thumbs-up emoji from someone called Amos Kerrigan.

Ned picked up his phone, looked at the message, then drained his glass. 'You'll need to switch your phone to flight mode,' he said, turning his off. 'We'll be taking off soon.'

I turned off my phone, thinking how surprised Carolyn would be to get my message. Ned pushed his chair back and yawned.

'I'm going to sleep,' he said. 'Feel free to do the same.'

But I couldn't, I was too excited.

We arrived in Las Vegas, and everything was like a dream. Ned had booked us into a mega hotel–casino complex. If I'd had to stay in my room all day, I wouldn't have minded. It was enormous, with sliding doors that led onto a balcony almost as big as my studio apartment.

'What do you think?' Ned asked from the doorway as I peered over my balcony at an enormous swimming pool below.

'It's amazing.' I turned to him. 'Thank you for inviting me along, it's so kind of you. You won't regret it, I promise.'

Ned smiled. 'I'm sure I won't. In fact, I already know that you're going to be a great help. Why don't you unpack? Then we can have lunch. I'll meet you in the lobby in thirty minutes.'

I unpacked quickly and sat down to send a message to Carolyn. I felt suddenly bad that I'd come all the way to Las Vegas without telling her. I'd had to pack in a rush – but was it because I thought she might dissuade me from coming that I hadn't found two minutes to call her? I didn't know why she might have tried to dissuade me, because she barely knew Ned. But the feeling was there, and I knew I would only feel better once I'd spoken to her.

But my phone wasn't in my bag. My heart sank; I remembered putting it into the seat pocket after I'd switched it to flight mode. I must have left it there.

Aware of Ned waiting for me, I took the lift down to the lobby. There were so many restaurants to choose from that I was happy to let Ned decide.

'I think I left my phone on the plane,' I admitted, once we were sitting down.

'Don't worry, when the plane lands in London, I can have it couriered back here.'

I paused, my glass halfway to my mouth. 'You can't do that, it would cost too much! It's my fault I left it on the plane.'

He smiled. 'I don't mind. But it might take two or three days to get here, and we'll probably be on our way back by then.'

'Don't worry, it's fine. If I need to contact anyone, I have my laptop.'

But later, when I was alone in my bedroom, I opened my laptop to email Carolyn and the screen was completely blank. I tried holding down the power button, but it didn't make any difference. Without thinking, I picked up the hotel phone and dialled Ned's room number. He answered after only three rings.

'Hello?'

'Hi, Ned, it's Amelie. I'm sorry to call so late, but I can't get my laptop to work . . .' I trailed off, realising that he probably wasn't going to be able to help.

'Did you knock it or drop it?'

I blushed, suddenly remembering dropping my bag on the floor in the bathroom at the airport. 'Not that I know of,' I lied, because I didn't want to seem too much of a liability after having left my phone on the plane.

'Let me make a few calls, see if we can get it fixed. If not, I'll get you a new one.' He paused. 'Don't sound so worried, it's not a problem.'

'But what if you need me to do any work?'

'Relax, it's the weekend. And to be honest, I don't think there'll be much for you to do until I meet Paul Martin, and that won't be until Monday now. But can you make sure to stay within the confines of the hotel for when I do need you? Until then, you're free to enjoy yourself.'

'Really?'

'Of course. Use the pools, go to the spa, have a couple of treatments. Just give them my name and it will be taken care of. If I need you, I'll send someone to find you.'

After breakfast together the next day, Ned disappeared into the business lounge. I wanted to use the pool, but I hadn't thought to pack a swimsuit, so I headed to one of the hotel shops and bought a red bikini. I also bought myself a pair of black aviator sunglasses and spent the morning swimming lengths and lying in the hot desert sun. At lunchtime, a young man came with a message from Ned, asking me to meet him for lunch.

'Paul Martin is now saying he can't meet until Tuesday or Wednesday.' Ned looked different today. His face was unshaven and there were dark circles under his eyes. He was playing with his salad and there was an edge to him I hadn't seen since the journalist had tried to talk to him at the party. 'He knows that I came out specially to interview him. I've told his agent it has to be Wednesday at the latest, because we'll be flying back on Thursday.'

'That's my birthday,' I exclaimed. 'I'll be twenty.'

'Twenty?' He raised his wineglass. 'We'll have to celebrate that before we leave.'

Despite his darker mood, I liked being with Ned. He was funny and charming, and when he asked me to tell him about myself, I ended up telling him that both my parents were dead. He couldn't believe that I was all alone in the world.

'You must have relatives somewhere in France,' he protested, taking a drink of wine.

'I don't think so,' I said, glancing around the room at the other guests. 'My father was an only child and my French grandparents died before I was born.' I swapped my wineglass for my water glass and took a sip. Ned had persuaded me to try the wine he'd ordered but I wasn't sure I really liked it. 'My English grandmother died a few years ago. My mother had a cousin somewhere in Scotland, I think, but I'm not sure she ever met him. Even if I do have relatives, I wouldn't know where to begin searching for them.'

He gave me a sympathetic smile. 'I'm an only child too, now. Although my father does have another child, the Hawthorpe Foundation.'

'You must be proud of it, and of your father.'

Ned twirled the stem of his glass between his fingers. 'Yes, I am. But to be honest, the foundation has turned out to be a bit of a disappointment on a personal level.'

'Why is that?'

He shifted in his chair. 'It was supposed to be something my father and I could do together. He was just about to launch the foundation when I got into a bit of trouble – had a fight with someone, wrapped a car around a tree, that sort of thing. Of course, because of who I am – because of who my father is – it made it into the press, and he had to put the whole thing on hold because some of the potential benefactors got cold feet, muttering that the foundation would be tarnished by my "indiscretions". My father was furious and when he finally launched the Hawthorpe Foundation ten years later, he refused to let me have anything to do with it.' He paused, drained his glass and signalled to the waiter to bring more wine. 'When I told him that I knew people who would be happy to make substantial donations, he said he didn't think the people I had connections with were the sort of people he wanted associated with the foundation. The fundraiser I did in September is a case in point. We received millions in donations, but he wouldn't take it, so we donated it to another charity.' He waited while the waiter poured him wine. 'The truth is, my father cares more about the foundation than he does about me.'

'I'm sure that's not true,' I said, feeling sorry for him.

'It is.' He couldn't hide the bitterness in his voice. 'Enough about me, let's talk about something else. How are your plans for college coming along?'

'I received an offer from King's College, but I deferred it for a year.'

'Why?'

'Because I haven't saved enough yet.'

'And you want to be a lawyer, right?'

'Yes. My mum died in childbirth in a hospital in Paris, through negligence. I watched my dad fight for justice for years, but we never had enough money or the right people on our side to get anywhere. It made me determined to be not just a good lawyer, but a great one for people who can't afford to pay for representation.'

'That's very noble, but you'll never be rich.'

I laughed. 'I'm not interested in being rich, all I'm interested in is not being poor. I've been there, and it's horrible.

It's why I don't want to take out a huge loan to pay for college, in case I can never pay it back. But I might have to.'

'I remember what it was like when my father decided to put most of our money into the foundation,' Ned said, his face suddenly grim. 'If my grandfather hadn't stepped in, my life would have been very different from the one I have today.'

But still comfortable, I wanted to say to him. *Still wealthy and privileged.* But I didn't say anything, because he was my boss and because I didn't think he had any idea of what it was like to be any other way.

25

Present

Pains cramp my stomach. I stop walking, knead it with my hands. I haven't had anything to eat since the bread and cheese the night before my escape attempt, and that was ages ago. If I could sleep, it would take my mind off my hunger. But with the cramps and the cold, it's impossible.

I go to the bathroom, fill my empty stomach with water, so much of it that I vomit it up. I can't stop shivering as I score another line on the wall, because another day must have gone past by now. Eleven days; why has nobody come for us?

I return to the main room, manage to doze a little. At one point, a noise wakes me and I raise my head and look hopefully in the direction of the door. But no one comes walking across the room towards me and suddenly I'm furious, furious that they think they can starve me.

I push myself from the mattress, make my way blindly to the door.

'I'm hungry!' I yell. 'I need food!' I find the handle, rattle it. 'Did you hear me?' I thump on the door with my fists. 'I'm hungry!'

I stop, put my ear to the door, hoping to hear someone approaching. But there's nothing. I thump on the door again. 'Did you hear me? I need food!'

'Shut up!'

The high-pitched scream transcends the sound of my thumping. I stop, my fist halfway to the wall, paralysed by the violence in the scream. For a moment, I think it's the man who caught me when I tried to escape, that he's in the hall-way outside, yelling at me to stop. Then, I realise – it came from below. Ned. He's heard me hammering on the door.

I sink to the ground, my eyes smarting with tears of frustration and my leg knocks against something. I reach out, it's a tray. Relief floods through me; they must have brought it while I was asleep. I grope clumsily for food, find a sandwich, and begin to eat, searching at the same time for the bar of chocolate. But there's nothing else, not even a piece of fruit.

I finish my sandwich, sit with my back against the wall, thinking about the tray left just inside the door. No more chocolate or fruit. No more human contact. That is going to be the hardest to bear. And what about Ned? He knows where I am now, he knows I'm being kept in a room some-where above him. Which means he can invade my space whenever he wants.

Better for me to be quiet.

26

Past

On Thursday, our last day in Vegas, Ned took the afternoon off. We went out for lunch, and he ordered yet more champagne to celebrate both my birthday and Paul Martin finally agreeing to an interview for *Exclusives*. We'd had to stay longer than Ned had intended to secure it; by the time we flew out the next day, we would have been gone for six days.

'Justine is going to be thrilled,' I said, when Ned told me. 'Have you told her yet?'

'No, because I want to be able to see her face. So, no letting the cat out of the bag.'

'I won't,' I promised. 'I bet you can't wait to get back.'

He drained his glass. 'Actually, no. I wish I could stay here forever.'

'Why?'

He twirled the stem of the flute between his finger and thumb, a habit of his. 'Because my parents are pressuring me to marry a girl that I don't want to marry. They've invited her and her parents to stay next weekend and they're expecting me to propose to her. She's a nice girl, I've known her for years. But I'm not going to marry her, even for the sake of the Hawthorpe Foundation.'

I frowned. 'What do you mean?'

He signalled to the waiter, who brought over the red wine that Ned had asked him to decant into a carafe.

'She's Isobel Algerson, Steve Algerson's daughter,' Ned explained as the waiter poured a little wine into his glass. 'He and my father are great friends, and Steve has donated millions to the foundation. My mother and Priscilla Algerson are best friends, their son, Matt, is my best friend, so our marriage would be a win-win situation for everyone.' He took his glass, breathed the scent of the wine in through his nose, then nodded to the waiter. 'Except me,' he added, as the waiter filled our glasses.

I smiled my thanks to the waiter. 'How does Isobel feel about you? If she doesn't want to marry you, that would make everything all right, wouldn't it?'

'Unfortunately, she's been told from an early age that I'm her destiny.' He raised his glass towards me. 'Here's to my marriage.'

We clinked our glasses together.

'But nobody can force you to marry her,' I said.

He gave a grim laugh. 'Have you met my father? I'm already a huge disappointment to him because of the magazine, and to my mother, because I'm still unmarried at thirty-three.'

'Don't you want to get married?'

'Yes, but not to Isobel Algerson. She's not the sort of girl I want to marry.'

'What sort of girl do you want to marry?'

'Someone my parents would disapprove of, just to annoy them and get them off my back. That's why my father is so against the magazine. He's afraid I'm going to end up marrying a pop star or actress, which wouldn't be in keeping with the image he wishes to portray for his precious foundation. He thinks that everyone I meet is a drug user, and he has told me that my future wife can't have any history with regard to drugs.' He gave a dry laugh. 'It makes Isobel the perfect wife for me. Not only has she never touched drugs, but she also works as a volunteer for an addiction and mental health charity.' He looked at me. 'Have you ever used drugs?'

I shook my head. 'No.'

'Not even smoked a joint?'

'Not even. What about you?'

'Believe it or not, I haven't. I vowed I wouldn't after my brother died.' He held up his wineglass. 'This is my vice.'

'I don't really drink either. In fact, I've probably drunk more this lunchtime than I have in my whole life.'

He lapsed into silence, and I didn't know whether he hadn't heard what I said or if he was thinking about it. I took a sip of wine, so smooth and velvety that I took another sip.

'It's a Château Margaux,' he said, and I realised he'd been watching me.

I laughed. 'I have no idea what that is.'

He smiled. 'A very nice wine.'

'Then I'll make sure to remember the name.'

'Actually Amelie, the reason I mentioned my marriage is because I have a proposition for you. A business proposition,' he added, stressing the word *business*.

'Oh?' I said, intrigued.

'From what you've told me, you've been working for the last couple of years to be able to pay for yourself to go to college.'

'That's right.'

'How much does it cost to go to college nowadays?'

'Without a grant? Around twenty thousand a year, for fees and accommodation, maybe more. Then there's living expenses and books. So, between twenty-five thousand and thirty thousand.'

'And how many years are you planning on being at college?'

'A basic law degree is three years. And then I'll hopefully have a two-year training contract with a good law firm.'

'So, you're looking at an outlay of around a hundred thousand for three years.'

'Not quite,' I said, wincing inwardly at the amount. 'But I hope to get a grant, and I'll have to get a part-time job to cover the rest.'

He leaned back in his chair. 'Okay, so here's my proposition. I'll give you the hundred thousand you need to go to college if you marry me now, here in Las Vegas.'

I stared at him. 'Marry you?'

'In name only,' he said firmly. 'And for the shortest time possible. As I said, it's a business proposition, not a proposal.' Now he leaned forwards. 'Think about it, Amelie. We get married, I give you a hundred thousand. My parents are furious but powerless. I'm off the hook regarding Isobel Algerson and you can go to college without having to worry about money. A couple of weeks later, we say that we got carried away by the whole Las Vegas vibe, we've realised now that our marriage was a silly mistake, and that we're separating. Then we file for divorce.'

I couldn't believe he was serious. 'We couldn't,' I said. 'It wouldn't work.'

'Why not?'

'Because nobody would believe it. I mean, why would we get married? I work for you, you're my boss. It's not as if we've hung out together or anything.'

'We can say we've been seeing each other secretly.'

I laughed. 'You really think that people would believe that?'

'Why wouldn't they?'

'Because no one would believe that you would actually marry me, not when you are who you are, and I'm who I am.'

He shrugged. 'Stranger marriages have happened. Beautiful models marry old men, young men marry old women, ladies marry tramps. Marriages of convenience.' He paused. 'No strings, I promise. I don't expect anything, except for you to act as if you're happy to be married to me for those first few weeks until we announce that we're separating.'

I shook my head, trying to rid it of the absurdity of what Ned was proposing. But somewhere, I felt the stirrings of excitement at the thought of taking control of my life, of being able to fulfil my dream of going to college so easily. I tried to imagine what it would be like to not have to work part-time to supplement my grant – if I managed to get one – and be able to devote myself fully to studying. It would be total luxury. But.

'I couldn't,' I said.

'Because?'

'Because it wouldn't be right. We'd be tricking people.'

'Who are you concerned about tricking? You said you don't have any family.'

'Well, Carolyn, for a start. I couldn't lie to her, I'd have to tell her the truth.'

He nodded, sat back. 'In that case, let's forget this whole conversation.'

I looked at him, startled. 'Oh.'

'I'm sorry, Amelie, but for it to work, you'd have to agree not to tell anyone that it was purely a business transaction, even once we've separated. But if you feel you have to be straight with Carolyn, I respect that.' He paused. 'Although, if you're worried what Carolyn might think of you, wouldn't she be more understanding if she thought you'd made a silly mistake, rather than a calculated decision?'

It bothered me that he was right. Carolyn would think less of me if I admitted that I'd only married Ned because he offered to give me one hundred thousand pounds.

'She would still wonder where the money came from,' I said.

'I've thought of how to explain that to everyone. Shall I run through it for you?'

'All right. But I still think it's crazy.'

'So, we leave this bar, we go and get married. We need a licence, which I already have.'

I frowned. 'How come?'

'Because yesterday, I had a particularly fraught phone call with my father. He was incensed that I'd come here without telling him, and accused me of trying to escape the weekend with the Algersons. That's when I came up with the whole idea. I made enquiries, discovered that we'd need to get a licence twenty-four hours before the event, and arranged one in case I decided to tell you what I'd been thinking. Because, as you rightly said, it's a pretty crazy idea. But a crazy idea that could work in both our favours.' He paused. 'So, once we're married, I release the news to the press. Tomorrow, when we arrive in England, we go to my house in Wentworth where you'll have your own rooms. At some point, the press will want an interview, during which we'll play the happy couple. A few weeks later, we announce that we've realised our marriage was a mistake and are separating, pending our divorce. We file for divorce, I pay you the hundred thousand that people will think is our divorce settlement, you move back to your apartment. That way, people will never be able to say that you married me for my money.'

'I'm glad you thought of that,' I said. 'I'd hate people to think that of me.'

'But please know that I'm happy to give you more if you want.'

'No.' I shook my head quickly.

'Does that mean you agree?'

'I'll need to think about it.'

He shot back his cuff, glanced at his watch. 'You have approximately forty-five minutes. The ceremony, if you decide to go through with it, is booked for four o'clock.'

'Wow,' I said, my heart racing. 'No pressure then.'

'Actually, no pressure at all. It's entirely up to you.' He nodded to somewhere over my shoulder. 'See that chapel? That's where the ceremony will be. Why don't you go for a walk and think it through? If you decide it's something you'd like to go ahead with, I'll meet you outside at five to four. Wear something nice so that we can take a picture for the press. If not, I'll see you back at the hotel.'

27

Past

I woke up in my hotel room in Las Vegas, and the events of the previous day came flooding back. Had I really gone through with it? I held up my hand, saw the gold band that Ned had placed on my ring finger, and a terrible doubt took hold.

It's fine, it's a business arrangement, that's all. You thought it through and decided that the chance to go to college without having to worry financially was worth the risk.

Now, in the cold light of day, I thought about that risk. But when it came down to it, I couldn't see that it was so very great. I wasn't worried that Ned wouldn't pay me; a hundred thousand pounds was nothing to him. Nor was I afraid that he might want sex, despite telling me that it was purely a business arrangement. In all our time here, he had never done anything to make me uncomfortable, or made a remark that was out of place. People might judge me for being stupid enough to get married on the spur of the moment to a man I barely knew, but the story Ned and I had agreed to tell – that we'd been secretly dating for a few months, and that he whisked me off to Las Vegas with the intention of asking me to marry him – would make it more understandable.

If it hadn't been for Carolyn, I wouldn't have had any misgivings at all. She would be hurt that I'd kept a supposed relationship with Ned from her. It bothered me that I couldn't tell her the truth. But if I did, she'd be angry that I'd married him for money. Except that I hadn't, not really, because I'd given him something in return, a way out of what to him was an impossible situation. To be honest, I couldn't see why he didn't just stand up to his father. But maybe, in wealthy families like his, there were certain things that had to be done out of duty.

I pushed myself up on my pillows, looked at the ring on my hand again. Once I told Carolyn that our marriage was a stupid mistake, it would be fine. And she wouldn't be angry with me for long – I'd be able to tell her in a month, because yesterday was 1 August and Ned and I had agreed that we'd announce our separation on the first of September. Once we had, I'd move back to my apartment and carry on with my life. I'd have to leave my job at *Exclusives,* because no one would expect me to continue working there once we'd separated. But then I'd look for another job to take me through to next September, when I'd finally be able to go to college.

It had actually been fun yesterday. When I arrived at the chapel, Ned had been waiting with a bouquet of flowers and two witnesses. The ceremony was over in fifteen minutes. Outside, we'd posed for a photograph and Ned had joked that his parents were about to get the shock of their lives. We'd walked back to the hotel, had more champagne and a celebratory dinner, then Ned had gone to his room, and I had gone to mine.

I stretched my limbs, sorry that I was going to have to leave this luxurious bed, this beautiful hotel. But I needed to get up, the taxi was coming at ten to take us to the airport.

The hotel phone on the bedside table rang and I smiled that Ned was acting like a husband, checking I was ready.

'Amelie?'

My heart leapt into my mouth; it wasn't Ned, it was Carolyn. If Carolyn was phoning me here, at the hotel – how did she even know I was here? – something must have happened.

'Carolyn, is everything all right?'

'Amelie, thank God. Why haven't you been answering your phone?' She sounded close to tears and my panic increased.

'I left it on the plane; I'll get it back later today, when we land. We're leaving this morning. What's happened, are you all right, is Daniel all right?'

'Yes, yes, what about you, how are you?'

'I'm fine,' I said, puzzled at the urgency in her voice.

'I didn't know where you were; I tried to find out. I phoned *Exclusives,* spoke to Ned's PA, but she wouldn't tell me which hotel you were staying at; she said Ned had left instructions not to be disturbed, and it was more than her life was worth. Amelie, I have to ask, how has Ned been towards you? He hasn't tried to pressure you into anything, has he?'

My heart started thumping. Had she already heard about our marriage? 'What do you mean?' I asked.

'It's just that – Amelie, he assaulted Justine.'

'Assaulted her? Ned assaulted Justine?' I sat down on the bed, my legs suddenly weak. 'I don't understand. He can't have.'

'He did, he turned up at her apartment late at night, he said he needed to speak to her about her contract. She didn't want to let him in but he said he wouldn't be long as Hunter was waiting downstairs in the car. He asked if he could have a coffee and while she was in the kitchen – well, he cornered her, began grabbing her, saying she had teased him for years, that she was an ungrateful bitch, that she owed him for giving her a job in the first place.'

My head was spinning, I could hardly understand what Carolyn was saying.

'But – when was this? Ned's been here with me for the last few days.'

'Last Friday.'

I drew in my breath. The day before we left for Las Vegas.

'It was awful, Amelie,' Carolyn went on. 'She only managed to stop him by grabbing a knife and threatening him with it.'

I clapped my hand over my mouth. 'How is she, how is Justine?'

'She was very shaken, obviously, but she was angry more than anything. She called me as soon as Ned left, and I went over. But you should know, Amelie – she filed a complaint against him, for sexual assault. She didn't want to at first, she said the police wouldn't believe her, and that they would ask her why she let him into her apartment to discuss her contract instead of asking him to wait until they were in the office – which she did, but Ned insisted he needed to see her that night. She said it would be her word against Ned's. But then she realised the seriousness of what he'd done and that if she hadn't grabbed the knife, it could have ended in rape, so we went straight to the police station, and she reported it.'

'I'm glad she did,' I said fiercely. 'He can't be allowed to get away with it.'

'I can't tell you how worried I was when I got your message saying you were on your way to Las Vegas, because I guessed you were with Ned. He hasn't tried anything, has he, made you do anything you were uncomfortable with?'

I swallowed hard. *Uncomfortable with.* The words echoed in my head. I couldn't tell Carolyn about the marriage, not now, not like this. 'No, nothing at all. I'm so sorry you've been worried. I would have told you I was going, but it was a last-minute thing. He said he needed to go to Las Vegas on urgent business and asked if I'd like to go with him. If I'd known about Justine, I'd never have agreed.'

'Vicky said she'd let Ned know that I was trying to contact you and ever since, I've been waiting for you to call. I couldn't get hold of Lina either, and Justine hasn't been answering her phone since I took her home. It's such a mess, Amelie!' Her voice broke and shame flooded through me. 'I needed to find you, make sure you were all right, so I started phoning all the hotels in Las Vegas.'

'Carolyn, I'm so sorry. I didn't know you'd been trying to contact me, Ned didn't tell me. Maybe Vicky didn't tell him.'

'Even if she had, he probably wouldn't have passed the message on in case I told you about his assault on Justine,' Carolyn said, her voice heavy with disgust.

'This is awful.' I was shaking so much I could barely hold the phone. 'I don't know what to do, I don't even want to see him.'

'Just come home, but don't tell him that you know what he did; it's better if you don't say anything for now. I'll keep trying to find Justine. She's not at her apartment, I've been over.'

'Maybe she's with Lina,' I said. 'Maybe Lina has taken her away for a few days, you know, for a change of scene.'

'That's what I've been trying to tell myself. But why aren't either of them answering their phones?'

My eyes flicked to the clock on the bedside table. 'I'm going to have to go, Carolyn, I'm meeting Ned downstairs in the lobby in ten minutes. When you get hold of Justine, please tell her I'm sorry and give her my love.'

28

Present

Something wakes me, the sound of the door closing. I sit up and something falls from my shoulders. My blanket. It's back.

I stretch out my hand and find a tray. The last four had been left inside the door. Does this mean that my punishment is finally over? My spirits lift. I wish I hadn't been asleep when the tray was brought. I've missed my captor, missed his presence.

Maybe it's because my punishment appears to be over, and I no longer need to obsess about lack of food or human contact, my mind keeps returning to the past. So far, I've managed to bury the absolute horror of the few days before Ned and I were kidnapped somewhere deep inside me, terrified that if I gave in to it, grief would make me lose my mind. But now their faces – Justine, Lina, Hunter – loom in the darkness. *Please, not now. Don't let me break now.*

I do everything I can to block them out. I pace the room, counting furiously in an attempt to focus my mind on something other than those memories. When that doesn't work, I lie under my blanket, my eyes shut tight, my fingers in my ears, not wanting to see, not wanting to hear. But nothing works, and sobs rack my body. Aware of Ned being able to hear me, I jam my hand into my mouth so that no sound escapes.

By the time my captor brings my evening tray, despair and loneliness have morphed into a burning resentment.

'Do you even see me?' I spit. 'I mean, do you *see* me – Amelie? Or do you see some poor stupid girl, some poor, stupid, collateral-damage girl? Because that's not who I am. And I want you to know that. And now that I've told you, you can leave. Go back to your worthless life working for violent men who seek to extort money by imprisoning women. I hope you feel good about yourself.'

He has already moved away, and I can't bear that my words have left him unmoved. Groping for the tray, I pick it up, knocking everything off it, and aim blindly for his departing back. I hear a thud, then a grunt.

'Got you!' I yell.

The door slams shut, and I burst into fresh tears.

29

Past

In the hotel room, I dressed quickly, struggling to process what Carolyn had just told me. I couldn't believe that the man I'd spent six days with – the man I'd just married – could have done something so terrible. But Justine wouldn't have made it up.

My fingers were shaking so much I could barely zip up my dress. What would Carolyn think when she heard that Ned and I were married? I needed to tell her face-to-face – and in spite of what Ned had said, I would tell her the truth. There was no way I was going to pretend that Ned and I had been in a secret relationship and that I was so in love with him I'd said yes when he proposed. Our deal was off. I didn't want his money; the thought of it made me sick.

I'd have given anything to be able to say that I hadn't been thinking straight when Ned had put his proposition to me, that the champagne and wine I'd drunk had clouded my judgment. But I couldn't lie, not to myself, not to anyone else. I had gone into our arrangement with my eyes wide open, and my head turned at the idea of living a life of luxury for a month. Waves of shame rolled through me. How could I have been so stupid?

And now there was Justine to worry about. Carolyn had said that she wasn't answering her phone. I suddenly remembered what Ned had said, that she had gone to Paris to interview Ophélie Tessier. Maybe that was why she wasn't answering Carolyn's calls. Or had she never gone, after Ned assaulted her? Because if she'd filed a complaint against Ned, why would she continue working for him? On the other hand, why should she give up a job that she loved, or hide herself away, when she had done nothing wrong? And what about Ned? Did he know about the complaint Justine had filed?

A knock at the door made me jump; it would be someone to collect my luggage. My suitcase was still open on the bed, I closed the lid quickly and opened the door.

Ned was standing there.

'Good morning,' he said, then stopped. 'Is everything all right? You look as if you've seen a ghost.'

I had to stop myself from backing away from him. 'I – I thought we were meeting downstairs,' I stuttered, my heart crashing in my chest.

'It wouldn't look very good if we arrived in the lobby separately,' Ned said, amused. 'Now that we're married.'

I couldn't look at him. I moved to the bed, zipped my suitcase shut. I wanted to attack him, tell him that I knew about Justine, shout and scream at him. But Carolyn had said not to mention anything, and I couldn't make it worse for Justine, so I bit my tongue.

'We need to go,' he said, coming into the room and taking my suitcase from me. 'The car is waiting.'

In a trance, I followed him out of the room. We got into the lift and as it descended to the lobby, I stared at our reflections in the mirrored wall. I recognised Ned but I didn't recognise the girl standing next to him. It looked like me, but it wasn't me.

30

Past

On the flight home, the hostess congratulated us on our marriage.

'A glass of champagne for you, Mrs Hawthorpe?' she asked.

I flinched. I was not Mrs Hawthorpe. And then I realised that in the eyes of the world, I was.

'No, thank you,' I said stiffly.

I pretended to sleep during the flight so that I wouldn't have to talk. When we touched down in Farnborough, Hunter was there to meet us.

'Congratulations, Mrs Hawthorpe,' he said, his voice devoid of emotion. 'On your marriage.'

I frowned, confused by his unfriendliness, until the enormity of what I'd done hit me. How could I have forgotten about Hunter, about the drink we were going to have together? My stomach churned. I wanted to grab his hand, tell him that my marriage to Ned wasn't real, that it was just an agreement. But Ned placed a hand firmly on my back and pushed me towards the open car door.

As I got into the car, I tried to catch Hunter's eye. But without looking at me, he handed Ned a newspaper, open to one of the inside pages. Ned glanced at it and then showed me, and I saw the photograph of me and Ned outside the chapel, and the caption Hawthorpe Heir's Secret Wedding.

Ned smiled. 'Perfect,' he said as Hunter slammed my door shut.

Ned got into the back of the car next to me.

'Straight home, please,' he said, and my heart fluttered. I was sure we'd be going to my apartment first to pick up my clothes and I'd planned to lock the door and refuse to come out.

'Can we go to my apartment to pick up the things that I'll need?' I asked.

'Hunter already has them, they're waiting for you at the house,' Ned said.

My stomach knotted. Again, I tried to catch Hunter's eye, this time in the rearview mirror, but his attention was on the road ahead.

'How did you get my key?' I asked.

But they both ignored me.

Ned's phone rang. He cursed under his breath and let it ring out. It rang again immediately. I glanced at the screen and saw *Dad*. With another curse, Ned answered it.

Jethro Hawthorpe's voice was so loud and angry that I could hear every word he was saying. Realising, Ned turned away from me. But it didn't make any difference.

What the hell do you think you're doing?

'I'm in the car,' Ned said tersely. 'I'll call you when I get home.'

I'm coming over to the house.

'No, don't come over, I said I'll—'

Jethro Hawthorpe had cut the call.

Ned's phone rang again, and again, and again, and again. Eventually, he snatched it up.

'Stop phoning me, all right?' he said angrily, and I was shocked that he would speak to his father like that. 'I mean it, Lina,' he added, before cutting the call.

My heart sank. If I'd known it was Lina, I would have grabbed the phone from him, asked her how Justine was. Except I wasn't meant to know what Ned had done. I glanced at Hunter – did he know? That must have been why Lina was calling, why Ned hadn't wanted to take her call.

Thirty minutes later, we arrived at the house in Wentworth. Hunter dropped us at the door, then drove the car around the side of the house. I walked up three wide steps to the black front door and waited while Ned punched a code into a panel on the right. There was a click, and the heavy door swung open.

I followed Ned into a marbled entrance hall. In front was a vast staircase with a hallway on either side, one to the right and one to the left.

'Your room is on the left at the top of the stairs,' Ned said. 'Hunter will bring your luggage. I'll see you later.'

He walked off down the right-hand hallway. I watched until he was out of sight, then turned and headed for the door. But there was no handle, just a panel on the wall; I would need the code to be able to open it. I tried not to panic. Ned couldn't keep me here against my will. I would phone Carolyn, she would know what to do. Except, I realised, we hadn't picked up my phone at the airport.

I looked around; there had to be a phone somewhere. There wasn't one in the entrance hall so I walked down the left-hand hallway, determined to search until I found one.

There were three doors; behind the first two were a huge sitting room and an equally huge dining room, with internal doors between so that they could become one vast reception area. I moved quickly between lavish sofas and low tables, then moved to the dining room, checking every surface I could see. But there wasn't a phone anywhere.

The third room along was a large kitchen with doors that led onto a terraced seating area. It seemed to have every gadget anyone could wish for except a phone. At the end of the hallway, a door led to a garden at the side of the house. There was one more door; I opened it and saw stairs leading down to a basement.

Back in the entrance hall, I stood for a moment, debating whether to go in search of Ned to ask him where I could find a phone, or continue looking myself. Making a decision, I ran up the marble staircase, counting as I went. I always counted steps, it was something I'd always done – the house where I lived with my father had eleven, Ned's had twenty-four. I arrived on a wide landing with a polished wooden floor, partly covered by an ornate green-and-red runner.

Remembering what Ned had said about my bedroom being on the left, I opened the first door. Like every other room I'd seen, it was huge. My luggage from the trip to Las Vegas was already there; Hunter must have brought it up while I was downstairs. Deflated, I sank onto the king-sized bed. Now I'd missed my chance to explain to him about my marriage to Ned.

Gradually, I realised that all the objects decorating the room – a wooden box, a couple of china bowls, the books, a photo of my mother and father – belonged to me. It felt too much, too intrusive and controlling. I got to my feet and found an en suite shower room, the toiletries from my apartment laid out. There was also a dressing room with my clothes already hanging neatly on the rails. Opening the drawers, I found my T-shirts and underwear, and my cheeks reddened at the thought of Hunter handling my underpants and bras. Anger took hold; he had no right to enter my home and remove my things. I needed to find a phone, fast.

At first, I thought the bedroom next to mine was Ned's bedroom, but its colours – shades of yellow – and a dress neatly draped over the back of a chair, plus two pairs of sensible shoes tucked under it, told me a woman slept there. A live-in housekeeper, maybe? There was no phone on the bedside table and when I continued my search, I found that the two doors on the other side of the landing were locked.

Even angrier now, I ran downstairs and took the right-hand hallway, looking for Ned. It was identical to the other hallway, with three main doors and at the end, a door that led to the outside. I heard Ned's voice coming from behind the middle door. He was on the phone, and from his irritated tone, he was having an argument with someone.

I paused, waiting, listening. But I couldn't hear anything clearly, so I stepped away from the door and traced my steps back down the hallway. I opened a door and found myself in a beautiful wood-panelled library, its shelves filled with hundreds of books, maybe thousands. There were two sets of carved wooden steps on wheels, for reaching to the higher shelves and, in the far corner, two beautiful high-backed armchairs, placed to face the tall windows that looked onto the front of the house. Along the left-hand wall, a set of panelled double doors led to the room where Ned was; I could hear his voice clearer now.

'Look, I've sorted it out,' Ned was saying. 'It was a misunderstanding, I told her I was terminating her contract and she took her revenge.'

His words brought me to a halt. Who was Ned talking about?

I crept closer to the set of doors.

'I don't know how it was leaked to the press, but I've taken care of it, she's not going to press charges.' Ned's voice had risen and there was an edge to it. 'Well, God forbid that your precious foundation should be touched by it . . . No, there's no truth in it, I've already told you and no, there won't be any repercussions – Dad? Dad?' A silence, then a curse, and behind the double doors, I was filled with an impending sense of dread.

Something wasn't right.

31

Present

'I'm sorry,' I say to the man when he arrives. 'I'm sorry for throwing the tray at you, for the things I said. I know it's not your fault, I know that someone is forcing your hand and that you probably hate what you're doing. I know that you'd help me if you could. You're as much a victim in this as I am. If I ever get out of here—'

The door closes, and the room is silent again.

I sit in the darkness and blink so hard I see the edges of star patterns behind my lids. The pads of my fingers pinch at the skin of my arm. To my abductors I barely exist. But I am still here. I'm still alive.

In the bathroom, I score another line on the wall. Two weeks, we've been here two weeks. Why is nothing happening?

I'm in the middle of my first circuit of steps when I hear footsteps in the hall outside. If I can hear them, it means he's wearing shoes. If he's wearing shoes, it means he's coming for me.

I dart back to my corner and huddle under the blanket just as the door opens. I try to make my breathing deep and even, but in my heart, I know that pretending to be asleep won't make him go away.

I'm right. The blanket is removed from me, he pulls me to my feet.

Instead of resisting, I let myself be moved; I need him to think I'm somehow helping him. In return, a hood is put carefully over my head, my hands tied more loosely behind my back. He guides me from the room with hands that feel almost gentle on my shoulders.

The air smells different in the hallway; even through the hood I can sense that it's heavier, dense with sunlight maybe. The skin on my arms prickles as he takes me down the twelve stone steps to the cooler air of the basement, to the room where Ned is being held. I hear the door slam, allow myself to be placed on the chair, then tied to it.

Like before, the hood comes off, and light scorches my eyes before I'm quickly blindfolded. In those few seconds there's no time to see anything, just a flash of light, then darkness again. A hand, hard, ruthless, grips the back of my head, keeping it facing forward. I know it's the other man. It's always the other man who holds me still.

It reaches me then, the same sour smell, but stronger. Ned. He's here, next to me. They've lined us up, side by side.

'State your name, say you have a message for Jethro Hawthorpe. The message is that if he doesn't pay up, his son will die.' A pause. 'Speak.'

'No.'

The voice becomes threatening. 'State your name—'

'No.'

'Give the message, for fuck's sake, otherwise they'll kill us,' Ned snarls.

'I don't care if I die,' I say.

'Well, I do, so just give the fucking message!'

The hand tightens its grip. 'Speak!'

I can feel the muscles in my neck going into spasm and fear flickers inside me.

'My name is Amelie Hawthorpe,' I say, trying to keep my breath even. 'This is a message for Jethro Hawthorpe. If you don't pay up, your son will die.' I take another breath. 'So don't pay up, he deserves to die, he's a m—'

The air shifts in a flash of movement as Ned slams into the side of me. I feel my chair toppling, hear the man cursing as my neck is ripped from his grasp. I hit the floor and stars explode in my head.

When I next open my eyes, I'm in my room. I groan, close them again. Despite the pain in my head, I smile. Ned isn't coping; his privilege and wealth, so powerful in the outside world, mean nothing in here. Here, we are equal. But I am mentally stronger.

I sit up, wincing. My face throbs with heat and when I touch my fingers to my skin, I find the puffiness of a large bruise down the left-hand side of my face. And farther up, above my temple, a lump the size of a small egg, the result of being knocked to the ground by Ned. It hurts, but it was worth it. My only regret is that the video they were filming will never be sent.

I grope for the blanket, glad it's still there. After my performance, they could have taken it from me. I wrap it around me, stand up. But I'm so dizzy that I quickly crouch down, and crawl to the bathroom on all fours. Perching on the rim of the toilet, I wet the washcloth, lather soap into it and wipe my face, wincing at the feel of rough towel against tender skin. It's only now, in the dim light, that I realise my vision has been affected by the fall. Everything is hazy, as if I'm looking through a piece of gauze. Concussion, I have a concussion.

I want to weep. My act of defiance means I'll have to postpone my next escape by several days. I realise something else:

what I said in the basement might have felt good, but it was foolish.

When the man comes with my tray, I appeal to him.

'Just promise me one thing. When Jethro Hawthorpe pays the ransom, don't release me with Ned. Take him to wherever you agree to take him but drop me off somewhere else.' He's moving away, I reach for his arm, my fingers brush his sleeve, then dangle in midair. 'Because if you release me at the same time as him,' I call after him desperately, 'he'll kill me!'

The key turns in the lock. He's gone.

32

Past

I waited silently in the library, giving Ned time to calm down, thinking about what I'd overheard. If it was Justine he'd been talking about, why did he say that she wasn't pressing charges? Had she changed her mind? Ned said he'd sorted it out; had he pressured her into withdrawing the statement she made to the police by threatening to fire her if she didn't?

Leaving the library, I turned right in the hallway and knocked at the next door along.

'Yes?' Ned called.

I went in. The room was huge, with the same tall windows as in the library, and two sets of double doors, a pair to the left, and a pair to the right leading to the library where I'd been a moment ago. Ned was sitting behind a desk the size of a ping-pong table, slouched in a black leather chair.

'We forgot to pick up my phone at the airport in Farnborough,' I began. 'Is there a phone I can use? I'd like to tell Carolyn I'm back.'

'Sure.' His phone was on the desk. He picked it up, held it out to me. 'Here you are.'

I hesitated. I wanted to tell Carolyn about the conversation I'd just overheard between Ned and his father, but if I walked out of his study with his phone in my hand, he might be suspicious. And I didn't want him to guess that I knew what he'd done.

'Thanks,' I said, taking the phone from him.

I tapped in Carolyn's number, glad that when she'd first given it to me, it had meant so much to have someone's phone number that I'd learned it by heart. I waited for her to answer, planning to ask her, quite casually, if she'd seen Lina and Justine recently, if she'd been for a coffee with them. There would be nothing suspicious in that and at least I'd know that they were okay without asking Carolyn outright.

But she didn't pick up.

'No answer?' Ned asked, and I realised he'd been watching me.

'No,' I said. 'I'll send her a message.'

I added Carolyn as a contact in Ned's phone, selected WhatsApp from his menu, and typed:

Hi Carolyn, it's Amelie, on Ned's phone. Just wanted to let you know I'm back from LV, safe and sound. I wanted to add that if she'd heard that Ned and I were married, I would explain everything when we met. But how could I, when Ned might check what I wrote? I thought for a moment, then typed, I can't wait to tell you all about it, maybe you can come and see me at Ned's? I added two kisses and handed the phone back to him.

'Anything else?' he enquired, when I stayed where I was.

'Yes. It's about my apartment.'

'What about it?'

'Everything that was in it is here. You didn't give notice on it, did you?'

'No, of course not.'

'So I can move back into it, once we've said that we're separating?'

'Yes. Now, is that all? I have work to do.'

'No, that's not all.' He looked up at me, surprised by my tone. 'What about my job?'

'You work for me, don't you?'

'Yes.'

'Then, until we separate, you'll work for me from here.'

'I don't have a laptop; it broke, remember?'

'I'll sort it out.'

'Can I go and pick up my phone? Maybe Hunter can take me.'

He turned his attention back to his computer screen. 'No, I'm afraid not, I need him to run some errands for me.'

I flushed at his dismissive tone, and at the use of the word *errands*.

'I'd like to go out anyway.'

'I'm afraid that's not possible, not today. The press is already camped outside the gates. The minute you walk through them, they'll be on you like a pack of vultures. We agreed we'd meet the press together, so that's what we'll do. But not today. Now, go and rest, have a swim, do whatever it takes to get over the jet lag. It's a nice house, it has a swimming pool and a gym. Think of it as an extended holiday. I'll see you later for dinner. My housekeeper has gone to see her family in Hungary for a few weeks so perhaps you could prepare something. Or I can order in. Seven-thirty, in the dining room, in the left wing.' He raised his head, and for the first time, I saw steel in his grey eyes. 'And by the way, Amelie, don't come down here again. You have the run of the rest of the house and the gardens, but the rooms in the right wing are my private quarters.' He paused. 'I trust you understand.'

33

Present

There are voices in the basement. I move the mattress and lie on my stomach to listen.

'. . . wasn't a clever move on your part.'

'She deserved it. Stupid bitch.' Ned's voice.

'It's set us back several days. We needed that recording.' A pause. 'So, what are we going to do, Ned? Your dad's not paying up and your wife won't beg for your life. Seems nobody cares if you live or die.'

'Kill her.'

'Your wife?'

'Yes. Kill her and deliver the body to my father. He'll pay up then.'

'I'm not so sure. After all, what is she to him? Better to send him something of yours, an ear or a finger.'

'I think that would be a mistake.'

'I'm sure you do.' The voice is mocking, amused. 'I'll be back, Ned. And who knows, maybe I'll have a knife with me.'

I lie there, furious. How dare he tell them to kill me?

Jumping to my feet, I begin thumping on the wall above where he's being held. I want to infuriate him, I want him to be crazy with rage, I want him to know what it is to be at the mercy of someone else, to be unable to stop something from happening.

It seems that Ned is at the end of his tether too. He reacts quickly and violently to the thumping.

'Shut up!' he screams from below.

But I don't stop. His anger drives me on, I feed off it, so that when my arms are tired and my fists bruised, I use my body, throwing myself against the wall repeatedly, using each of my shoulders in turn. I don't stop until, exhausted, I collapse onto the mattress – and then, when I feel I've waited long enough to lull him into a false sense of security, I devise a new torture, and begin a slow, evenly spaced thump against the wall with the heel of each foot in turn – *thump-thump, thump-thump, thump-thump*. It feels so good.

When the man comes with my tray, I'm still *thump-thump*-ing my heels against the wall, and Ned, hoarse from shouting, is weeping uncontrollably. I don't stop as he crosses the room and places my tray on the floor, and when he leaves, without the slightest indication that he has witnessed anything out of the ordinary, I retaliate with a drumroll of fury, acknowledg-ing that the thumping hadn't only been for Ned. During all those hours, I'd been expecting one of the men to burst into the room and make me stop the incessant noise. But no one had come; either they were in a different part of the house where the noise didn't affect them, or they were happy to let me continue enraging Ned.

I bring my feet down from the wall, hating my invisibility, hating again my inability to provoke a reaction in them, in him. My heels are throbbing, I imagine them red and blis-tered, like when I walk too long in heels. An image pushes its way into my mind, red high-heeled shoes, scrabbling uselessly on a marble floor. I rush to blank it out, but it stays, and a solitary tear glides down my cheek.

34

Past

Ned called me; the press was waiting for us at the gates. It was five days since we'd arrived back from Vegas and I still hadn't been able to leave the house.

Ned always had an excuse as to why I couldn't. I never saw him during the day, only in the evening for dinner. I didn't mind making it; I'd always enjoyed cooking and it gave me something to do.

Ned was waiting in the hall below and as I walked down the marble staircase, he ran a critical eye over me. I was wearing a pink sleeveless dress and my hair hung loose around my shoulders. He nodded approvingly, took an engagement ring from his pocket.

'Here,' he said, taking my hand and sliding it on my finger, next to the gold wedding band that I only usually wore when I went down to dinner. I hadn't at first, I couldn't bear to see it on my finger. But when Ned saw me without it the first evening, he'd made me go back and fetch it.

I shuddered internally at his touch, automatically thinking of Justine. She would know by now that I had married Ned and would see it as a terrible betrayal. If only I could see her, see Carolyn, explain to them what had happened. I'd hoped that Carolyn might call me back on Ned's phone but so far, there hadn't been anything and I was scared that she couldn't bring herself to speak to me.

There had been so many times when I'd wanted to ask Ned about Justine, ask him if her interview with Ophélie Tessier had gone well. But an inner voice – the same inner voice that told me to be very, very careful, that I didn't know the true nature of the man I'd allowed myself to be caught up with – warned me not to.

'It's not real, is it?' I asked, staring at the biggest diamond I'd ever seen, and Ned laughed.

I pulled my hand away quickly and we moved to the front door. Ned turned his back to me and tapped the code into the panel. I tried to lean around him to see the numbers, but he sensed my movement and bent over the keypad, blocking my vision. The door clicked open, and a clamour of voices reached me. Ned took my hand and instinctively, I tried to pull it away.

'We need to keep up appearances,' he reminded me, holding it firmly.

Hunter appeared. I hadn't seen him since the day he'd picked me and Ned up at the airport, and I could feel his eyes on my back as he followed us down the long gravel drive. As we approached the gates, they swung open and I saw twenty or so reporters waiting, with cameras and microphones. They surged forward and Hunter stepped quickly in front of us, spreading his arms, motioning at them to keep back.

The questions started.

'Mr Hawthorpe, can you tell us about your new wife?'

'Apart from the fact that she's perfect?' he said. 'As you can see for yourselves,' he added, turning to me with a smile.

'Amelie, you worked for Mr Hawthorpe?'

'I still do,' I replied. 'Nothing has changed.'

'Were you surprised when he proposed?'

I blinked in the flash of lights from the cameras, suddenly overwhelmed.

'Yes, she was,' Ned said smoothly.

'It seems to have been a whirlwind romance. You only met four months ago, is that right, Amelie?'

'We met nearly a year ago, at a party,' Ned said, stepping in again. 'And I knew straightaway that there was something special about Amelie. I couldn't believe my luck when she started working at *Exclusives*. It seemed like destiny.'

'Can you tell us about your trip to Vegas? Did you intend to ask her to marry you or was it a spur-of-the-moment decision?'

Ned shook his head. 'I planned it weeks ago. But I didn't want Amelie to guess what I was up to, so I pretended I had to go on a sudden business trip, and told her I needed her to come with me to sit in on the meetings. Even when I didn't take her along to any meetings she still didn't guess. There were no meetings, of course, I used the time to choose the rings, get the marriage licence, find witnesses and sort out all the other things.'

The lies tripped off his tongue so easily.

'Can we see the ring, Amelie?' someone shouted.

Ned pulled my hand forward and the diamond sparkled in the sunlight. He put his arm around me as the reporters took more and more photos and I stared emotionless into the crowd as they called to me, asking me to smile. And then, out of the corner of my eye, I saw Carolyn.

Relief washed over me as our eyes locked. I moved to go to her, but Ned's arm tightened around my waist. I tried shifting away from him, but his grip was so strong that it pinched my skin.

Carolyn held up her phone and pointed to it with her other hand. 'I don't believe you!' she called over the noise of the reporters.

'Mr Hawthorpe, is there any truth in the rumour that a charge of sexual assault was recently filed against you?' another voice shouted, drowning out Carolyn.

There was a sudden silence as everyone turned to look at the woman who'd asked the question. Some of the reporters moved aside to give her a direct view of Ned, and I recognised her as the woman who had approached him at the *Exclusives* party. Beside me, Ned froze.

'I'll ask you again, Mr Hawthorpe. Can you confirm that a charge of sexual assault was recently filed against you?' the woman repeated.

Chaos broke out as journalists began thrusting their microphones towards Ned, asking the same question, until Hunter stepped hurriedly in front of us, protecting Ned. As the gates began to close, I heard Carolyn call out again.

'Her name is Justine Elland! The woman Ned Hawthorpe assaulted is Justine Elland!' She tried to push her way through the throng of journalists. 'Where is she, Mr Hawthorpe? Where is Justine?'

My mind was spinning as Ned walked me back to the house. Justine was still missing. And what had Carolyn meant, she didn't believe me? She'd been pointing to her phone, but the only message I'd sent her since my return was the one from Ned's phone, saying that I'd arrived back safe and sound, and suggesting that she came to Ned's so that I could tell her about the trip. There had been nothing for her not to believe. Unless Ned had sent her another message, pretending to be me.

'Find out who that journalist is,' Ned snapped to Hunter.

'The one who asked about the sexual assault. She's already bothered me twice; there won't be a third time.'

He let go of me then, and I ran upstairs. I tried to get into the two rooms that led out onto the front of the house, so that I could shout down to Carolyn. But they were still locked. I ran to my bedroom and rushed to the window, because if I shouted loud enough, she might hear me. But when I pulled at the handle, the window wouldn't move. My chest was pounding; what was I doing here? I took a breath, calmed myself. Now that Carolyn knew something was wrong, she would come and rescue me.

35

Present

The silence around me is suffocating, the loneliness heavier today.

My fingers pick at the blanket; I can feel dried food, porridge probably. When am I going to get out of here? Why hasn't Jethro Hawthorpe paid the ransom yet? Even if he is angry with Ned, wouldn't he still want him back? He's lost one son already, and I know from the foundation that he cares about people. Does he know I'm here too? He must. For a moment I imagine what it would be like to be rescued, the police storming in, the shouts and searchlights blinding me. It feels so real that I squint in the darkness.

I move to the window. It reminds me that there is a world out there and I feel even more stifled than I did before. I need to see daylight. I run my hand down the left-hand side of the board, remembering how I tried to jam my spoon between it and the window frame to widen the gap. If only there was something else I could use.

I think for a moment, then go to the bathroom, tear the cardboard lid from the box of tampons, then tear it in half, and in half again. Clutching the four pieces of cardboard, I go back to the window, wishing there was a way to keep the light on in the bathroom once the door was open, so that I could see what I was doing.

Taking one of the pieces of cardboard, I locate the weak spot – the place where I managed to pry the nail out – and push it into the minuscule gap between the board and the window. It goes in quite easily, so I push another piece on top of the first one. Bending, I put my eye close to the cardboard and squint. Nothing, not even the tiniest glimmer of daylight. I force another piece in, take another look. My heart leaps – is that a pinprick of light I can see or is it my imagination? I take the fourth piece of cardboard, fold it in half, jam it in on top of the others, determined to widen the gap a little more. I squint again; it's daylight I can see, I'm sure of it.

I remove the cardboard, grab hold of the edge of the board, wedge my fingertips into the gap, and pull as hard as I can. I don't feel it's made any difference until I take another look. I can definitely see daylight.

The thrill is incredible. I know I'll never be able to get the board off the window, I've accepted that. But to be able to visibly see that time isn't standing still, to be able to track the passing of day into night through the tiny gap I've made feels like a huge achievement.

I take another look, drink in the sliver of daylight. Then, worried that my captor might arrive and see what I've done, I take the pieces of cardboard back to the bathroom and hide them in the cupboard.

36

Past

I heard a commotion in the hallway below and jumped off my bed. Hurrying to the top of the stairs, I looked over the balustrade. A man I recognised as Jethro Hawthorpe was standing just inside the front door, immaculate in a dark suit and tie, a pristine white shirt visible under his jacket. Ned, his arms outstretched, was trying to stop him from coming any farther.

'What are you doing here, Dad?'

'What the hell was that about?' Jethro Hawthorpe thundered, pushing past him. 'That fiasco with the press? It's all over the news. I thought you said those charges against you had been dropped?'

'They have been,' Ned said.

'So how come the press got wind of it?'

'Let's talk in my study, shall we?'

I waited until they were no longer in sight, then ran down the stairs and tiptoed along the hallway to the library. Closing the door carefully behind me, I moved quietly to the double doors.

'It's an occupational hazard, Dad,' I heard Ned saying. 'When I terminate contracts, people get upset.'

'Let me get this straight – this woman decided to accuse you of sexual assault for no other reason than revenge?'

'That's right.'

'And you think the press is going to accept that?'

'Why shouldn't they? I told the police what happened, and they accepted it.'

'For now,' Jethro Hawthorpe said darkly. 'What if this woman changes her mind about not pressing charges?'

'She won't. I paid her off, she's gone back to France, where she's originally from. Nobody will go to the trouble of contacting her there.'

'You paid her off?' I could hear the frown in Jethro Hawthorpe's voice.

'That's right.'

'But I thought there was nothing to her accusation?'

'There wasn't. There isn't! But what else was I supposed to do, let a court case drag on? Imagine how that would have affected your precious foundation.'

'The stench of sexual assault will still linger,' Jethro Hawthorpe snapped. 'You did see the article in the *Mail*, didn't you, while you were away getting married? "Ned Hawthorpe: Mr Nice Guy, or Sexual Predator?" They're not going to leave it alone. And what about this ridiculous marriage of yours? Don't insult me by telling me you married for love.'

'It's none of your business, Dad.'

'Well, I hope you had the sense to get her to sign a prenup.' There was a silence. 'Are you completely crazy?' Jethro Hawthorpe exploded. 'Have you any idea how much she would be entitled to if you divorce?'

'We have an agreement. In case of a divorce, she gets fifty thousand, nothing more.'

I took a step back. Fifty thousand?

'She agreed to that in writing, did she?'

'No, but I'm going to get Carr to draw something up.'

'And you expect her to sign it?'

'Yes.'

Jethro Hawthorpe snorted. 'Then you're even more stupid than I thought.' There was the scrape of a chair being pushed back. 'I need to go.' Then a pause. 'Remember, Ned, the slightest whiff of anything that could harm the foundation, I'll publicly disown you.'

37

Present

Deep in sleep, I barely have time to register his hands on my shoulders, the hood coming over my head, my hands being tied behind my back before being hustled from the room.

The need to focus on going down the stairs to the basement jolts me to the reality of what is happening. Isn't it the middle of the night? Why would he come for me in the middle of the night? My heart pounds when I remember the door Ned and I came through three weeks ago, that led from the outside to the basement. Is that where we're heading, outside? Has their patience run out? My mind spins as I imagine being made to kneel, then shot. I falter, stumble, almost fall down the stairs. But his hands steady me, and the firm but gentle pressure on my shoulders feels oddly reassuring.

I hear a door being unlocked and feel a rush of relief when I'm pushed inside and the usual routine follows: bound to a chair, my hood removed, my eyes blindfolded.

'Ned thinks we should kill you,' a voice says, the voice of the second man. This time, it doesn't come from behind me, it comes from directly in front of me.

'If you think Jethro Hawthorpe will pay up if my body is delivered to him, you're making a mistake.' My voice is strong, but my hands are shaking.

'Why is that?'

'Because I'm nothing to him. Better to cut off something of Ned's and send it through the mail. But, as nobody seems keen to have him back, you might be wasting your time.'

To my right, I hear muffled sounds. Ned is here too. They must have gagged him.

I hear the sound of something being ripped off. Tape.

'What do you have to say about that, Ned?' the other man asks.

'Kill her,' Ned snarls. His voice is muffled but the hatred still clear. He must be hooded. My nose picks up his smell, but fainter. They've placed him farther away from me this time.

'Do you know why he wants you to kill me?' I say. 'It's to save him from doing it himself. I know something about him, something he did, something that would send him to prison for a very long time. If you let me go, I'll tell you—' A strip of tape comes over my mouth, silencing me. I twist my head away, but it's no use.

'I think she has something, Ned,' the other man says. 'I mean, why would your father pay up if we send her body to him?'

'Because he'd be worried that I'd be next.'

'But she has a point when she says that your family doesn't seem to want you back. It's been three weeks. Your father is playing a dangerous game. He knows the score, he knows the longer he takes, the more he'll have to pay. Yet, he's in no hurry to pay, in no hurry to get you back.' There's a pause. 'Do you know what your mother did yesterday, Ned? She played tennis. Not only did she play tennis, but she also won at tennis. I have photos to prove it. Does that strike you as the behaviour of someone whose son is missing? Either your father hasn't told her you've been kidnapped, or she doesn't seem particularly bothered. Which is it, do you think?'

I almost feel sorry for Ned.

Ned doesn't answer, so the man continues talking.

'I have to ask, Ned – did you do something to piss off your family? Is that why they're not keen to get you back?'

'They don't believe you're serious, that's all,' Ned says. 'That's why you should kill her. They need to know you're ruthless.'

'Maybe you're right.'

'I know I am.'

'So, you won't mind if we kill her?'

A harsh laugh from Ned. 'Be my guest.'

'All right.'

To my horror, I hear a gun being cocked. Panic courses through me; I don't want to die like this, I can't die like this, tied to a chair. I strain against the cord that binds me, try to shout out from behind the tape, but I am held still. And then, an almighty bang, and a terrible ringing in my ears, followed by silence so deathly I think I've been shot. I wait to feel pain – but there's none, just a hand that comes over my mouth, silencing me further, pulling my head back against him, making sure I can't move. Did they shoot Ned?

'Shit.' Ned's voice reaches me. 'Did you really do it?'

'You told us to.'

'Is she dead?'

'I'd say so. A bullet to the head is usually fatal.' A pause. 'Get her out of here before she bleeds all over the place. Make sure she's dumped on Jethro Hawthorpe's doorstep. If you can't get near enough, throw her body over the fence. He'll see it soon enough.'

The cord holding me to the chair is cut, shock has set in, my body is limp, I'm dragged from the room as a body would be dragged from a room, arms hooked under my shoulders, my feet dragging on the ground until I'm in the corridor outside and the door slams behind us. I feel myself being lifted from the floor and as I am carried swiftly up the stairs, he scrunches me into him, making me small so that my feet don't smash off the walls.

In the room, he lowers me to the mattress, quickly rips the tape from my mouth. Shock has set in, and I begin hyperventilating. I curl into a ball, trying to shut out the pain in my chest, but he pushes me upright, leans me against the wall. Tears stream from my eyes as I gasp short panicky breaths, trying desperately to get air into my lungs. But it's impossible. My mind spirals; I'm going to die.

And then, something penetrates my fear – his breathing deep and slow so close to my ear I can feel the warmth of his breath. I latch onto it, try to match him breath for breath, a long inhale, a long exhale. It takes a while, but I get there. My breathing slows, the pain in my chest lessens. Tremors run through me; vomit pushes up into my throat. I swallow it down and continue to breathe, slowly, calmly.

'Thank you,' I whisper, when I can speak again.

He places a finger against my mouth, a sign to make no noise. Something settles around my shoulders, my blanket. And then he leaves.

38

Past

I sat under the shade of an oak tree, my back resting against its trunk, my body exhausted with a mix of stifling heat and desperation. I'd spent the morning trying to look nonchalant as I walked around the grounds, when I was in fact desperately seeking a way out of Ned's property. It was surrounded, on all sides, by a twelve-foot-high wall; the only way out was through the front gates, which were worked electronically, like the front door. It was hard to accept that for the moment, I was a prisoner in this house, and I was becoming increasingly panicked.

Last night, during dinner, Ned had become impatient when I'd asked again if I could go out.

'Those journalists are still hanging around,' he'd said. 'If you go out, you'll be mobbed. I'm used to dealing with the press. I know what to say, how much to give them. I think you'd find it overwhelming facing them on your own.' He'd paused. 'I'm only protecting you, Amelie. I don't want you saying anything you shouldn't be saying.'

Or contradicting his version of events.

'But I really want to see my friends.'

'You can, in three weeks' time.'

'Have there been any messages from Carolyn?'

He dabbed his mouth with a napkin. 'If there had been, I would have told you.' He leaned across the table towards me.

'Look, I'm only insisting that you don't leave the house until we announce our separation. Then you're free to leave, go back to your apartment, tell the world we made a mistake.'

'What about my computer? Has it arrived? You said you'd ordered me one two days ago.'

'I'll get Hunter to chase it.' He hardened his gaze. 'I hope I don't have to remind you, Amelie, that you went into this with your eyes wide open.'

He was right, I had. The thought of the money made my face burn with shame. I would take it, then give it to a charity that had nothing to do with the Hawthorpe family.

I picked up the sun hat I'd been wearing and fanned myself with it. There was no air today; even the birds were quiet, their energy sapped by the intensity of the sun's rays. The gentle sound of water trickling from one of the garden's many water features was a welcome distraction. If it hadn't been for Ned's attack on Justine, I realised, I would probably have been happy to wait out the month in this beautiful house. But now, that horrific reality aside, it also dawned on me that the marriage I'd entered into so casually would always be with me. It was something I hadn't considered: that my past would always include that I was married and divorced by the age of twenty.

I hated that I still hadn't said anything to Ned about his attack on Justine; it made me ashamed, almost complicit. But I didn't trust Ned, the lies he told. Justine hadn't gone to Paris to interview Ophélie Tessier, as he had said. She was in France, but she'd left because he'd paid her off in exchange for dropping the charges against him. If it was true, it was understandable that Justine hadn't been answering Carolyn's phone calls. She would have been too embarrassed to admit that she'd allowed Ned to buy her silence.

I shifted uncomfortably on the straw-like grass. I could hardly judge Justine for dropping charges against Ned in exchange for money. I wondered if she had been offered a hundred thousand like me. I remembered Ned's conversation with his dad, and his lie about our agreement having been for fifty thousand pounds. *Good luck with that, Ned,* I thought grimly. Because if he tried to cheat me out of even a penny of the hundred thousand – well, thanks to my father, I had a plan.

39

Present

Tears of bewilderment and exhaustion fall from my eyes. I've tried to make sense of what happened in the basement, but I can't.

I've replayed it so many times in my head that the sound of the gunshot ricochets incessantly in my ears. And I still don't understand. Why did they pretend to kill me? Why do they want Ned to think I'm dead?

Remembering how Ned didn't care that I was supposedly dead, my tears flow faster. There was no remorse that his wife of a few weeks – his damage limitation wife, because that's all I ever was to him – had been shot. There were no recriminations, just a question – is she dead?

There'd been an argument after; I heard shouting from somewhere in the house, the kitchen, I think. One of the voices was the other abductor's, the other was deeper, did it belong to the man who usually came to my room? Who had placed his finger against my lips, so that I would be quiet? I close my eyes and fall asleep.

When I wake, he's in the room.

'I don't understand,' I whisper. 'Can you explain what happened down there, why you pretended to shoot me?'

But, as always, he doesn't answer. If I could scream, I would. My fingers itch to hurl the tray after him again as he leaves the room.

It hits me then, that I've had this weapon all along. Why hadn't I thought of it before? I play it out in my mind. The man stoops to place my tray on the floor and I upend it, sending the porridge over him. And while he's trying to work out what has happened, I grab the tray and smash it over his head. Then the same scenario as before – I get out of the room, lock him in, except that this time, instead of edging my way down the hallway, I run. I know my way now, I know there's nothing to trip me, I know that once past the double doors of the room farther along the hallway, I'll be able to see light under the kitchen door. I know that it won't be locked, I know there are French windows, I know there are things I could use in the kitchen to smash them open if I had to. And in the kitchen, there will be knives, to protect myself with.

My captor might have showed me kindness, but I will hurt him if I need to. I'm angry with him, angry that despite seemingly saving my life, it's made no difference. He is still keeping me in this room, in the dark. And if Jethro Hawthorpe does pay up, and my captor doesn't do as I asked, and I'm released with Ned, I'll never be safe. Because Ned will come after me, and when he finds me, he will kill me.

40

Past

I could feel Ned's eyes on me across the table.

'Is something wrong?' he asked.

'I was just wondering how Justine's interview with Ophélie Tessier went,' I said. 'The day we left for Vegas, you told me she was going to Paris to interview her.'

He did his usual thing of taking his napkin and dabbing at his lips, buying himself time. Was he going to continue lying to me, or would he tell me the truth?

'I'm afraid I wasn't quite truthful with you,' he admitted. 'But it came from a good place. I knew how much you liked Justine so I didn't want to upset you by telling you that I had to let her go.'

'Let her go? You mean, you fired her?'

'Yes, I'm afraid so.'

'Why?'

'Because I found out something unsavoury about her, something that would tarnish the reputation of the magazine.'

'Unsavoury? Like what?' I had to play along; he held the key to my freedom. 'It's just that I know Justine, and I can't imagine her doing anything that would hurt the magazine. It's not as if she gets drunk, or does drugs, or—'

A light went on in Ned's eyes. 'That's exactly it,' he cut in. 'I found out that she'd been taking drugs. And, as you know, we have a no-drugs policy at the magazine, because of what happened to my brother. I had no choice, I had to let her go.'

I felt suddenly sick. When he had been speaking to his father, Ned had never said why he had terminated Justine's contract, and Jethro Hawthorpe had never asked. I didn't know what Ned would have come up with if he'd been put on the spot – but now, I'd supplied him with the perfect excuse for firing her.

'I don't believe it,' I said loudly. 'I know Justine, she wouldn't touch drugs.'

Ned pushed his chair back. 'Well, there's a lesson for you, Amelie. We don't always know people as well as we think.'

'Don't worry, it's one I've already learned,' I hissed, as he walked from the room.

41

Present

I walk to the window, the strips of cardboard in my hands, and wedge them in the gap between it and the wooden board. I bend to look through the gap, but there's no glimmer of light. I straighten up, puzzled. It's not been long since I was brought my porridge, I should be able to see a sliver of daylight. I jam my fingers into the gap, make it a little wider, as I've done before. I still can't see daylight. Was it my imagination, those other times?

Voices reach me, they're talking downstairs. I move to my corner, push the mattress from the wall.

'I have news, Ned,' I hear his abductor say. 'Dumping your wife's body on your father's doorstep seems to have had the desired effect. He wants to talk.'

'You should have killed her earlier,' Ned says.

'Maybe. But if we had, we wouldn't have got such a great payout.'

'What do you mean?'

'Do you know how much we initially asked for?'

'No.'

'Take a guess.'

'I don't know – a million?'

'We asked for a pound, Ned. One pound to get you back. And you know what? Your father refused. Imagine that.'

I frown at the mention of a pound. Why would they only ask for a pound?

The same thought has occurred to Ned.

'You expect me to believe it?' he sneers. 'That you asked for a pound and my father refused to pay it?'

'It's true. When we told him that if he didn't pay the pound, we'd double it to two pounds the next day, and continue doubling the amount for every day that he refused to pay, do you know what he did? He laughed.'

My heart almost stops.

'What the fuck?' Ned says, his voice rising. 'Who *are* you? What did that bitch tell you?'

I flinch at the fury in his voice, my mind reeling, echoing Ned's question. Who are these people?

'Yes, your father didn't take us seriously at first,' the man goes on, ignoring Ned's outburst. 'Which, considering you've already been here twenty-three days, is going to end up costing him a lot of money.'

'And you think my father can't afford a few thousand pounds?' Ned is all bravado now.

'Work it out, Ned. Twenty-three days. I think you'll find it comes to a lot more than a few thousand pounds.'

The door below slams shut, I hear Ned curse. I stay as I am, too stunned to move. How is it possible? They can't know about the postnup, it must be a coincidence.

42

Past

Ned called me to his study. There was a man with him in a smart suit and tie, polished shoes, black-rimmed glasses, a black bag on the floor beside him. He sat across from Ned, his laptop perched precariously on the edge of the desk, as if he was worried about taking up too much space.

'Darling, this is Paul Carr, my father's solicitor. He has a document for you to sign.'

The *darling* – a warning that I needed to play the game – set my teeth on edge.

'What is it?' I asked.

'A postnup,' Ned explained. 'In case we ever divorce.'

I sat down in the chair next to Paul Carr, and took the paper Ned held out to me. It stated that Ned and I were married on Thursday, 1 August, 2019, in Las Vegas and the terms were simple: if we separated, I would receive fifty thousand pounds.

Fifty thousand. I kept my head bent over the document so that Ned couldn't see my anger. How dared he? But I had prepared for this, I knew exactly how I was going to play it.

I looked up. 'I'm sorry, darling, I can't sign this.'

'What do you mean?'

'It's just that I don't think fifty thousand is very fair.'

His face tightened in annoyance. 'How much do you want?'

'A million.'

His mouth dropped open. 'A million! You're joking, aren't you?'

I forced a laugh. 'Yes, actually, I am. Even if we separate, I don't want any of your money.'

Another frown. 'You need to accept something.'

I'd been expecting him to say that. If it came down to it, he needed to be able to prove that I'd agreed to marry him for money, that he hadn't coerced me into it.

'Why?' I asked innocently.

'Because we need to have a written agreement. In Las Vegas, we agreed that I would draw up a document for you to sign when we got back, mentioning a settlement in case of separation.'

I looked him square in the eye. 'I don't remember it being fifty thousand, though.'

'That is what we agreed,' he said, daring me to contradict him.

I allowed him to hold my gaze for a moment longer, then dropped my eyes in defeat.

'All right, then. If I must accept something, I only want a pound.'

He stared at me. 'A pound?'

'Yes. A pound doubled for every day that we are married, before we separate.'

'Doubled? I don't follow.'

'It's simple,' I explained. 'A pound on day one. On day two, my pound is doubled to two pounds, on day three, my two pounds becomes four pounds, on day four, eight pounds, day five, sixteen pounds, day six – today – thirty-two pounds—'

'I can count,' Ned said. He looked at me in amusement. 'Is that really what you want?'

'Yes.'

Beside me, Paul Carr frowned. 'But if you remain married for some time, it could add up to quite a—'

'A month,' I said quickly. 'I would only want it for the first month of our marriage.'

Ned gave a small nod of understanding. A month was the length of time we'd agreed to stay married before separating. Paul Carr, however, raised an eyebrow.

'A month? We stop the clock, so to speak, at thirty days. Is that what you mean?'

I thought of my father, my inspiration for this. I didn't know what the doubling thing would come to but I remembered how he'd laughed and told me I was clever when I'd asked for an extra day. Maybe that was the key.

'Thirty-one days,' I said. I looked pointedly at Ned. 'After all, some months have thirty-one days.'

He gave me another nod of understanding. August had thirty-one days, and we had married on the first.

'Done,' Ned said. 'If that's really what you want.'

'It is.'

Paul Carr shifted in his chair. 'I think it might be prudent if I make a few calculations—'

'I haven't got time,' Ned said impatiently. 'Just draw it up.'

'I really—'

'Now,' Ned barked.

Five minutes later, two copies of the amended document whirred out of the printer by Ned's desk. He ran his eye over one of the copies, then signed both and passed them to me. I read carefully, checking the wording.

'In the event of a separation between Ned Jethro Haw-thorpe and Amelie Maude Lamont, Amelie Maude

Lamont will receive the total amount after the following calculation has been made: a pound for day one of their marriage, doubled to two pounds on day two, the resulting totals to be doubled thereafter for each consecutive day of their marriage, for a duration of thirty-one days.'

I read it through again. How did they know my middle name was Maude? Then I saw my passport, which I'd last used at the airport, lying on the desk in front of the solicitor. I signed the two copies, Paul Carr verified our signatures, added his own signature and handed one of the copies to Ned.

I reached across the table and took my passport, my eyes fixed on Ned. But maybe because his father's solicitor was there, he didn't stop me. 'You can go now,' Ned said. I could feel his eyes on my back as I walked out of the study.

43

Present

I pace the room, counting, doubling. I need to know how much Jethro Hawthorpe will have to pay the kidnappers if he pays the ransom tomorrow, day twenty-four of our kidnap.

The first days are easy: one – two – four – eight – sixteen – thirty-two – sixty-four – one hundred and twenty-eight – two hundred and fifty-six – five hundred and twelve – one thousand and twenty-four – two thousand and forty-eight – four thousand and ninety-six – eight thousand, one hundred and ninety-two – sixteen thousand, three hundred and eighty-four – thirty-two thousand, seven hundred and sixty-eight.

I've been counting the days off on my fingers, and already at day sixteen, over halfway through the month, I'm not sure I'll get to a million pounds by day thirty-one. But I owe it to my father to work it out.

I carry on. Sixty-five thousand, five hundred and thirty-six on day seventeen; one hundred and thirty-one thousand and seventy-two on day eighteen; two hundred and sixty-two thousand – without warning, the rest of the total slips from my grasp. Without a pen and paper, it's going to be difficult to hang on to the figures.

I might not have a pen, but I have a nail. In the bathroom, I start doubling again from the beginning. When I get to day eighteen, I hang on to the number – one hundred and thirty-one thousand and seventy-two – while I scratch *19* on the back of the door. Then, in my mind, I double the number I've been holding onto and scratch the number *262,144* next to the *19*.

I carry on; underneath the *19*, I scratch a *20*, then next to it, the number *524,288*. I'm about to double it when I realise that I've already reached the half-million mark.

I sit down on the toilet seat, frowning at the door. I must have made a mistake, it's not possible that by the next day, day twenty-one, the total will already be more than a million. I go back over everything, from day one, and arrive at the same figure. A thrill of excitement takes hold. I carry on calculating.

21 – 1,048,576
22 – 2,097,152
23 – 4,194,304
24 – 8,388,608

I stand back, staring in disbelief at the number I've just scratched on the back of the door. If Jethro Hawthorpe pays the ransom tomorrow, on day twenty-four of our kidnapping, he will have to pay our abductors over eight million pounds.

My fingers are sore from the effort of scratching legible numbers with a nail, but I push on. Twice the light goes off, twice I reset it.

25 – 16,777,216
26 – 33,554,432
27 – 67,108,864
28 – 134,217,728
29 – 268,435,456
30 – 536,870,912

My body trembles as I make the last calculation.

31 – 1,073,741,824

My breath catches. Day thirty-one: over one billion pounds.

44

Past

I was in the sitting room, reading a book, when I heard Ned's car in the drive. Jumping from the sofa, I ran to the window and saw him sitting up front next to Hunter.

It was the first time Ned had left the house since we'd come back from Vegas. Seizing my chance, I ran out to the garden, then around the side of the house, my bare feet stinging as I reached the drive. But the gate had already closed. I hurried to it, trying to find a way to climb up the smooth steel. But it was impossible to get traction.

'Carolyn!' I shouted.

There was no reply. Even the press seemed to have gone, despite Ned's insistence that they were camped outside. Another of his lies.

I tried again. 'Help! Can somebody help?'

But there was still nothing. I called again and again, moving to different parts of the wall, but nobody came to my rescue. Deflated, I returned to the house.

Every day, I had sat at the top of the stairs, hoping to hear Carolyn at the front door, calling my name, demanding to see me. Maybe she'd tried and Hunter hadn't let her past the gates. And then there was Hunter himself. In the eight days since I'd been here, he'd never come to check on me. It hurt that I couldn't explain everything to him. But why would he seek me out if he believed I was happy being married to Ned?

I consoled myself that Carolyn wouldn't have given up on me. If she had been turned away, it would only reinforce what she already knew, that something was wrong. She would be back, and next time, she would bring Daniel with her, or better still, the police.

I was about to go back to the sitting room when I decided to borrow a book from Ned's library. I had never asked him if I could, because I wasn't meant to know he had a library. I went in and began exploring the shelves. There were books on the universe, books on art, books on the history of the world.

I was pushing the moveable wooden stairs along the library floor so that I could reach the books on the higher shelves when I heard the car coming up the drive. I hurried to the window; they were already back. Panic surged; I needed to leave, get back to my bedroom before Ned caught me here. But before I could move, I saw someone squeezing in through the gates as they closed shut. I recognised her instantly – Lina. My heart leapt; had Carolyn sent her, hoping she would have more influence with Ned?

The car braked to a stop at the front door. Hunter jumped out, pulled Ned's door open, and without waiting for him to exit the car, he ran down the drive towards Lina. She was shouting something at Ned as he stepped out of the car and Hunter took hold of her arm, preventing her from going any farther.

Ned didn't bother looking at Lina, he just walked into the house as if she wasn't standing there, shouting at him. As I watched, Lina shrugged off Hunter's hand and ran after Ned, her signature red tote bag clutched to her chest, her red high-heeled sandals a splash of colour against the grey gravel.

Hunter caught up with her as she reached the front door. He was talking urgently to her, trying to steer her away from the house. But Lina was shouting over him.

'Let me in, Hunter, I want to speak to him!' Unlike Hunter's, her voice carried all the way through the open front door and down the hallway to the library.

'It's all right, Hunter, let her in!' I heard Ned call.

I'd been so busy watching the drama unfolding between Lina and Hunter that I'd forgotten I needed to leave the library. But it was too late; Ned was already coming down the hallway. The door was open; if he looked in, he would see me.

I ran to the door, slid myself behind it, my heart hammering in my chest as Lina's stilettos clattered on the marble floor of the entrance hall. Through the gap between the hinges, I could see Ned approaching the library.

'Hey!' I heard Lina call. 'I want to talk to you!'

Ned stopped in his tracks, just feet away from me, then turned slowly, waiting for Lina to catch up with him. He was so agonisingly close that from my hiding place, I could see the flare of anger on his face.

Lina came into view and stopped inches away from Ned, her hands on her hips, her eyes like daggers.

'Where's Justine?' she snapped.

Her question threw me. She wasn't here for me, she was here for Justine. Shame flooded my body. Did she really believe that I'd married Ned for love, that I'd been in a secret relationship with him, that I'd lied to them all?

'Haven't you heard?' Ned said smoothly, masking his anger. 'She's gone back to France.'

Lina's eyes flashed. 'I don't believe it. She would never have left without saying goodbye to me.'

Ned shrugged. 'Seems like she did.'

'No.' Lina was adamant. 'Her life is here in England. Where is she?'

'I suspect she was too embarrassed to tell you why I terminated her contract.'

'Why would you fire her? She managed to get some of the best interviews ever, you said so yourself. You were happy with her work.'

'I was, until I found out she'd been taking drugs.'

'Drugs? Justine?' Lina laughed. 'Are you crazy?'

Ned's face darkened. 'Have you forgotten who you're talking to?'

'A liar, that's who I'm talking to.'

Please be careful, Lina, I implored silently. But her eyes narrowed.

'I know what you did; Carolyn told me. You went to Justine's apartment on the pretence of discussing her contract, and sexually assaulted her. I also know that she filed charges against you. So, you know what I'm going to do? I'm going to go to the police station and tell them that since filing the charges against you, Justine has disappeared, and that when we call her phone, it's been disconnected. I'll tell them that you said she's in France and I'll ask them to check the ports and airports to see if she actually arrived there. I'll tell them how you were always pestering her, I'll show them the numerous messages she sent to me, complaining about your continual harassment. And while I'm there, I'll also tell the police about the off-the-record payments I've had to make as your accountant, to the young women you silenced after you sexually assaulted them. Except that they are not as off-the-record as you would like them to be, because I have copies of everything, I even have those girls on tape saying that they accepted the money because you threatened them with—'

It happened so fast. Ned grabbed Lina by the arms and pushed her against the wall, pinning her there with one hand while he covered her mouth with the other. I saw Lina's eyes widen, heard her muffled protests as she twisted her head, then her body, trying to break free. She tried to grab Ned's arm, dislodge his hand from her mouth, but her red tote slipped from her shoulder and dropped to her elbow, dragging it downwards. She kicked out with her foot but Ned pressed his hand harder against her mouth, and her nostrils flared in and out in rapid movements as she tried to draw in air. I tried to move but my whole body was paralysed by a mix of disbelief and denial – this wasn't happening, what was Ned doing, why was he now pinching Lina's nose with his fingers, his other hand still pressed over her mouth?

Lina's feet started scrabbling on the ground, the pointed heels of her bright red sandals slip-sliding on the polished marble floor as she tried to get purchase. Realising that it was real, it was actually happening, I tore from my hiding place and launched myself at Ned.

'Get off her! Leave her alone!'

The force of my body crashing into his knocked him away from Lina. She crumpled to the floor, clutching her throat, making terrible sounds as she struggled to draw in breath.

'Lina!' I crouched down next to her, tried to get her to sit. For the briefest of moments, our eyes met and I saw that hers were filled with fear and warning.

'It's all right, I—'

From the corner of my eye, I saw Ned's shadow looming over me. A blow to my head knocked me off my feet. My head hit the floor and there was an explosion of stars before my eyes. Then everything went black.

*　　*　　*

The sound of laboured breathing reached me. Lina. I snapped open my eyes and lay for a moment, fighting the pain in my head. I was crumpled along the bottom of the wall and realising that Ned was there, just inches away from me, I became very still, only my eyes moving as I looked desperately for Lina. She was lying on her back not far from me, her body skewed at a strange angle, her long legs bent, her arms spread wide. I couldn't see her face because Ned was bent over her. It was only when he straightened up, breathing heavily, that I saw her eyes were wide and staring, saliva pooling from her slack mouth. And, in that moment, I realised she was dead.

A scream rose up from inside me but terror trapped it in my throat. Ned was picking up Lina's bag from the floor. I saw him dump it on her stomach, then move to stand behind her head. Stooping, he put his hands under Lina's arms and began dragging her body down the hallway, towards his study. I stared in horror as first Lina's head, then her legs, then her feet disappeared slowly from my view. I heard the door to Ned's study open, followed by the sound of Lina's body being dragged inside. Then Ned's voice.

'Amos, I need your services, you need to come now.' His voice was urgent, commanding. 'Come to the side door, I'll get rid of my security guard.' A pause followed by the sound of something clattering onto his desk. 'And Amos, I'll need you to find her passport, it's not in her bag. We need to be more thorough this time.'

Then a short silence, then his voice again. 'Hunter, I need you to go to the office, there's a file I need urgently. Call me when you get there, I'll tell you where it is.'

The air around was suddenly charged with danger. I needed to move – but when I tried to lift my head, the dizziness was so bad I had to close my eyes. I waited for it to pass and when I opened them again, Ned was there, crouched down beside me.

'No!' I began scrabbling away from him, using my heels to push my body back. But he reached out and pressed a hand down on my chest, stopping my movements.

'Listen to me very carefully, Amelie.' His eyes found mine. I wanted to look away, look at anything but him, but I couldn't. 'In a minute, I will take you to your room and you will stay there until the month is up and then we will announce our separation as agreed. And you will be free to leave. But if you mention to anyone anything of what you might have witnessed today, if you even think of going to the police, I will kill your friend Carolyn, and then I will kill you. Do you understand?'

A terrible shaking took hold of me, so violent that my teeth chattered with it. Ned watched dispassionately for a moment, then asked me again.

'Do you understand?'

Speech was impossible, so I nodded, my head wobbling against the floor.

'Good.' He stood, pulled me to my feet. I fell against him, too dizzy to stand and he half-carried, half-dragged me up the stairs to my room.

45

Present

Today, Monday, the ninth of September, is my last day in this room. Now that I know what the kidnappers have asked for, it seems unfathomable that Jethro Hawthorpe will stall any longer.

The abductor told Ned that his father didn't take their ransom demands seriously at first – which suggests that now, he does. I need to leave before he pays, before I'm released with Ned.

The man comes, I'm ready. I've gone over it a hundred times; I know his movements, the way he always puts the tray down in the same place.

'Hey,' I say as he approaches. 'How are you today?'

I sense him stoop, my hands are on my knees, the palms upturned. As he places the tray on the floor, I shoot them out and with all my strength, upend it over him. There's a clatter of bowl and cup, I hear the whispered 'Fuck,' I sense him stumble back and I scramble for the fallen tray. It's in my hands. I leap to my feet, swing it hard, aiming for where I think his head is. There's an almighty *thwack* as it connects, a clunk against his goggles. I hear his grunt of pain; I swing again, the force of the blow shuddering up my arms. Another curse; I dart to the right, throw the tray hard in his direction and run for the door.

I'm almost there, my outstretched fingers are touching it, when a hand locks around my ankle. I stumble, grab hold of the door to stop myself from falling, and kick out with my leg, trying to loosen his hold. His fingers grip my ankle tighter, they're like iron, I can't lift my foot from the floor. I kick out with my other foot, feel the mass of his body, and kick harder, again and again and again.

He still won't let go. I have no choice, I take my hands from the door, bend to pry his fingers from my ankle. But his other hand comes up, he pulls me down, I'm on top of him, his arms a vise around my body. In one quick movement, he flips me onto my back, traps my legs between his thighs, and holds me down with one giant hand on my chest. I open my mouth to scream but he silences me with his other hand, clamping it over my mouth. I twist my body, trying to free myself, trying to move him off me. But I'm powerless against his strength.

Wrenching my mouth from under his hand, I bring my teeth down and bite as hard as I can. He curses again, tries to free his hand. I bite harder, taste his blood, but I don't let go. He removes the hand from my chest, and my body released, I surge up, still clenching his other hand between my teeth. And then, somehow, he spins me around, he's crouched behind me now. I feel the heat of his body as he locks me against him with his free arm, and with his fingers, pinches my nose. My lungs tighten, I reflexively open my mouth for air. He pulls his other hand out from between my teeth and clamps it hard over my mouth. With my nose still pinched between his fingers, I can't breathe.

Images flash through my mind, Lina's heels scrabbling on the ground, her eyes rolling back in her head as Ned began to suffocate her. Panic grips me in its iron fist. *This is it, I'm going to die, I'm going to die like Lina.*

But I am not Lina, and he is not Ned. His hand is still over my mouth, but his fingers are no longer pinching my nose.

My breath comes hard and fast, he is breathing hard too, the sound of it fills the room. I remember then, the day I had the panic attack, how he helped me, breathed with me, and tears spill from my eyes, down my cheeks, onto his bloodied hand. My body shudders with silent sobs; he doesn't move, how can he? If he releases me, takes his hand from my mouth, Ned will hear my wails of frustration, of hopelessness, and remorse. So, he waits, he waits until I'm calm.

And then he leaves.

46

Past

Ned came to my room. I kept my eyes closed, my body still.

'You need to get up,' he said. 'We've been invited to lunch.'

I didn't reply and he moved nearer to my bed. My skin crawled.

'Did you hear what I said?'

'I can't,' I muttered. 'I can't eat lunch.'

'Too bad, I need you there. It's a potential business contact and he wants to meet my new wife. Besides, you haven't eaten in days.'

I lapsed back into silence. He had brought me food; I'd heard him place trays on the table next to my bed. But I hadn't touched any of it. I couldn't.

I sensed him bending towards me and my body flinched in response.

'You want this to be over, don't you? It would be a shame if it had to drag on for more than a month.'

I heard his threat, and something withered inside me.

'Be ready in thirty minutes. And bring a swimsuit.'

I heard him leave, the click as he locked the door. I fought down the ever-present nausea and tried to push the memories of Lina from my mind. They were always there; her feet scrabbling on the ground, her head twisting and turning as she tried to break free, her eyes as she looked back at me when I was crouched down beside her. She had been alive at that point, I should have sprung up, attacked Ned again. But Ned had been quicker than me.

I pushed the bedcovers off, suddenly desperate to be under a scalding shower. My head spun and I gripped the chest of drawers, closed my eyes a moment. I didn't want to go to this lunch, I wanted to hide, block everything out. I couldn't even begin to think of Justine. I was so scared for her. Ned's words to the man on the other end of the phone, the man he had addressed as Amos – *We need to be more thorough this time* – played on a loop in my mind. Lina had said that Justine had disappeared – and now that I knew what Ned was capable of, I was filled with dread that she hadn't been paid off, she had been killed. I felt so helpless, so powerless. Without a phone, unable to get out of the house, this room even, I couldn't do anything.

A sob pushed up from inside me. I needed to warn Carolyn that she might be in danger. I took a breath. Maybe, at this lunch, there would be other people there. I would play along for now, then find a phone, find a moment to escape.

I showered, dressed, squashed the red bikini that I'd bought in Las Vegas into my bag.

I heard Ned opening the door and as always when he was near, my body started its terrible shaking. I fought it down, walked down the twenty-four marble steps, aware of him close behind me. We arrived at the front door; Ned opened it, and when I saw the car waiting, I instinctively stepped backwards. But he reached out, gripped my wrist tightly, and walked me through the door and down the three steps to the car. Hunter was holding the door open and my heart leapt. *Hunter will help me, he'll know what to do.* I tried to catch his eye, signal to him that I needed help. But as Ned bundled me into the car, he stared straight ahead, and fear flashed through me, that he was part of it all.

Ned slammed my door shut, then got in the front next to Hunter.

The car pulled away from the house. Unable to look at either Ned or Hunter, I stared out of my window. But all I could see was Lina running up the drive, her red heels hitting the gravel like spots of blood.

47

Present

My captor comes, and I sit with my back to him. I can't bear for him to see me, not after my disastrous attempt to escape.

I hear him gather my breakfast tray from the floor, pick up the bowl and cup from where they fell. I hear the floor being wiped, smell the tang of disinfectant, imagine him scooping up the gloopy porridge with a wipe of some kind. He does all of these things, and I stay facing the wall.

But it's not enough. He can still see me. The next time he comes, I won't be here, I'll hide in the bathroom until he leaves.

I can't face any more humiliation. I want it to end. I don't care how, but I want it to end.

48

Past

We arrived at the gates of a large, detached house. Just before we'd turned onto the road where the house stood, I'd seen a sign for Haven Cliffs.

The gates slid open. Hunter drove through and drew up in front of the house. I got out of the car before he could open the door for me, and smelled the tang of the sea in the air.

Our host, a man in a white suit and black shirt, came to meet us. He was tall and broad with jet-black hair, and introduced himself as Lukas. He led us around the back of the house to a beautiful paved terrace, and I looked in dismay at a table set for three; there were no other guests. He spoke English with a slight accent and told us he was from Lithuania.

My thoughts flew to Lina, and maybe Ned's did too because I immediately felt his unease.

'I understood you were from the States,' he said.

'I live there some of the time, in Los Angeles, which is why I can be of interest to you,' Lukas said smoothly. 'But I also have a home in Vilnius; in fact, I am going there tomorrow. This house' – he swept his arm around – 'does not belong to me. I rent it whenever I have business in the UK. I think of it as my home away from home.'

'It's beautiful,' I said, looking around the terrace, where sun-loungers were grouped around a stunning infinity pool.

He nodded, pleased. 'Yes, I love it here, it is very different from both Los Angeles and Vilnius.'

Over lunch, served by Lukas, Ned told him about our trip to Las Vegas and our wedding. It was less than two weeks since that fateful day, but it seemed a lifetime ago. It was excruciating to have to pretend that everything was fine, to smile, to let Ned take my hand across the table.

Ned pushed his chair back and stood up. 'Could I use the bathroom, please?'

'Of course. There is one in the pool house,' Lukas replied, pointing to it.

'Please excuse me.'

As Ned began to walk across the terrace, I reached for a bottle of water; was this my chance, could I say something to Lukas? I wasn't sure. He seemed nice but how would he react if I blurted out that my brand-new husband had killed my friend? I looked towards the pool house. Ned had stopped in front of it and was looking back at me and as I watched, he took his phone from his pocket and held it in his hand. It was a warning, a warning that Carolyn's fate was just a phone call away.

'Please, let me.'

Startled, I pulled my eyes away from Ned. Lukas took the bottle from my hand and filled my glass. In moments Ned was back, and I realised he hadn't even gone into the pool house long enough to use the bathroom. He had been testing me, a warning not to say anything.

'Now,' Lukas said when lunch was over. 'Your husband and I have something to discuss, so perhaps you would like to use the pool while we speak.'

The burst of hope, that it might be my chance to escape, was quickly extinguished when he and Ned came with me.

They sat at the poolside bar on high stools, watching me as I swam up and down, and I wished I'd had something other to wear than my red bikini. Self-conscious, I got out of the pool, wrapped a towel around me, and moved to one of the grey-and-yellow-striped sun-loungers. I was desperate to find a phone, but I had no excuse for going into the house as there was a toilet in the pool house. But no phone; I had already checked when I went in to change.

I listened as Lukas told Ned about a famous actor, who lived next-door to him in Los Angeles, and who was willing to be interviewed for *Exclusives* along with her actor husband, almost as famous as she was. Ned was excited about the possibility of a double interview, something *Exclusives* hadn't yet had. Lukas also mentioned a politician he knew well.

I closed my eyes, as if I were asleep. My head was turned away from them but I was listening to every word, waiting for my moment, because there was no way I was getting back in the car with Ned.

'So, what happened to Lina?' I heard Lukas say.

My eyes snapped open. Despite my heart hammering in my chest, I kept very still, made my breathing deep and even.

'Lina?' Ned said, a frown in his voice. 'She went back to Lithuania. But – how do you know Lina?'

'We have mutual acquaintances,' Lukas replied smoothly. 'And I know that she went back to Lithuania, because one of those acquaintances works at your magazine and she received a text from Lina saying that she was happy to be back in her country.'

'That'll be Vicky, my PA,' Ned said. 'She mentioned that Lina had messaged her. But – you also know Vicky?'

'What I would like to know,' Lukas said, ignoring Ned's question, 'is why Lina decided to go back to a country she left many years ago, just like that.' There was a snap of finger and thumb. 'Rumour has it that she went to see you at your house the day she left so suddenly.'

'You're right, she did,' Ned said, and I marvelled at his ability to keep his voice even when he had to be wondering how Lukas knew about Lina's visit. 'She wanted to see me because I had recently fired one of her friends.'

'That friend would be Justine Elland, I think,' Lukas interjected.

My fingers curled into my palms, my nails pressing so hard into the skin that pain sparked.

'Yes. Lina wanted to know why I'd had to let Justine go, so I told her the sad truth, that I'd discovered Justine was using drugs. And that is something I can't tolerate because my brother died from a drug overdose. We have a zero-tolerance policy at the magazine, it's in everyone's contract my staff know the consequences if they abuse it.'

'That is very sad about your brother,' Lukas said. 'And it is perfectly understandable that you responded this way.' He paused. 'It seems that Justine is also in Lithuania,' Lukas went on. 'I know this because your assistant – Vicky – received a second message from Lina, and in that message, Lina told Vicky that she was very happy, because Justine had flown from France to see her.'

'Yes, Vicky mentioned that to me too,' Ned said. 'Lina and Justine are good friends, it's nice that they are staying in touch.'

'So why did you terminate Lina's contract?' Lukas asked. 'Was she also using drugs?'

'Not that I know of.' I couldn't believe how calm Ned sounded. 'Although, as she was friends with Justine, she may have been influenced by her. But that wasn't the reason

I let her go.' He paused. 'Perhaps you know, Lina was my accountant, and I had recently discovered, after an audit, that she had been putting in false claims for expenses. They were small amounts and I decided to say nothing; I preferred to wait and see if the amounts would become more substantial if she thought she'd got away with it. But when she came to the house – which in itself is a sackable offense, she had no right to turn up uninvited at my private residence – she was extremely rude to me, demanding that I reinstate Justine. So, I told her that I knew she'd been stealing money from the company and that I was terminating her contract with immediate effect.' Another pause. 'I also told her that I would tell everyone exactly why I was letting her go.'

'If she was stealing money, you did the right thing,' Lukas said.

'But do you know what? Despite those messages to Vicky, there are some who don't believe that Lina is in Lithuania, because she left so suddenly, without saying goodbye to anyone, not even her friends, and without collecting her belongings. So, to put an end to those rumours, I called a friend in Immigration at Vilnius Airport. And he confirmed that Lina did indeed arrive there, three days ago now.'

'There you are, then,' Ned said coolly. 'I admit, she was very upset when I fired her, because she knew she would never be able to get another job here once it became public knowledge that she was a thief. She begged me to reconsider and when I refused, she said she had no choice but to return to Lithuania. She wanted to leave at once; she said that she didn't want to see anyone, because she'd be too embarrassed to tell them why I had fired her. She asked me if I could book a flight for her and although it wasn't my job to do so, she was so distraught that I felt sorry for her. I found a flight leaving a few hours later and booked her a ticket.'

'That was very generous of you. May I ask how she got to the airport? Did she take a taxi?'

'No, I asked Hunter to take her.'

'Hunter?'

'My driver.'

'The one who brought you here today?'

'Yes,' Ned said.

'Hmm. So, your driver was the last person to see Lina before she left?'

'That's right.'

'And he dropped her off at the airport?'

'I believe so. That is what I asked him to do.'

I heard someone come onto the terrace and for a wild moment, I thought that Lukas was an undercover policeman, and someone had come to arrest Ned.

'My apologies for interrupting.' I heard Hunter's voice and came crashing back to reality. 'I have a call for Mr Hawthorpe.'

I heard Ned leave the pool area with Hunter. My mind was spinning with what I'd heard. How could Lina have gone through Immigration at Vilnius Airport when she was already dead? I turned on my sun-lounger so that I was facing the pool bar where Lukas was sitting. I needed to tell him that Ned had murdered her.

I wrapped my towel around myself and quickly made my way over. Lukas had his head bent over his phone, messaging someone. As I approached, he looked up. He was wearing dark sunglasses and I wished that he wasn't because if I could have seen his eyes, they might have told me if I could trust him or not.

'Please,' I said hurriedly, noticing the grey flecks in his hair. He was older than Ned, mid-forties perhaps. 'I need to tell you something.'

'Of course.' He put his phone down on the table. 'What is it that you want to tell me?'

I was so close to him that I could smell a lovely grassy scent, his aftershave perhaps. My eyes fell on his phone.

'Could I use your phone, please? It's urgent. I need to call the police.'

'The police?'

My heart sank. I shouldn't have mentioned the police.

'Yes,' I said quickly. 'It's about Lina—'

'What are you two talking about?'

I spun around. Ned was standing behind me.

'This and that,' Lukas said.

Ned held my gaze, waiting for my answer. My heart thumped – how much had he heard?

'I was telling Lukas what a beautiful house this is,' I said.

'Again?' Ned said, and Lukas laughed.

'Go and get dressed,' Ned barked to me. 'We're leaving.'

Lukas raised his eyebrows. 'So soon?'

'Yes. I've been called away on urgent business, I'm afraid.'

'Well, that is a shame.'

I hadn't moved, I couldn't. This was my last chance to get help.

'Hurry, please, Amelie.' There was an edge to Ned's voice. 'If we delay any longer, you won't be able to see Carolyn.' He took out his phone. 'Maybe I should phone ahead.'

I found my voice. 'No. That won't be necessary.'

I walked to the pool house and dressed quickly, a knot of dread in the pit of my stomach. There was nothing I could do. I couldn't risk Carolyn's life. I was trapped.

Ned appeared, gripped my arm. 'I hope you're grateful that I saved you from yourself.' He paused. 'You, and Carolyn.'

Outside, Lukas extended his hand to Ned. 'I hope I can be of help to you.' He turned to me. 'Goodbye, Amelie, it's been a pleasure.'

He picked up his phone. Thinking he was going to give it to me, right now, in front of Ned, I forgot to breathe. But he didn't, he just held it in his hand and I realised that his focus wasn't on me, but on Hunter, waiting at the side of the pool to escort us to the car.

I let out the breath I'd been holding. Lukas hadn't given me away. That had to mean something.

49

Present

The sound of the door in the basement being unlocked rouses me from my apathy. Pushing the mattress aside, I lie on my front to listen.

'Good news, Ned. Your father has decided to pay the ransom.'

'Thank God.' Ned's voice is shaky. 'Today, will it be today?'

'That's up to your father. Did you work out how much he'll have to pay to get you back?'

'What do you mean?'

'Come on, Ned, I told you how it worked, I told you that for every day your father refused to pay, we doubled the amount of the ransom. You've been here nearly four weeks; today is day twenty-six. If he paid today, how much do you think he'd owe us?'

'I don't know – a few hundred thousand, a couple of million?'

I can almost see Ned shrugging his shoulders at the unimportance of such an amount.

'More than that, Ned, much more. Have another guess.'

'Ten million?'

'More.'

'It can't be more, it's not possible, not just from that doubling thing.'

The man laughs. 'I tell you what, Ned, take the time to

work it out. I'll come back in a while for your answer.'

The door closes, Ned curses. And then I hear it, Ned counting, doubling, trying to hang on to numbers, cursing when they slip away from him.

I give up listening, pull my knees to my chest. If Ned's abductor is telling the truth, they'll be releasing him soon. What about me? Ned thinks I'm dead but that doesn't mean they'll release me somewhere else. Maybe they want to play a trick on him, say, 'Look, she's alive, we just made you think she was dead.'

Anxiety gnaws in the pit of my stomach. If that is what is going to happen, I don't want to be released. I am safer here, in this pitch-black room, than I am in the outside world with Ned.

50

Past

On the way back to Ned's house, I stared straight ahead. Ned was riding up front next to Hunter, and I was sitting behind Hunter.

Had I done enough? Would Lukas call the police? My heart was racing, terrified that he might phone Ned and tell him what I'd said. But the car stayed silent. Perhaps, at this very moment, Lukas was phoning the police.

'There's an accident on the A31,' Hunter said from the front of the car. 'I'll take the back roads to avoid it.'

'Whatever, you're the driver, just get me home.' Ned's tone was so dismissive that my hatred of him deepened. The thought of going back to his house made me breathless. I felt my panic rising and desperately tried to focus – when we arrived, I'd refuse to get out of the car. I'd wait until Ned had got out, I'd lock my door from the inside, then lock his so that he wouldn't be able to get to me.

There was a sudden screech of tyres and I saw a flash of black, a car overtaking us at tremendous speed. Our car swerved violently; I flew forwards and was snapped back against the seat by my belt as the car braked to a stop.

'What the fuck!' Ned cursed.

'Sorry about that, Mr Hawthorpe. I don't know what that idiot—'

Hunter's voice broke off, and looking through window, I saw that the car that had overtaken us had pulled in front of us, blocking our way. My heart leapt. *It's the police, Lukas must have phoned them, they've come to arrest Ned.* But a man, dressed all in black, a balaclava over his head, got out of the car and walked towards us. He had a gun in his hand.

'What the—'

'Turn around!' Ned screamed, cutting Hunter off. 'Back up! Now!'

Hunter gunned the car but before he could reverse, the gunman, who had continued walking calmly towards us, pulled open Hunter's door. Hunter tried to close it, but the man reached in, stunned Hunter with his gun, snapped off his seat belt and began dragging him from the car.

'NO!' I unclipped my seat belt, and threw myself over the seat, trying to grab hold of Hunter. But I was too late. His body thudded to the ground, I saw his arms and legs flail. Then three gunshots rang out, *bang, bang, bang.*

'HUNTER!' His name ripped from me, I twisted to the window and my heart stopped. He was lying facedown, blood pooling from his head.

'NO!' I screamed again. The gunman's head jerked up. He looked straight at me and then, moving around Hunter's body, he began walking towards my door. Suddenly, the car jerked forwards, throwing me into the footwell. Ned had managed to get into the driver's seat. But the car had stalled.

Ned gunned the car again, and as it shot forwards, the gunman lunged for my door. But he was too late.

I climbed back onto the seat, looked out of the back

window. Blood was seeping from Hunter's body, a red pool on the black tarmac of the road.

'Stop!' I cried. 'We need to call an ambulance!'

'Are you crazy?' Ned snarled.

'We can't just leave him!'

Ned's eyes flicked to the rearview mirror. 'He's dead.'

'No, no.' My teeth were chattering as I shook my head in denial. 'We need to go back. The gunman's gone, I saw him drive off.' I threw the top of my body over the seat, made a grab for the steering wheel. 'Stop the car! We need to go back!'

Ned's hand lashed out and I felt a crack of pain. My head snapped back, and I slid between the seats, so dizzy that I began retching. I closed my eyes. *Hunter is dead, Hunter is dead, Hunter is dead.*

I didn't realise I was sobbing until Ned yelled at me to shut up. I jammed a fist into my mouth, scared to anger him further. He was already driving too fast; from where I lay on the floor, trees flashed past in a kaleidoscope of green.

The journey was interminable. My mind was all over the place. The gunman had been coming for me, I would have been shot like Hunter if Ned hadn't driven off, and Ned would have been shot too. I wished we had been, it would have been a way out from this horror. I tried to focus on what I would do when I got to the house – as soon as Ned released the doors, I'd jump from the car, run towards the gates; if I couldn't get through them before they closed, I'd scream for help. Someone would hear me, someone had to hear me.

At last, the car slowed; we had arrived at the house. Ned pulled to a stop at the front door. I pushed myself up from the floor and onto the seat, my hand on the door, my eyes fixed on the gates, which were already closing. I waited for the clunk of the doors unlocking as Ned got out of the car. But it didn't come. I turned to look at him and saw him watching the gates, his face grey with fear. It was only when they juddered shut that he began to relax. He thought he was safe, behind his closed doors. But he wasn't safe because I was seething with rage.

He got out of the car, slammed his door shut, and began to walk off. I tried to open my door but the latch clicked uselessly as I moved it back and forth. He was leaving me locked in the car.

'Let me out!' I yelled, thumping on the window. 'Let me out!'

He continued walking towards the house, so I leaned over the seat, found the horn, and jammed my hand down on it. The noise was deafening. It brought him running back.

He pulled open my door and I leapt out, lunged at him.

'Get off!' he yelled, raising his arms to protect himself. 'Get off me!'

But I didn't stop, I kept on attacking him, hitting him with my fists, clawing at his face. He stumbled under the force of my anger, and I aimed a kick at him. He grabbed my leg.

'Let me go!' I yelled, hanging on to the door. 'Help! Help!'

'Shut your mouth!' He had managed to stand. Blood oozed from his gouged cheeks and there was fury in his eyes as he yanked me away from the car, up the steps, and in through the front door. His strength was overwhelming; each time I managed to grab on to something, he wrenched me away.

'Let me go!' I yelled again.

I swung my arm and my fist connected with his face. He gave a howl of pain, grabbed my shoulders, and slammed me against the wall, pinning me there with his body. He was panting, cursing, squashing the breath from me. His hand came over my mouth, and he raised his other hand, pinching my nose with his fingers. I couldn't breathe; my eyes bulged. I thought of Lina and my body went limp.

51

Present

Ned's abductor is back in the basement room.

'So, what have you got for me?' I hear him ask.

'Around a million on day twenty-one, so probably ten million if he paid today, exactly like I said.' Ned sounds pleased with himself. 'But don't worry, my father can pay it.'

'You're right about the million on day twenty-one but I'm afraid he owes us a lot more than ten million today. Let's work it out, shall we? What would he have owed if he'd paid us on day twenty-two?'

'Two million.'

'Day twenty-three?'

'Four million.'

'Day twenty-four?'

'Eight million.'

'Day twenty-five?'

'Sixteen million. Look, do we really have to do this?'

'Humour me, Ned, humour me. Today, day twenty-six?'

'Thirty-two million.' Then it hits him. 'Wow, that's a lot of money. Are you really asking him for thirty-two million pounds?'

'No, Ned, we're not.'

'Thank God for that. I mean, my father's rich but—'

'You misunderstand me. He's not paying us today, so he'll have to pay us more.'

'But—'

'Let's carry on. And by the way, because you've been rounding down, the actual figure your father would owe us today is around—'

'Thirty-three million,' I whisper.

'Thirty-three million. In fact, the exact figure is thirty-three million, five hundred and fifty-four thousand, four hundred and thirty-two pounds. So, let's carry on. What will your father owe us if he pays us tomorrow?' A pause. 'You can just double the millions, if you like.'

'Sixty-six million.' Ned's voice is sullen now.

'And the next day?'

'A hundred and thirty-two million.'

'The next day, day twenty-nine?'

'Two hundred and sixty-four million.'

'And day thirty?'

'Five hundred and twenty-eight million.'

'The thing is, Ned, we've asked your dad to pay us on Monday, which will be day thirty-one of your captivity.' Another pause. 'So, how much is your father paying us for your life?'

'I – I don't know.'

There's a crack, followed by a cry from Ned.

'DON'T BULLSHIT ME! HOW MUCH IS YOUR FATHER PAYING US FOR YOUR LOUSY LIFE?'

'Um – over a billion pounds?'

'That's right, Ned, over a billion pounds.' The man is no longer shouting, his voice is quiet, I have to strain my ears to hear him. 'Except that it's not for your life. Your life is worth nothing. We know who you are, we know what you did. The billion isn't for your life. It's for Lina's.'

52

Past

I woke in the dark, felt a hard floor beneath me. It took me a while to work out that I was lying on my bedroom floor in Ned's house. My chest hurt, my throat was on fire. I remembered then, Ned suffocating me.

I swallowed painfully. He mustn't have wanted to actually kill me; he could have if he'd continued blocking my airways for just a few seconds more. But he needed me until the end of the month, he needed me available for the outside world.

The events of the previous day came flooding back and my cry of anguish echoed through the silent house. Images hurtled through my mind: the gunman dragging Hunter from the car, his pistol pointing downwards, the bangs of three bullets being fired. The gunman raising his head, looking at me, then walking around Hunter's body to get to me.

I curled my body into itself. I had misjudged Lukas. Hunter's murder was down to him, I was sure of it. So many things pointed to it, from the message he'd been sending on his phone as I went to speak to him, to the way he had stared at Hunter as we were leaving. Lukas had assumed that Hunter was responsible for Lina's murder. Except he wasn't the one who had killed her.

My mind jumped to the thumbs-up message Ned had received in the plane, just before we left London for Las Vegas, from someone named Amos Kerrigan. Ned had spoken to someone called Amos after he'd murdered Lina; it had sounded as if he was asking him to come and remove her body from the house. Had Ned murdered Justine, and the thumbs-up from Amos Kerrigan was to let Ned know he'd disposed of her body? Nausea surged into my throat, and scrambling to my feet, I ran to the bathroom.

My stomach emptied, I wiped my mouth, then sat on the bathroom floor, my head on my knees. There were things I didn't understand. How had Lina passed through Immigration at the airport in Vilnius? I remembered overhearing Ned telling Amos Kerrigan to find Lina's passport, and his comment that they would have to be more thorough this time. Had he paid someone, someone who could pass for Lina, to travel to Lithuania using her passport? Then, that person, or Ned himself, had used Lina's phone to send the messages to Vicky?

But Lukas had taken the trouble to check that Lina had actually arrived in Vilnius. Had he also checked that the person using her passport really was Lina and discovered that she was an impostor? And because Ned had pointed the finger at Hunter – by effectively telling Lukas that Hunter was the last person to see Lina alive – Lukas had had him killed.

So, who was Lukas? Lina was an orphan, but maybe he was a family friend, someone who'd looked out for Lina when she was orphaned – someone who would avenge her murder. It would explain why he'd had Hunter killed. Revenge. Which meant that it wasn't over yet. Lukas would come after Ned, and he would come after me; he would finish the job his gunman had failed to do.

53

Present

I've spent the last three days walking around the room in circles. It hadn't taken me long to work it out, once I knew our abduction was about Lina. Lukas is behind our kidnapping. I had known he would come after us, but I didn't think we'd be kidnapped. But maybe he had seen it as a way of extorting money from Jethro Hawthorpe before having us killed.

Exhausted from walking, I move to my mattress, wrap my blanket around me. The day I met Lukas, he said he was returning to Vilnius the next day. Is that where he is, masterminding our abduction from his home there, giving orders to the two men holding us?

Has Ned worked out that Lukas is behind our kidnapping? He must have, now that he knows this is about Lina. He will know, then, that he'll never get out of here alive. Once the kidnappers have the money, they'll kill him. They might spare me, but they'll kill him.

There's a noise from the basement.

'Wake up, Ned, the day has finally arrived. Your father has paid us, so we're releasing you early.'

'What?' Ned's voice is groggy with sleep. 'Did you say you're releasing me?'

'Yes, we're letting you go. There's a couple of hours before the agreed drop-off time, so you've got time to clean yourself up. We can't let your father see you in such a disgusting state, can we?'

Ned makes a sound somewhere between a sob and a laugh. 'Can I have a shower?' he asks. 'Some clean clothes?'

'Absolutely. You can even have a coffee, if you like.' A pause. 'There's just one thing: if anyone asks you about your wife, you'll tell them you don't know what happened to her, that she was held apart from you. If you tell them that we killed her, we'll tell them that you were the one who asked for her to be killed. And in case you're wondering how we'd do that – well, we have the recording of you telling us to kill her. All we have to do is drop it off at a police station, or broadcast it on social media, for you to spend the rest of your life in prison, especially when we add in Lina's murder. So, don't forget, Ned. Nothing about your wife, and no pretending you were a hero.' Another pause. 'Your wife tried to escape, did you know that? But you – nothing. You did nothing to try and help yourself.'

'Yeah, well, look where it got her,' Ned sneers.

'And that's exactly what will happen to you if you say anything, or do anything, to displease us. We'll be watching you, Ned, from all angles.' There's the sound of the door opening. 'Right, let's get you into a shower.'

In the room upstairs, I'm trembling. It's over. They're releasing Ned, he isn't going to be killed. But I'll be safe, because he truly believes that I'm dead. My shooting wasn't about playing a trick on him, as I'd feared.

My abductor has done what I asked.

54

Past

Ned was in my bedroom. He had brought me a supper tray. I refused to be scared of him, so I kept my eyes fixed on him as he put it down on the table. His face was a mess; he still had the marks from when I'd attacked him three days before, and I was glad.

'Make sure you eat it this time,' he said. 'I don't want you looking emaciated when we announce our separation.'

I didn't answer, just kept on staring at him. There was something else on his face, a sort of wariness. It told me he was living in fear of his life, and I was glad about that too. Whatever he had coming to him, he deserved it.

There was a call on the intercom and he jumped so badly I nearly laughed out loud. He hurried from the bedroom, leaving the door open in his haste, and I imagined him hovering at the top of the stairs, waiting for his new security guard to open the front door below. I had heard the new guard's voice in the hall the day after Lukas's lunch, and I'd felt a rush of anger at the way Hunter had been replaced so quickly.

'I'm Carl, sir,' I heard the security guard saying to the guest at the door. 'I'm Mr Hawthorpe's new hire.'

'Then please tell my son I would like to see him.'

I heard Ned clattering down the stairs.

'Dad, what are you doing here?' I heard him asking.

I leapt from the bed and went to crouch at the top of the stairs.

'What's happened to your face?' Jethro Hawthorpe barked. Again, he was immaculately dressed, in contrast to Ned, who looked dishevelled in his jeans and half-unbuttoned shirt. 'Have you been in a fight?'

'It's nothing.'

'It doesn't look like nothing to me. Where have you been? I came to the house on Tuesday and there was no one here. And why haven't you been answering your phone?'

'I've been busy. Look, Dad, why are you here?'

'In your study,' Jethro Hawthorpe said, glancing at the security guard who was still in the hall. He was dressed all in black, his head was shaved, his arms held rigid at his sides. I just had time to get a glimpse of his face before he turned towards the door.

I wasn't sure why I thought I might be able to appeal to Ned's father for help. Maybe it was because each time I'd heard him speaking to Ned, he'd been angry. I waited until the security guard had moved outside, to his post on the front step, and ran down the stairs to the entrance hall. I faltered at the start of the hallway leading to Ned's study, then, fighting down a rush of tears, I hurried to the library, my head up, my eyes away from the floor where Lina had lain. Closing the door behind me, I moved silently to the double doors that led to the study.

'Where's Hunter?' Jethro Hawthorpe was asking. 'Why have you got a new man on the door?'

'I had to get rid of him,' Ned said. 'He wasn't doing his job properly. Carl is his replacement.' There was a pause. 'I'll ask you again, why are you here?'

'Because of this ridiculous marriage of yours. Why did you do it? I want the truth.'

'You needn't worry, we're separating.'

There was a snort of disgust. 'Already? After what – little more than two weeks?'

'All right,' Ned said. 'You want the truth, here it is. I'd been seeing her for a while, and I took her to Las Vegas because she said she'd never been on a plane before and I felt sorry for her. Then, while we were there, she told me she was pregnant, and yeah, it was a shock but I thought I should do the right thing by her and my future child. So, I married her.'

'What?' Jethro Hawthorpe sounded as if he was about to have a heart attack. 'She's pregnant?'

'No,' Ned said. 'She tricked me, Dad, she tricked me into marrying her. She was after my money, so she made up a story about being pregnant.' His voice rose to a whine. 'Do you see now, do you see what it's like for me?'

'Are you serious?' Jethro Hawthorpe thundered. 'You let yourself be taken in by some slip of a girl?'

Ned's voice hardened. 'You're missing the point. When I tell the press why we're separating, they'll realise what it's been like for me, they'll see that women will try anything to get money out of me, whether it's pretending I sexually assaulted them, or pretending that they're pregnant. Don't you see, that accusation against me – it will go away. The press won't be gunning for me anymore, they'll be sympathetic.'

I clapped my hand over my mouth to smother my gasp of shock. Even though I had guessed it, to hear Ned actually admit that he used me to protect himself against Justine's accusation of sexual assault, to hear his vicious lie about my character, was brutal.

'You did sort out a postnup with Paul Carr, I hope?' Jethro Hawthorpe said.

'Yes, of course I did, I'm not stupid.'

'How much? How much did she want?'

'I offered her fifty thousand if we separate but she refused it,' Ned said. 'She said she only wanted a pound for each day that we stayed married.'

'Hold on.' I imagined Jethro Hawthorpe holding up his hand, his palm facing Ned. 'That doesn't make sense. If she tricked you into marrying her to extort money from you, why would she only ask for a pound for each day of your marriage? Even if you separated in two years' time, that adds up to little more than seven hundred. There must be more to it than that.'

'It's not exactly a pound for each day,' Ned said. 'There's a doubling thing involved.'

'What do you mean, a doubling thing?'

'Well, it's a pound for the first day, then doubled for every day after that,' Ned explained. 'You know – she gets a pound for day one of our marriage, two pounds for day two, four pounds on day three, eight pounds on day four—'

Jethro Hawthorpe cut him off. 'You didn't agree to it, did you?'

'Of course,' Ned said.

'Are you completely crazy? Did you even bother to work it out?'

'No, but don't worry, she only wants it for the first month of our marriage.'

'The only thing I'm worried about is how I raised such an imbecile! You could end up owing her millions!'

The door to the study opened, then slammed shut. I heard Jethro Hawthorpe stride past the library door, his footsteps loud and angry. I stayed where I was, in case Ned decided to go after him. But there was a crash, the sound of something smashing against the wall.

'BITCH! FUCKING BITCH!'

I recoiled, ran from the room. In my bedroom, I paced up and down, seething at the way Ned had used me. There was no last-minute trip to Vegas, he had planned our marriage before we left. He had found my Achilles' heel and used it to protect himself from the fallout of his assault on Justine. In the eyes of the world, if Ned and I had been in a secret relationship for the last few months, if he'd been about to propose to me, would he really have assaulted one of his employees the day before we left?

I thought for a moment, then crept downstairs to the kitchen and took a knife with a long, pointed blade from the drawer. I ran back to my room, closing the door behind me. It was almost dark. I waited for Ned to remember that he hadn't locked me in, but he didn't come. Good. Soon, he would go to bed, and once he was asleep, I would find his bedroom, I would hold the knife to his throat, I would take his phone and call the police. And if he so much as moved, well, I would kill him. I would kill him for Justine and Lina, and for Hunter.

But before I could do any of those things, I was kidnapped.

55

Present

I walk to the bathroom, trailing the blanket behind me. When will they come for me? Since Ned was taken from the room downstairs, there have been strange noises, sounds of things being moved around, furniture perhaps. It's put me on edge, this change from static to fluid.

I lock the door, activate the light. It jars my eyes, and I hold onto the wall a moment. I stoop to open the cupboard, take the nail from the toiletry bag and gouge a final line on the wall. And below the line, I scrape *14/9,* the date at which our kidnapping has come to end, exactly four weeks from the day we were taken.

I return to my mattress. I don't have to wait long before I hear the door opening.

'It's time,' a man's voice says.

It isn't the usual man, it's the other.

I stand up. He puts the hood over my head, but maybe because I'm holding my blanket, he doesn't tie my hands, but leads me from the room with his hands on my shoulders.

He takes me down the hallway. I know we're going past the double doors, towards the front of the house, and I imagine a car waiting to take me somewhere safe. But he stops, guides me into a room on the right; it will be the kitchen with the long table and the French windows at the end. He makes me sit. I smell coffee and my mouth waters.

'I want you to listen carefully,' he says. His voice comes from behind me. 'I'm going to take off the hood and put sunglasses on you so that your eyes get accustomed to the light. Do you understand?'

'Yes.'

'Close your eyes.'

I do as he says and the hood comes off. The light pierces my closed lids and I drop my head in reflex. Sunglasses are put on me. I raise my head, open my eyes a little, close them again.

'I'll be back soon,' he says. 'Don't move. Stay exactly where you are.'

The door closes. Muted sounds come to me, of hammering, of things being put down, picked up. While my eyes adjust to the light – I open them slightly behind my sunglasses for a couple of seconds, then close them again, gradually increasing the time of exposure – I wonder where my captor is. He must have left with Ned. Is Ned with his father now, does the world know that he's been rescued, that I'm apparently dead?

The man comes back, moves behind me.

'Don't turn around,' he says. 'On the table in front of you, you'll find a letter with instructions for you to follow. You'll need to read it at least three times, maybe more, but however strange the instructions seem, you must comply with them. Your help is in exchange for your life.' He pauses, giving time for his words to sink in. 'Do you understand?'

A tremor runs through me. 'Yes.'

'If there had been some other way, we would have taken it. But there's too much at stake. That's what you need to remember. What we need from you is a leap of faith.' Another pause. 'Are you willing to make that leap?'

'Yes,' I say again, because what choice do I have?

'Once you know the instructions by heart, put a match to them, burn the sheets of paper. Don't write anything down, or take notes. I'm going to leave now. Don't attempt to look at me. There's a clock on the wall in front of you. It's now six in the morning. Don't move for fifteen minutes, except to pour yourself a coffee. Once the fifteen minutes are up, you can read the letter.'

He leaves, and tears seep out from under my sunglasses. I'm out of the room. I'm alive.

56

Present

I lift my sunglasses, scrub the tears from my eyes, then put them back on and search for the clock on the wall. I study its face, my sight gradually adjusting. The black hands show it's five past six.

I lower my eyes to the table. Lying facedown are two sheets of paper. There's also a carafe of coffee, a bottle of milk and two mugs. I reach out, pour myself a coffee and take a sip, my hands shaking as I raise the mug to my lips. The taste is so strong that I hold the hot liquid in my mouth before swallowing it down. I stare at the sheets of paper. I feel detached from reality, as if my body is still locked away in the darkness and I'm watching this scene from above. I take another sip of coffee and this time I close my eyes a moment, savouring the nutty, slightly burnt taste.

I look again at the two sheets of paper. Everything written on them will determine the rest of my life. Will I have a new name? Where will I go? Will a car come to collect me, take me to a safe house somewhere? What about money? My stomach clenches. I am here because of money, because I wanted to make life easier for myself.

The black clock's hands now point to six-fifteen. I take a breath, exhale, take the blanket from my lap, place it on the table and remove my sunglasses. The light streaming in through the windows is too bright and I'm about to put them on again when something catches my attention. I look at the mugs more closely, turning them this way and that, squinting at them. They're mine, they're the ones I bought in Vegas. One of the abductors must have gone back to Ned's house after taking us. I put them down on the table, my mind too exhausted to think about it now.

Turning over the sheets of paper, I read the first line.

Today is Saturday, 31 August.

I frown. It must be a mistake. Today is Saturday, 14 September, day twenty-nine of our captivity. I know this. I continue reading.

Today, you have been married to Ned Hawthorpe for exactly thirty-one days.

My skin prickles. What is this? A joke of some kind?

You may think it's later, but your days here were not days of twenty-four hours. This is day fifteen of your capture.

Day fifteen? Stunned, I lift my head from the paper. I can't have been locked in that room for only fourteen days.

I continue reading.

The story you will tell when you are asked is that Ned rented this house for two weeks to escape from the media glare surrounding the claim of sexual assault made by Justine Elland, and to spend some quality time with his new wife. His Instagram account will confirm this. You can check it on his phone in the bedroom upstairs, in accordance with our instructions.

I read the paragraph twice more and even then, I'm not sure I've understood correctly. Ned rented this house? I read it again. No, that's the story I must tell, when I'm asked. But why? And who is going to ask me? I read the rest of the letter, then read it again, barely able to comprehend what I'm reading, what I've been asked to do. It's only on the third reading that I finally understand.

Our kidnapping wasn't a kidnapping at all.

PART TWO

The Reckoning

I

It's 7 a.m. I stand at the sink, holding the letter in one hand, a lighted match in the other. I push away the fear that I might not have memorised the instructions properly, that I might not be able to carry them out. I have to. I need to.

I put the match to the corner of the letter, feel the heat approaching my fingers as the yellow-blue flame gathers momentum, then watch, mesmerised, as the paper blackens and curls. At the last moment, I drop the sheets into the sink and quickly run water over them, washing the charred remains down the drain, along with the match. I replace the box of matches in the drawer where I found them and move around the kitchen, noting where everything is, the kettle, the fridge, opening cupboards and other drawers, taking in the contents.

I walk to the French windows that had presented such hope to me when I'd tried to escape, and look out. There's a large paved terrace with a swimming pool, and suddenly, I experience a weird sense of déjà vu. I know this terrace, this pool.

My heart racing, I pull open the sliding doors and step out, barely registering the fresh air, the warmth of the early morning sun on my skin. I see the distinctive grey-and-yellow-striped sun-loungers, the bar at the end of the pool, the stools tucked neatly under the counter, smell the tang of the sea in the air. Stunned, I sink onto one of the sun-loungers. This is the house in Haven Cliffs where Ned and I had lunch with Lukas. If I'd needed more proof that Lukas was behind our kidnapping, this was it.

Aware of time marching on, I go back to the kitchen and into the hallway. Opposite the kitchen is a door; I open it and find a dining room. Farther down the hallway, on the left, are the double doors I passed when I tried to escape. Behind them is what I'd imagined, a huge sitting room. On a low rectangular table inlaid with onyx, there are magazines and books, books that belong to me, taken from my bedroom at Ned's. One of my wraps is draped casually over the arm of the nearby sofa. There's also a mug, a stain of coffee still visible in the bottom.

Following the instructions, I familiarise myself with the rest of the house. Opposite the sitting room is a wide stair-case to the upper floor. I ignore it and move along the corridor and find a wood-panelled library with a study tucked behind it. And opposite the library, next to the sitting room, the room where I was held.

I open the door, stand in the doorway. The board has been removed from the window, the room is no longer in darkness. It's nothing like I had imagined. In my mind, it was shabby, its walls yellowed with age. But the walls are smooth, painted in the palest of greens, an echo of the foliage I can see through the window.

In front of the window there's a mahogany writing desk. An ornate lamp stands on it. In the corner where my mattress was, there's a comfortable armchair, upholstered in dark green, and a low wooden table with another lamp. A small bookshelf, filled with neat rows of books, stands against the opposite wall. It seems impossible that this beautiful study was my home for four weeks – two weeks, I correct myself. My mind is tripping on how they did it, why they did it. But I don't have time, not now.

I cross to the little bathroom. With the light streaming in from the window in the other room I don't need to go all the way in and lock the door to be able to see that the cake of soap is gone. I bend to look in the cupboard; it's bare. I check the wall behind the door; the scratches I made and my calculations on the door itself have been sanded away. There's nothing, no trace of me at all.

Except. Back in the main room, I walk over to the wall where I smeared my blood. It's still there. It did happen. It was real. There's still a trace of me in this room.

I return to the hallway. The door to the basement is farther along but I can't face going down to see the room where Ned was held.

I hurry upstairs, find the main bedroom. The bed is unmade, two suitcases, half-packed, lie open by the wardrobe. Clothes – some belonging to me, some to Ned, I presume – are draped on one of the chairs that sit in the bow window. I see my handbag, which I haven't seen since I arrived at Ned's house after Vegas, on the floor by the left-hand side of the bed, and on the bedside table on the right-hand side, a phone which I recognise as Ned's. The door to the en suite is tantalisingly open. More than anything, I crave a shower. But first, I lie down on the left-hand side of the bed, move my body around in the sheets, then get up.

The bathroom is damp and steamy; it must be where Ned had his shower. I touch the navy towel draped casually over the rack; it's still damp. There's a pile of clean towels. I throw one over the shower door, strip off my pyjamas. Stepping into the shower, I turn on the tap and position myself under the cascade of steaming water. I let it gush over me, into my ears, my mouth, down my body onto my feet, then reaching to the array of bottles aligned along a shelf, I shampoo my hair, soap my body, and scrub my skin until it zings. I don't want to get out, I want to stay under the water forever. But after a few more minutes I reluctantly turn off the tap, wrap the towel around myself and step out of the shower. Walking over to the mirror, I peer at my face. It looks thinner, paler, and there are dark smudges under my eyes. But I still look like me.

Next to the bathroom, I find a walk-in dressing room, one side with the amount of clothes – my clothes – that I would have brought for a two-week holiday, the other side with Ned's. I choose a pair of white shorts and a T-shirt, push my feet into a pair of my trainers, find my brush in the bathroom, detangle my wet hair.

Back in the bedroom, I sit on the bed, put my bag on my knees, and riffle through the contents. The first thing I see is a passport. I check the name quickly; even though I'll no longer be dead, I want to be sure I can still be Amelie Lamont. The photograph is one I took not long before Papa died.

There are other things in the bag, things that were there before – tissues, lip gloss, my purse, the keys I've always kept for my childhood house in Reading – and things that weren't – a set of keys with a remote attached, and my phone. I take my phone, switch it on, and see that it's fully charged. The only people I messaged on a regular basis were Carolyn, Justine, and Lina, and occasionally Vicky, if I was running late for work. There are countless messages from Carolyn. I scroll to the one she sent on the twenty-sixth of July, in response to the photo I'd sent her from the plane.

Amelie, if you haven't taken off yet, call me. It's urgent. Something has happened that you should know about x

It breaks my heart to read the following twenty or so messages, all from Carolyn, all asking me to call urgently. She must have been so worried when I didn't reply. But I understand now; I hadn't left my phone on the plane, Ned had taken it and, at the same time, had damaged my computer.

I find a message from Carolyn on 2 August, the day after my wedding to Ned, sent after she called me at the hotel to tell me of his assault on Justine.

Amelie, is it true? Did you really get married to Ned? It's all over the news.

Then, the following morning, other messages, followed by:

I know you're probably not getting these messages, otherwise you would have phoned me. But if you are getting them, please at least message me back. I need to know that you're OK.

And then a message, supposedly from me, sent to Carolyn from my phone two days after Ned and I arrived back in the UK.

Hi Carolyn, thanks for your concern but I'm sure you'll understand that I'm busy right now. Please don't worry, I'm fine, really happy to be married to Ned. I'll call you soon.

No wonder Carolyn hadn't believed it. I would never have told Carolyn that I was too busy to see her.

There aren't any messages from Justine, and I have to fight back tears. If what I think is true, she would have already been dead by the time I left for Las Vegas.

I move from the bed, aware that I need to finish my tour of the house. Taking my phone, and Ned's, I leave the bedroom, find another four bedrooms, all with en suites, and return to the kitchen. I check the clock: it's eight-fifteen, almost time to carry out the next part of the instructions. I falter a moment; it seems too enormous, what they've asked me to do. But I have no choice.

I make a quick mental check to be sure I've completed the first part properly.

First, look around you. Take note of where you are, familiarise yourself with the kitchen, then with the rest of the house. Walk around, open cupboards, touch things. Remember, for the last two weeks, you and Ned have been living here as man and wife.

In the master bedroom upstairs, you'll find your clothes. You will also see half-packed suitcases; today, you and Ned were heading back to his house in Wentworth.

Before you have a shower, lie down on the bed for a moment, as if you've been sleeping in it. Your phone is in your bag; look at the last messages you received once you've had your shower. Ned's phone is on his bedside table. When you leave the bedroom, take it with you to the kitchen. At 8.20 a.m. precisely, continue to the next part of your instructions.

2

It's 8.20 a.m. Pushing my chair back, I go into the hall, turn towards the main door. Taking a bunch of keys from a hook, I read the labels to find the right key, unlock the door and pull it closed behind me. I hurry to a small gate to the right of the main gates, recognising Ned's car parked in the drive. I press the buzzer to open the gate, step onto the pavement and start running to the right. At the end of the road, there's a barrier. Looking down, I see the beach below. I look for a way to reach it and about fifty yards to the left, find some zigzag steps leading to a promenade.

I run down the steps, jump from the low wall of the promenade onto the beach. There are a few people around and I hurry to a couple walking their dog along the sand.

'Excuse me,' I say, breathing hard. 'I'm looking for my husband, he told me he was going to the beach for a walk and he hasn't come back yet. He's medium build, dark hair, grey eyes, he's wearing knee-length navy shorts and a white polo shirt. Have you seen him?'

They shake their heads. 'We passed a couple of joggers—'

'No, he's not a jogger, he wouldn't have been jogging,' I say, already running off. 'Thanks anyway.'

I pose the same question to a man jogging along the water's edge, then to a young woman sitting on the sand with a toddler, then to an older woman walking a Dalmatian. None of them have seen a man matching Ned's description. I've been running along the beach for about ten minutes now; I see a pier ahead of me, it must be Bournemouth Pier. I keep on running, stopping some more people on the way, who all tell me that they haven't seen Ned. When I'm almost at the pier, I turn and run back the way I came, past the steps I came down, until I can't run anymore. I stop for a while to catch my breath, then go back to the steps and return to the house.

It's now nearly nine o'clock. Using my phone, I search for the number of the local police station.

'Hello, can you help me?' I ask. 'I'm worried about my husband; he went for a walk this morning at six o'clock, and he still hasn't come back. I wouldn't normally be worried, but he left his phone on the kitchen table.'

'Has your husband gone off on long walks before?' the responder asks.

'No, at least, not without his phone. But he's been under a lot of strain recently, he's been accused of something, allegations have been made against him, he's been hounded in the press—'

'What's his name?'

'Ned, Ned Hawthorpe, shall I spell that for you—'

'No, it's fine.' The woman's tone has suddenly perked up. 'And you are?'

'Amelie Hawthorpe – I'm his wife.'

'And your address?'

'I don't know it exactly, we're not at home. Ned rented a house for a couple of weeks, it's in Haven Cliffs. The house name is Albatross, but I don't know which road it's on.'

'Okay, madam, stay where you are. I'm sending someone to you, they'll be with you within the next twenty minutes.'

'Oh good, thank you.' I let relief suffuse my voice, then hang up.

I wait, my stomach a mass of knots. Fifteen minutes later, there's a ring on the bell. I use the control pad by the door to open the main gate. A police car drives through and pulls up at the front of the house. Two police officers get out, a man and a woman. I hurry to the door.

'Mrs Hawthorpe?' the woman says. 'I'm Officer Wendy Garrat and this is Officer Phil Allson. Can we come in?'

'Yes, of course,' I say, hoping I sound worried rather than nervous. 'Thank you for coming so quickly.'

I lead them to the kitchen, offer them a seat and repeat what I already said on the phone.

'You say your husband – Ned – has been under some strain recently?' Officer Garrat asks.

'Yes, he was accused of sexual assault.' I glance at them. 'You probably know about it. The accuser was one of his staff at *Exclusives* magazine; he fired her and she took revenge.' I twist my hands in my lap. 'But even though she dropped the charges, the press won't leave him alone and it's been getting him down; it's why he decided to rent this house, he wanted to get away for a while. I thought he was fine, a little depressed maybe, but he seemed to be coping. But last night I woke up and he wasn't in bed. I went to look for him and found him here, in the kitchen, sitting at the table with his head in his hands. He said that he had a headache and that I was to go back to bed.' I pause, slow my speech. 'I managed to persuade him to come with me but he couldn't sleep, and at around half past five, he took a shower and said he was going for a walk on the beach, that he'd have breakfast with me when he got back. He gave me a kiss and I went back to sleep.'

'You weren't worried about him at that point?'

'No. I was only worried about his headache, but I hoped a walk would clear it.'

'When did you become worried about him?'

'When I came downstairs after my shower, at about eight o'clock. And not straightaway, because of his phone being on the table.' I reach for it, pick it up, put it down again. 'I presumed he was in the pool, he's never far from his phone, so I made a pot of coffee and went to call him. But he wasn't in the pool so I thought he must be in the study or the sitting room. But I couldn't find him anywhere in the house and that's when I began to get worried, because it was almost twenty past eight and he'd left around six.' I swallow. 'Without his phone. So I went to the beach to look for him but he wasn't there either and I thought that maybe he'd come back to the house while I was out, that we'd somehow missed each other. But he wasn't here.'

'Did you have an argument, yesterday or this morning, maybe?'

'No, not at all.' I give an embarrassed laugh. 'We're still in the honeymoon period, we've only been married a few weeks.'

Officer Allson nods to Ned's phone. 'Have you checked it?' he asks.

'No, I don't know the passcode. But there wouldn't be anything on it anyway, he deleted his Instagram before we left to come here, he wanted a complete break from social media.'

Officer Garrat picks up the phone. 'You have no idea what the passcode is?'

'I think he once said it was his mother's birth date but I've no idea if that was true.'

'Do you know his mother's date of birth?'

'No. I've never met her. She wasn't too happy about our marriage, and he hasn't seen her since. He was upset about that too.'

Officer Garrat looks at her colleague, who's been typing on his phone. 'Have you found it?'

'Zero three two three five seven,' he says.

'Right, let's give it a try.' She types it into Ned's phone. 'Bingo.'

I watch, my heart thumping, as Officer Garrat scrolls around Ned's phone. After a moment, she shows it to her colleague, who immediately leaves the room.

'Have you found something?' I ask anxiously.

The policewoman hesitates, then passes Ned's phone to me. It's open to his Instagram account. There are only two recent posts: the last one, posted at 6.05 this morning, reads 'I'm sorry. Forgive me.' The one before that, from the previous Saturday, is a photo with the caption:

I know I said I was taking an Instagram break but I couldn't resist posting this photo of Amelie that I took earlier today. Isn't she beautiful?

I stare at the photo. I'm stretched out on a yellow-and-grey-striped sun-lounger, wearing my red bikini.

'I don't understand,' I murmur.

'Can you think of any reason why he'd be sorry?' Officer Garrat asks. 'You said you hadn't had an argument?'

I raise my head, cover my mistake quickly. 'No, that's what I mean, I don't understand what he had to be sorry about.' Officer Garrat doesn't say anything and in the ensuing silence, I let realisation dawn. 'You don't think . . .' My voice falters.

Officer Garrat is kind, she says that her colleagues are looking for Ned now, that she's sure they'll find him sitting on a bench somewhere, unaware that he's been causing me a lot of worry. She asks if she can make tea and I point to the cupboards and tell her where to find tea bags and mugs. While we drink it, Officer Garrat asks gentle questions about me and Ned, about our whirlwind marriage, about our relationship, about the allegation against him.

It must be about an hour later when Officer Allson puts his head around the door and calls Officer Garrat into the hallway. I hear the murmur of voices, wipe sweaty hands on my shorts. The waiting is unbearable.

At last, the two police officers come back to the kitchen.

'Mrs Hawthorpe,' Officer Allson says gently. 'We've had a development from our colleagues. I'm very sorry to have to tell you that a body has been found in the bracken at the foot of one of the cliffs leading down to the beach.'

I burst into tears. Officer Garrat finds a tissue, passes it to me. 'We don't know for sure that it's Ned,' she says. 'I'm sorry to have to ask – does he have any distinguishing marks?'

I nod. 'He's got a tattoo of an eagle on his lower back.'

'Anything else?'

'Um – a mole between two of his toes, between the big toe and the next one.'

'Can you remember which foot?'

I take a breath, rub my eyes. 'The left.'

'Anything else that might help us identify the body?' Officer Allson asks.

'No, I can't think of anything.'

And then I stare into space.

The wait until a phone call to Officer Garrat confirms that the body is Ned's is interminable. By the time it comes, already mentally and physically exhausted, it isn't hard for me to seem distraught. The relief is so huge I can't stop crying. Ned really is dead, he will never be able to harm me.

When I'm calmer, Officer Garrat tells me that I need to go with her to the police station to make a statement. Taking my blanket, I go upstairs to get my suitcase, gathering Ned's things together at the same time. Officer Garrat follows silently. She is coming across as kind, but I see her eyes skim the room, the detective in her searching for clues.

'We need someone to officially identify Ned's body,' Officer Garrat says respectfully, when we're in the police car. 'Is that something you think you'd like to do?'

I shake my head quickly. 'I – I don't think I could. Anyway, I think someone from his family would want to, I don't know, his father maybe.'

Later, much later, when I think I'll scream from the need to be alone, to have space to think and digest everything that's happened, Officer Garrat, who has remained by my side all day, drives me to Ned's house in Wentworth. I want to beg not to be taken there, but I can't. Even with Ned dead, I have to continue playing the loving wife.

I arrive at the house, take the set of keys from my bag, use the remote to open the gates.

'We usually have a security guard,' I explain, as we drive up to the house. 'But Ned gave him time off while we were away.'

'Is there anyone else here, someone who can be with you?' Officer Garrat says, glancing at me in the rearview mirror.

I shake my head. 'The housekeeper is away visiting her family. But it's okay, I have friends I can call.' Without warning, I start to sob and quickly push my hand against my mouth to try and stop myself.

B. A. Paris

'It's okay, Mrs Hawthorpe. You've had a terrible shock. I can stay with you until your friends arrive, if you like.'

'Thank you, but I think I just need to be with Ned's things. I still can't believe . . .'

She nods, stops the car. I climb out, thanking her, but she follows me into the house. For a moment, we stand alone in the empty hallway.

'If you need anything, think of anything, just call,' she says.

I nod my thanks and she leaves.

Finally, I'm alone.

3

Officer Garrat has only been gone a few minutes and I want to shout for her to come back. I wish I'd asked her to check that the house was secure before she left. Alone in this vast place, I feel horribly vulnerable.

Methodically, I walk through the rooms, pulling at the windows, tugging at the kitchen patio door, making sure everything is locked, then return to the kitchen. My phone is on the table. I reach for it, about to call Carolyn, when I remember the instructions and withdraw my hand. I can't, not yet. Turning my phone so the screen is facing down, I stare vacantly at the wall.

Light moves across the marble counters, marking the passing of time. I sit, numb, until it is dark and my stomach is grumbling with hunger. There's a little food in the fridge, the 'use by' dates still some ways off: a packet of smoked salmon, a box of eggs, a block of butter, and a loaf of bread. I make some toast, take a couple of bites, then put it down, no longer hungry. I can't relax in this house and there's a voice in my head telling me to run. But I can't, I'm stuck here until Ned is buried. Only then will I be free to leave.

Anxiety gnaws away inside me. What if somewhere along the way today, I messed up? Did the police believe everything I told them, did I do everything I was supposed to do?

I close my eyes and run through the second part of the instructions that I memorised.

At 8.20 a.m., leave the house. You'll find the keys for the door and the side gate on a hook in the hallway. Once outside, turn right and head down to the beach. When you get there, stop people, tell them you're looking for your husband, describe him – medium height and build, dark hair, wearing knee-length navy shorts and a white polo shirt. Run to the pier and back, then run the other way, towards Sandbanks, before returning to the house. Call the local police station, tell them that you're staying at a house named Albatross and you're worried about your husband, who went for a walk early in the morning, leaving his phone on the table, and hasn't come back. Tell them he's been under a lot of strain because of an allegation against him. Once you mention his name, they'll be interested. The chances are they'll send somebody to you, if they don't, call back an hour later, say you're still worried.

At some point the police will ask if you know the passcode for Ned's phone. Tell them you don't but that you remember him saying that it was his mother's birth date, which you don't know. They' ll search for it themselves and open Ned's phone to three messages, the first dated Friday, 16 August, saying he's taking a break from social media, the second posted last week, a photo that proves you were both here at the house, the third at 6.05 this morning saying, 'I'm sorry, forgive me.' Be worried by the last message, ask the police if they think Ned might have harmed himself. If his body hasn't already been found, they'll start a search. They'll eventually find it at the bottom of a cliff not far from the house, indicating suicide. It will be up to you to play the distraught widow. Do not offer to identify the body but when asked for identifying features, mention the tattoo of an eagle on his lower back and the mole between the big toe and the next on his left foot. It will be a while before a verdict of suicide is confirmed but once the police are happy to let you go, return to the house in Wentworth. The security guard has left, he received a message from Ned's phone telling him to take time off while you were away, until further notice. If the police ask if there are any other staff, mention that the housekeeper is away on holiday. Take time to absorb the events of today and prepare to undertake the next set of instructions.

I think about the photo of me in my red bikini, the one on Ned's Instagram account. Lukas must have taken it the day we went for lunch. He had been planning this for that long. Was it because he had met me that day that I was treated better than Ned, that I wasn't killed? Or was it because he needed me to be able to cover all his tracks?

I pace the kitchen. I don't know what to do with myself, I feel more trapped here than I did locked in a room in the dark. But I can't leave, the instructions had been explicit. All I can do is wait, in a house that I hate, for events to play themselves out.

4

At 9 a.m., there's a call on the intercom.

I haven't slept, I couldn't. I spent the night curled on the sofa. At dawn I'd gone outside wrapped in my blanket and stood watching the sun rise, the wet grass cool beneath my feet, and tried to find peace.

Going to the video panel by the door, I see Jethro Hawthorpe standing outside the gates, the driver's-side door of his car open. Without speaking, I find the button to activate the gates, watch as he gets back in his car. He starts to drive through, and I have a sudden desire to press the close button on the control pad and crush his car between the metal gates so that I won't have to see him.

He drives to the front door, the sound of expensive car tyres crunching on the gravel. He gets out of the car, sombre in his dark suit and tie. I smooth down the navy-blue shift dress I'm wearing for his visit, although I didn't know when it would come, or if it would come.

He walks up the steps and I silently open the door, stand back to let him in. We appraise each other a moment. His face is etched with grief, and my heart contracts in sympathy. I have no idea what to say, so I wait for him to speak.

'Let's talk in the study,' he says.

'I prefer the library,' I say, and he nods, realising maybe that it will be less painful than being in the room where he last saw his son.

I let him lead the way and follow, clenching my hands. I'm going to have to play this by ear.

'I'll get to the point – I don't believe my son's death was suicide, and I've told the police,' Jethro Hawthorpe says, without sitting down. 'I think he was murdered, and I think you' – he jabs his finger at me – 'were involved.'

Thrown by his accusation of murder, my heart leaps to my mouth. I'm not prepared for this.

'Why would I want Ned murdered?' I ask, my mind racing.

'For his money, why else?'

'I don't want his money, I—'

'Don't lie!' His dark eyes flash with anger. 'Ned told me you pretended you were pregnant, and about the terms of the postnuptial agreement. You tricked him on both accounts. I've worked it out – a billion pounds.' He gives me a look of disbelief tinged with disgust. 'It's unbelievable that you think you can get away with it.'

'Do you think I would take even a penny from a man who only married me as a damage-limitation exercise, to cover himself against sexual assault allegations by playing the victim card?' I can feel heat rising on my face as I step towards him. 'Do you think I would take even a penny from a man who would have told the world that I tricked him into marrying me, when it was he who tricked me? He told me that he wanted to get you off his back about a girl you wanted him to marry, and that if I agreed to marry him, he would pay me a hundred thousand pounds for my college fees.'

'What are you talking about? What girl I wanted him to marry?'

248

'Your son said our marriage was a simple business arrangement and that we would separate after a month, tell everyone we'd made a mistake. And yes, I believed it, because I was stupid and I'll pay for it for the rest of my life. But I did *not* trick him!'

I see the pain and confusion on his face and for a moment, I think he believes me. But then his face hardens again.

'You can say what you like, it will be your word against mine. I shall tell the truth, that you pretended you were pregnant to get your hands on his money, and that when he discovered you had lied, and challenged you, you pushed him off the cliff. Or had someone do it for you.'

Panic swells, I fight it down. 'That is not the truth, I did not pretend to be pregnant. And as I'll be donating any money due to me, in its entirety, to your foundation, your theory that I was after his money won't stand up.'

He falters and I feel a flash of victory. But he recovers quickly.

'Nice try. You would say that, of course, now that you know you're cornered.'

I'm unsure what to say next, unsure how much to tell him. But I have to make him believe that Ned died by his own hand.

'If we're talking of murder, Mr Hawthorpe, I think you should know that Hunter was murdered.'

'Hunter? Ned's security guard? What are you talking about? He wasn't murdered, Ned dismissed him.'

Consumed by doubt that I might be saying too much, I sink onto the nearest chair.

'No,' I say. 'That's what Ned told you. But the truth is that Hunter was murdered two days before your last visit here. Ned and I had been to lunch with a man named Lukas, and on our way back, our car was ambushed. Hunter was dragged from it and shot dead.'

'Where?' Jethro Hawthorpe is sceptical. 'Where did this happen?'

'Along a country road somewhere between here and Haven Cliffs, on the coast.'

'I don't believe a word of it. Why would someone want to murder Hunter?'

'He was murdered in retaliation for the murder of Lina Mielkutė, the accountant at *Exclusives*.'

'Hunter murdered Ned's accountant?' He barks a laugh. 'You are delusional. What is this, some kind of joke?'

'No, none of this is a joke! Hunter didn't murder Lina, your son did. Hunter's murder was a warning, a warning that Ned understood. It's why he hid himself away in Haven Cliffs. He knew they'd be coming for him and thought it would be the last place they'd look for him.'

'How dare you! How dare you accuse my son of murder!'

'I saw it with my own eyes, Mr Hawthorpe.' I stand and walk towards him. 'I saw him suffocate Lina with his bare hands right outside that door.' My eyes well with tears as I point to the hallway.

He moves away from me to stand at the window. 'Why would he murder this woman?'

'Because she threatened to tell the police about the payments Ned had asked her to make to staff members whom he had sexually harassed. She was a friend of—'

He holds his hand up. 'I'm not going to listen to any more of this. You need help, you're delusional and dangerous.'

'It's the truth!'

He walks past me, our shoulders almost touching as he heads towards the door. I can't let him go.

'Did you know that Justine Elland, the woman who accused Ned of sexual assault a few weeks ago, has disappeared?' My voice rings out across the room, stopping him in his tracks.

'She's in France,' he says, turning to face me. 'Like you, she was after Ned's money and when he offered it to her, she took it and ran.'

'That's what Ned told you. But when I go to the police and tell them that I saw your son murder Lina, I'll also tell them that he told everyone she'd gone back to Lithuania, just like he told everyone that Justine had gone back to France. I'll ask them to check that Lina actually arrived in Lithuania and when they find that she did, I'll suggest that they dig deeper. And when they do, they'll find that the person who went through immigration at the airport in Vilnius was not Lina Mielkutė, but someone travelling on her passport, someone who was paid to travel as Lina by Ned. That's how he hid Lina's murder, Mr Hawthorpe, by getting someone to fly to Lithuania using her passport. Lukas, the man we had lunch with on the day of Hunter's murder, knew Lina. He had discovered this cover-up and made Ned understand that he knew what had happened. Ned was worried and told Lukas he'd asked Hunter to take Lina to the airport, suggesting that if anything *had* happened to Lina, it was down to Hunter. We left soon after – and then Hunter was murdered.'

'If what you say is true, that you saw my son murder this woman, why haven't you been to the police?'

How can I tell him that in the month since I married Ned, I've had no access to the outside world? It would add to the fantasy he thinks I'm creating. I need him to drop his threat. I need him to listen.

'Because of your foundation,' I say.

'And why would you be concerned about the foundation?'

I take a step towards him. 'Mr Hawthorpe, I know how important the foundation is to you. If you persist with your claim that Ned was murdered, the truth will come out about the women he has killed, and your foundation will suffer. Do you think your benefactors will continue to donate if your son is accused of murder, even if he's no longer alive? The best thing, for everyone, is to accept the truth, which is that Ned took his own life because he knew that Lukas was coming after him for Lina's murder.' I pause, worried he's not buying it. 'There's another thing. The day before Ned died, I told him that I'd seen him murder Lina. I also told him about the letter I'd sent to a journalist detailing what I'd seen and instructing her that if she didn't hear from me within seven days, to go to the police and give them my letter. Ned knew then that one way or another he was going to have to pay for Lina's death. If Lukas didn't get him, the police would.'

'No.' He shakes his head. 'I won't believe it. My son wouldn't have taken his own life.' He's at the door, he walks through it, into the hall.

'I need to know by tomorrow morning what your intentions are, Mr Hawthorpe,' I call after him. 'If I don't hear from you, I'll go to the police!'

I hear the front door slam and running to the window, I see him get into his car and drive off. Once he's through the gates, I hurry to the hall and using the remote, close them behind him. I'm panting now, my breath raspy. But I did it. I feel a strange exhilaration, because there had been no instructions for this part, only guidelines.

At some point, you may have a visit from Jethro Hawthorpe. We cannot help you with this; we can't predict what he will say.

He knows the terms of the postnuptial agreement so he may accuse you of marrying Ned for his money. To put a stop to those allegations, tell him that you plan to donate any monies due to you to his foundation. You should know that Jethro Hawthorpe, unlike his son, is an honourable man who, through his foundation, works tirelessly to help others.

There's the possibility he may not want to accept that his son took his own life. If so, you may use any of the information contained in this letter to persuade him that Ned was depressed and feared for his life. If necessary, tell him that Ned was responsible for the murder of a young woman, Lina Mielkutė, and that he feared he would be killed in retaliation for her murder. He will not want to accept that his son was a murderer, but we know you witnessed the revenge murder of his security guard, so use this to your advantage.

You should also know that it's probable Ned also killed Justine Elland, the woman who accused him of sexual assault. You may use this information to persuade Jethro Hawthorpe that his son was guilty, not just of Lina's murder, but also of Justine's.

In the kitchen, I make a pot of coffee. My euphoria has disappeared and is replaced by an awful doubt. Was it terrible to tell a bereaved father that his son was a murderer, even if it was true? But Jethro Hawthorpe had accused me of murdering Ned, an accusation that, with his connections, he could make stick. It would be my word against his. I also have terrible doubts about insisting to Jethro Hawthorpe that Ned took his own life when I don't believe that he did. He was too happy to be finally free. Which means he was pushed. By whom?

As always, my mind circles back to Lukas. To the line in the letter of instructions – *we know you witnessed the revenge murder of his security guard.* The only way the kidnappers could have known that I witnessed Hunter's murder was from someone who saw me in the car with Ned. And the only person who had seen me was the gunman, sent by Lukas to kill us.

5

I'm nervous the next day, waiting for Jethro Hawthorpe's visit. I should have given him my phone number so that I wouldn't have to see him again.

The nonstop ringing at the gate doesn't help. Each time, I check via the video link to see if it's him. But it's always journalists, cameramen hovering behind them like flies.

The news of Ned's death broke last night. I watched it emotionless on the news, curled up on the sofa. I listened as they confirmed that the body found the previous day on the beach at Haven Cliffs was that of Ned Hawthorpe. I waited for the reporter to say that the police weren't looking for anyone else in connection with his death, and when he didn't, my heart had sunk. The bulletin had, however, mentioned the allegation of sexual assault against Ned, and the fact that he had been trolled on social media and targeted in the press because of it. Most people listening would probably think suicide. But the police weren't most people, and neither was Jethro Hawthorpe.

At midday my phone rings, a call from an unknown number. I'm in the kitchen, cleaning the already pristine cupboards. Packets of pasta and tins of food, piles of plates and bowls are scattered over the work surfaces. I stare at my phone, then press answer.

'For the sake of the foundation, I will accept that my son took his own life,' Jethro Hawthorpe says.

I close my eyes. 'Thank you. If you could give me the name of the solicitor who drew up the postnuptial agreement, I'll make my wishes known to him. In return, I'd like to be kept informed of the funeral arrangements. I'll need to be there, for appearances' sake. Once it's over, you won't hear from me again.'

'I hope not,' he says, and hangs up.

Within minutes, my phone rings again. There's a number listed this time, but not one I know. I pick up.

'Hello?'

'Mrs Hawthorpe,' a voice says. 'It's Paul Carr. I understand that you've spoken to Mr Jethro Hawthorpe.'

'Yes,' I say, moving to the table and sitting down.

'I'm very sorry for your loss.'

'Thank you.'

'I'm sorry to intrude, but I'm calling on the instruction of Mr Hawthorpe to confirm that the funeral of your husband will take place on Friday.'

Four days away. My stomach plummets at the thought of having to stay in this house another five days.

'Thank you, Mr Carr.'

'Mrs Hawthorpe—'

'It's not Hawthorpe,' I interrupt quickly. 'It's Lamont. But you can call me Amelie.'

'Then, Amelie, could I visit you tomorrow to discuss the postnuptial agreement you and Ned signed?'

'Yes,' I reply mechanically. 'Of course. Is ten a.m. okay?'

'Perfect. And can I bring anything for you? I imagine it's difficult for you to leave the house to go shopping.'

'Yes, there are journalists outside the gate.'

'Have you spoken to them?'

'No, and I don't intend to.'

'Good.'

I give him a small list of groceries to see me through the next few days. 'If you're sure you don't mind,' I add, when I get to the end.

'Not at all. I've been instructed to look after you until after the funeral. Goodbye, Amelie, I'll see you tomorrow at ten.'

6

I have trouble equating the man who strides through the front door at precisely ten o'clock the next morning, a box of groceries tucked under his arm, with the hesitant and nervous man I'd seen in Ned's study. He'd been pitiless to the journalists who'd tried to squeeze through the gate behind his car; I'd heard him via the intercom threatening them with legal action if they so much as put a toe onto the property.

'Amelie,' he says, placing his bag on the floor so that he can shake my hand. 'How nice to meet you again. And please, call me Paul.'

He insists on carrying the box through to the kitchen and when I suggest we talk in the library, he says he's perfectly happy in the kitchen, where we could perhaps have some coffee.

'Mr Hawthorpe Senior said that you wanted to talk to me about the postnuptial agreement,' he says, once I've placed two mugs in front of us.

'Is it actually valid?' I ask. 'What I mean is, when I asked for a pound doubled for each day that Ned and I remained married, I had no idea what it would come to because I'd never worked it out. I would never have expected him to honour it and I suspect he would have found a way not to, if it did happen to be valid.'

'It's absolutely valid. But as his spouse, you are the beneficiary of his estate in any case.'

'I don't want any of it. Whatever is due to me, I want to donate it to the Hawthorpe Foundation. I hope that won't be a problem.'

'That can certainly be arranged. I'll just need you to sign a document to that effect.'

'Do you have it with you? I understand that it might be months or even years before his estate is settled but I'd rather get it over and done with.'

'As a matter of fact, I do,' he says, delving into his bag.

I smile. 'I see Mr Hawthorpe has already informed you of my wish.'

He neither confirms nor denies it, and as he places a file on the table and slides out a document, another thought hits me. Maybe it was the kidnappers who told him. I'd already worked out that for the kidnappers to have used the doubling method on Ned, they must have known about the terms of the postnup – and the only person who could have told them about the postnup was Paul Carr. Maybe there's more to him than I first thought. Was he, and is he still, working for the kidnappers? I study him for a moment, but his face gives nothing away.

I read the document, sign it.

'You said you'd been instructed to look after me until after the funeral,' I say, passing it back to him. 'Can I ask by whom? I doubt it was Jethro Hawthorpe.'

He gives me a gentle smile. 'I'm afraid I'm not at liberty to say. However,' he goes on, and I look at him hopefully. 'I have some information for you.'

'What sort of information?'

'Soon after your marriage to Mr Hawthorpe, I was contacted by a solicitor, a Mr Barriston. He has a practice in

Reading and saw reports of Ned's marriage in the news-
papers. When he saw your name, he realised you were the
daughter of one of his clients, who died some years back.
Your father, Eduard Lamont. Mr Barriston was eager to
make contact with you and contacted me, as Mr Hawthorpe's
solicitor, to ask if I could tell him your whereabouts.'

'I didn't know my father had a solicitor,' I say, frowning.

'Mr Barriston has instructed me to tell you that the house
where you lived in Reading was left to you by your father in
his will, and is yours to do with as you see fit.'

I stare at him. 'My father made a will?'

'Yes.'

It's a struggle to understand. Why would Papa have made
a will when he didn't have anything to leave me? The word
house penetrates my consciousness.

'There must be a mistake. My father can't have left me the
house. It wasn't his, we only rented it.'

He draws a sheet of paper from the file. 'I have the details
here. It seems that he bought it with money left to him by his
mother-in-law, your maternal grandmother. If I understand
correctly, it took a while for her estate to be settled after she
died, but when the inheritance came through, your father
arranged with the landlord to buy the property.'

My head spins. 'I didn't know, he didn't tell me that he
bought the house. Are you sure he did?'

'Quite sure.'

'And he left it to me?'

'Yes.'

'I can't believe it. I mean, it's . . . it's wonderful, it means I
have somewhere to go. But I still can't believe it.'

'Will you go there after the funeral, do you think?'

'I don't know – I mean, can I? Can I just go there?'

'I don't see why not.'

'Today?'

'I'm afraid not.'

'But if I promise to come back for the funeral on Friday?' I persist.

'I would advise against that course of action,' Paul says, watching me. 'You're very much in the media spotlight because of Ned's unfortunate death. If you leave here, you'll be besieged. I don't know if you're aware, but this house belongs to Mr Hawthorpe Senior, and he's agreed to let you stay until the funeral. Once the funeral is over, you'll be able to go to Reading.' He pauses. 'When you're there, you should contact Mr Barriston. I have his details here.' He hands me a card. 'He asked if you have keys to the house.'

'Yes, I do, I kept them.'

'He also has a set, and he's asked if you would like for him to arrange for a company to clean the house before your arrival. He's concerned that it's been empty for three years. I don't know if you're aware, but he and your father were friends, and when your father became ill, he asked Mr Barriston to look out for you, be your unofficial guardian, so to speak. I think there was a boarding school involved. When nobody could find you after your father died, Mr Barriston had you registered as missing. When you still couldn't be found, he kept an eye on the house, hoping that one day you'd come back and claim it.'

'I don't understand,' I say, stunned. 'Why didn't my father tell me this? He never spoke of Mr Barriston, he never told me there was someone I could go to for help. When he died, I thought I had no one.'

'Perhaps he didn't want to worry you by admitting he was dying. Mr Barriston has always regretted that he was abroad when your father died, and that by the time he got back, you'd disappeared. He didn't realise that you had nobody at all. He presumed there would be friends or neighbours looking after you, at least until he returned.'

Momentarily overwhelmed, I take a sip of coffee.

'Thank you for telling me this,' I say, cradling my mug. 'It means a lot to know that my father provided for me.' I meet his eye. 'Are you sure I can't go to Reading and come back for the funeral on Friday? I'm not comfortable in this house. I've never been comfortable here,' I add, wishing I could tell him everything that had happened.

'Quite sure,' he says firmly. 'The journalists would follow you, they'd be camping on your doorstep. Once the funeral is over, Mr Hawthorpe will quickly become old news. It's a sad truth, but there will soon be something else to make the head-lines. We aren't remembered for long after our deaths, only by those who carry us in their hearts.' He takes the file from the table and puts it in his bag. 'Now, as your late husband's solicitor, it's fitting that I should attend the funeral. May I suggest I pick you up at eleven on Friday, and we can go together?'

'I'd like that, thank you.'

'I'll also arrange for a car to take you to Reading after the funeral.' He takes a card from his inside pocket and hands it to me. 'In the meantime, if you need anything at all, just call.'

7

I close my eyes, and memories from the house in Reading reach out from the past. I see Papa sitting in his chair in our sitting room, his eyes closed, his mouth half-open, smell his medication on his breath. I see the brown front door, the narrow hallway, the stairs with the patterned carpet.

Tears well. Papa had provided for me, he'd presumed that Mr Barriston and I would meet in the first few days after his death. He couldn't have foreseen that the end would come so swiftly, and while Mr Barriston was away. My life could have been so different. I would have gone to boarding school, I would have had Mr Barriston looking out for me. By now, I'd be in college, in the second year of my degree. I would have had friends, partners; I would have lived, loved, backpacked around Europe during the holidays. Instead, I had witnessed two murders, and been kidnapped.

It's strange how much I long to be in the house in Reading. I need to be away from here, I need to be free. Except I will never really be free. The kidnappers will always be there, somewhere in the background of my mind.

I think of Paul Carr, and what they had said about him.

At some point you will be contacted by Paul Carr, Ned's solicitor. He will have information for you, you can trust him. In case of a

*problem, he's the only person you may contact. Do not contact
anyone else.*

The last line of the instructions echoes through me. *Do not
contact anyone else.* I hadn't – but now that I've done everything they've asked of me, surely I can phone Carolyn?

The need to speak to her is urgent, visceral. She is all I
have left, she's the only one left. I find my phone and call her
number.

I'm nervous as I wait for her to pick up. How can I explain
any of this? I'm not allowed to tell anyone what I know, or
what I saw, I'm not allowed to tell anyone about my fake
kidnapping. I can tell Carolyn that Ned tricked me into
marrying him, but I'll have to pretend that we really did go to
Haven Cliffs for a two-week break, that he really was
depressed, so depressed that he took his own life. The thought
that I'll never be able to speak about what I actually went
through makes me horribly anxious.

It's almost a relief when an automated voice answers, telling me that Carolyn's number is no longer in use. Then I
frown; Carolyn wouldn't have changed her number without
telling me. But that was before. My heart sinks. What if she
doesn't want to have anything more to do with me because I
didn't tell her I had married Ned?

I call her office. A man answers and when I ask to speak to
her, he tells me that he's very sorry, but that Carolyn was the
victim of a hit-and-run accident a few weeks before, and
sadly passed away. The phone drops from my hands, I fall to
my knees, and my wails of grief and despair echo around the
silent house. I think I will die from the pain of it, I think I will
die from the guilt. But most of all, I think that if Ned wasn't
already dead, I'd kill him with my bare hands.

8

The sun bursting through the clouds sends shafts of light shooting across the room. I blink my eyes open, lift my head from the kitchen table. *Carolyn is dead.*

Was I never meant to know that she was dead? Is that why I was told not to contact anyone, in case I found out? Or don't the kidnappers know?

I stand slowly, move to the patio doors and stare into the garden without seeing it. Since leaving the house in Haven Cliffs on Saturday, I've barely been outside. I feel a spark of anger – do the kidnappers realise what they've asked of me, insisting I stay here, in this house, until the funeral? And I realise that they don't, because nobody except Jethro Hawthorpe knows I saw Lina being killed.

Where are they now, the kidnappers? Have they gone back to wives, children? Or are they plotting another kidnapping that isn't really a kidnapping? What about Lukas, where is he? I need to find him because if I don't, I'll never have the answers that will allow me to move on. I need to know why; why I had to lie to the police, tell a man that his son was a murderer. Why I had to be a part of it.

All I want is to leave. With Carolyn gone, there is nothing left for me in London. But I need to wait for Ned's funeral. I don't want to play the grieving widow but it's the price I must pay to be free. And when I am, I will find Lukas and I will get to the truth.

9

Ned's funeral, a service followed by a cremation, is mercifully short. I stand apart from his parents and pretend not to notice the stares of the Hawthorpe family.

I don't think of Ned, I think of Carolyn. I don't have proof but I know her death was murder and I know Ned was behind it. Tears seep from my eyes when the words *cruelly taken from us before his time* are pronounced; nobody watching could doubt the sorrow I feel at Ned's passing. Paul must wonder, though. He must know more; I'm sure he is somehow linked to the people behind our kidnapping.

This morning, when he remarked that I looked pale, I wanted to tell him about Carolyn. But if he knew I'd tried to call Carolyn, he might have told our abductors, and their instructions had forbidden me from contacting anyone except him.

Last night, I googled Carolyn's death and found a news bulletin from 11 August about a hit-and-run accident the previous day. It mentioned Carolyn's name and that she'd been hit during an early morning run. I'd had to work backwards – the interview with the journalists had been on the seventh, the hit-and-run on the tenth. It fitted: Ned had had three days to track and trace Carolyn.

When the service is over, Paul drives me to his offices in London. A taxi is waiting to take me to Reading.

'Good luck,' Paul says, once he's transferred my suitcases from his car boot to the taxi. He shakes my hand. 'If you need anything, you have my number.'

'Thank you.' I attempt a smile. 'I thought you were only meant to look after me until the funeral.'

He smiles back. 'I'm not averse to going above and beyond the call of duty.'

'Thank you,' I say again.

On the journey to Reading, I'm grateful that my driver is silent. The movement of the car makes me drowsy and I'm soon asleep.

'Mrs Hawthorpe—'

I open my eyes and see the face of the driver, turned in his seat.

'Lamont,' I correct automatically.

'Apologies, ma'am . . . we're here.'

I look out of the window at the brown front door of my childhood home. Shrouded in neglect, it stands out among the other houses, but only because of its shabbiness. In the three years since I left, the street feels different. The doors of the houses on either side of ours have been painted, one red, one blue. They also have new windows. The home that Papa and I lived in for eight years seems to have been frozen in time.

My fingers curl around the set of keys in my hand. The driver opens the car door for me and insists on carrying my suitcases into the house. He follows me into the dark, narrow hallway and puts them down on the floor.

'Thank you,' I say.

He leaves, closing the door behind him.

I push open the door to the right; it opens onto the sitting room where Papa spent most of his days, and an image comes to me, of him sitting in his chair, getting progressively weaker as the illness took hold. I move along to the small dining room, where we had our meals and where I used to study and dream of being a lawyer. At the end of the hallway, there's the tiny kitchen. I step inside, look around. The old wooden clock is still on the wall but it's no longer working. Through the window, I can see that someone has recently mowed the small rectangle of lawn.

I go upstairs. A bedroom – mine – sits above the sitting room, another, where Papa slept, above the dining room. It's only now that I realise that I had the bigger room. The avocado-green bathroom, which I always hated, sits above the kitchen. With the cupboard under the stairs, that's it: a traditional terraced house.

There's an envelope on the kitchen table. I open it and draw out a sheet of paper.

Dear Amelie,

First of all, please accept my sincere condolences for your recent loss.

Secondly, welcome back. I hope you find the house clean and comfortable. I had the water and electricity supplies reconnected ahead of your arrival. I also took the liberty of purchasing a new kettle and toaster, and have stocked the fridge and cupboards with food for the first day or two, in case you don't feel up to going out.

May I suggest that we meet at my office on Monday at 11 a.m.? If for any reason this doesn't suit you, please let me know at the following number and we can reschedule.

I very much look forward to meeting you.

Regards,
Anthony Barriston

I place the letter back on the table, and in the silence of the house, make a mug of tea. I add the hot water, watching the tea bag twisting in the scalding liquid, then pour in some milk. Suddenly, it all becomes overwhelming, not just Anthony Barriston's kindness, but being back in the house where I lived for so many years with my father, making tea in the mug that he used to use. Laying my head on the kitchen table, I let the tears come, and cry until I'm empty.

The tea is cold. I make another cup, and drink it leaning against the countertop, the steam thick in my nostrils, looking through the window above the sink. Putting the mug down, I find the key to the back door in the same place, in the same drawer. I unlock it, push it open and step outside. The smell of freshly cut grass reaches me, and I'm instantly taken back to the pitch-black room, and my captor stooping to place my tray beside me.

I pull myself back to the present, look around: the small paved area just outside the door is grey and bare, the grass patchy, the fences leaning inward. I have no memories of playing in this tiny garden except perhaps once, with a shiny green skipping rope Papa gave me for a birthday.

I make myself something to eat and carry it through to the dining room. It's been a long day, I can feel my body shutting down. Maybe here, in my childhood home, I'll finally be able to sleep.

Upstairs, I find bed linen in the chest of drawers in Papa's room, where I'd stored them before leaving. They smell musty. I don't know if the washing machine still works and I'm too tired to find out so I lie down on the mattress in my childhood bed and pull my blanket over me. The curtains are drawn and the door closed, but I can still see the shelf on the opposite wall, the line of books wedged between my jewellery box and an old biscuit tin, where I kept other treasures. I close my eyes; it's been a week since I was freed and I've barely slept more than an hour or two at a time.

Tomorrow, I decide, I'll walk to the local shops, buy bin bags, go through the house, sort out the clothes I left behind, take what I can to charity shops, and put the rest into recycling. After my meeting with Mr Barriston on Monday, I'll go into the centre of Reading and buy new everything: bed linen and towels and crockery and cutlery. I'll strip the wallpaper from my bedroom and paint the walls the palest of blues, to remind me of my room at Carolyn's.

Tears burn my throat. I can't think of Carolyn without wanting to cry so I turn my thoughts to Lukas, about my plans to find him. And then I think of my abductor, wondering where he is, and what he is doing.

IO

I'm curious to meet Mr Barriston, to have this connection to my past. He knew my father; Paul said they'd been friends. I wish I'd known that Papa had had a friend; it would have made me happy to know that he hadn't spent all day, every day in his armchair in the sitting room, that sometimes he'd met with Mr Barriston. And then I feel guilty; I can't remember ever asking Papa about his day. Maybe if I had, he would have told me.

Anthony Barriston ushers me into his office, offers me a seat, and coffee, which he makes himself from a machine behind his desk. This gives me time to study him. He seems to be about the same age as Paul Carr, late forties or early fifties, with a full head of thick black hair and matching eyebrows. He has a kind, open face that makes me instantly warm to him.

'I'm so glad to meet you at last, Amelie,' he says, once he's served the coffee. 'I'm very sorry for your recent loss and of course, about your father. I'd seen him about a month before he passed away. I had no idea the end would come so swiftly. I was away on holiday at the time and I feel terrible that I wasn't there to tell you about your father's will. We searched for you extensively, and I had you listed as missing. But not one person came forward to say that they'd seen you.'

'I'm sorry,' I say. 'If I'd known about you, and the house, I'd never have left.'

'And you managed on your own in London?'

My throat tightens. 'I was lucky, I met some lovely people, they were like family to me.'

He smiles. 'I'm glad you didn't have to face any real hardship. Especially when your father provided so well for you.'

'He never told me he'd bought the house, so it was such a shock to know it was mine. I think I'll probably end up selling it. I want to go to college to study law, and with the money from the house, I could hopefully do it next year.'

'Then, in that case, I'm delighted to tell you that if you don't want to sell the house, you won't have to. Your father also left you a substantial amount of money.'

I stare at him. 'Money?'

'Yes. I don't know if you're aware, but your father sued the hospital in France for negligence, in relation to the deaths of your mother and baby brother.'

'Yes, of course. But nothing ever happened.'

'Well, I'm delighted to tell you that the hospital finally admitted liability, and that you were named as the beneficiary of any settlement.'

'But – when did that happen?' I ask, my mind spinning. 'When did they settle?'

He shifts uncomfortably. 'About a month after your father died.'

'So he never knew?' Tears fill my eyes and I dig in my pocket for a tissue. 'This is awful. That's all he wanted, an acknowledgment from the hospital that they had been negligent. Why couldn't they have accepted responsibility sooner? They must have known he was ill, I'm sure his lawyer in France would have told them.'

'I'm sorry, Amelie, I don't know the full circumstances.'

I scrunch the tissue in my fingers, fighting anger and frustration.

'What I don't understand is why he never told me he'd bought the house. It would have made so much difference.'

'I think he would have, if he'd known the end was imminent. Would you like me to go through the details of the settlement from the hospital trust with you?'

'Please, if you have the time.'

I spend another hour with Mr Barriston, and by the end of it, I'm so tired I can hardly think straight. I have money, more than I'll ever need. I should be happy, Mr Barriston had expected me to be happy, but I'm not. I'm too angry, angry at the hospital for taking so long, angry that Papa died never knowing he had won. I don't deserve this money anyway, not after what I agreed to with Ned.

'Take care of yourself, Amelie,' Mr Barriston says as I leave.

'I will, thank you.' I turn to look at him. 'Can I ask you something? Did you ever come to the house? It's just that it would make a difference if I knew that my father had had a friend.'

'No, not to the house. But we were definitely friends. I saw him on several occasions, here in the office, and we sometimes had lunch. He was a very good man.'

I nod. 'I should go, I've taken up a lot of your time.'

'Not at all,' he says. 'But you probably want some time to think everything through. I imagine it's all been rather a shock. Would you like me to call a taxi to take you home?'

'Thank you, but I'm going to go shopping. There are a few things I need for the house.'

I walk to the shopping area, wishing there was someone I could talk to about how I feel. But there's no one left; everyone I cared about is dead.

11

I stand outside the DIY shop, my arms crossed over my body, waiting for it to open. It's out of town, so I had to take the bus here. I could feel panic rising inside me as the bus became fuller at each stop, everyday people going about their everyday lives.

On paper, my own life has changed from nightmare to fairy tale in the space of a few weeks. I'm no longer a prisoner, I am safe, I have money. But it is still a nightmare. I can't eat, I can't sleep. And when I'm awake, my mind is so full that I find it hard to focus on anything. If only I could stop thinking about the kidnapping, about my abductor, the man I fought and scratched and bit.

Twice now, when I've been out shopping, I was so sure that he was close by that I actually spun around, thinking I would find him standing behind me. It was only my imagination, but it had felt so real. I will never be rid of him, I realise. For the rest of my life, I will imagine him walking towards me in a pitch-black room with a boarded-up window.

A man unlocks the doors to the shop.

'You're eager,' he says, giving me a smile. He has an orange name tag clipped onto his black T-shirt, the name Scott embossed on it.

'Do you sell chipboard?' I ask.

'Sure,' he says. 'Let me show you.'

I follow him through the store, its high ceilings echoing our footsteps.

'What's it for?' he asks.

The question throws me. 'Sorry?'

'The chipboard. What are you making?'

'I just need it,' I say.

We arrive at an area of divided sections, with different sizes of chipboard leaning against each other.

'What size?' he asks.

I tell him and he drags one out.

'Do you need anything else?'

'Yes, I'll need a hammer and nails.'

'To put the chipboard up?'

'Yes.'

'This way.'

He lifts the sheet of chipboard and I follow him to another aisle where he picks out a black-handled hammer, and farther along, a box of nails.

'Two-inch nails,' he says. 'That should do it.'

'Great, thanks.'

We walk to the register, I pay, put the hammer and nails into my bag, and pick up the chipboard.

He looks at me doubtfully. 'Sure you can manage?'

'Yes. Thank you.'

He nods. 'Have a nice day.'

The chipboard isn't heavy, but its size makes it awkward to carry between my hands. I make it to the bus stop, and when the bus comes, I manoeuvre it down the aisle and slide it into a seat, then sit down, my knees jammed awkwardly against it. Back at home, I push it through the front door and lean it against the wall while I catch my breath, then drag it up the stairs into Papa's bedroom. A company came yesterday and took away the bed, the chest of drawers, and the single wardrobe, so the room is completely empty of furniture.

I take the hammer and nails from my bag, lift the chipboard off the ground, and hold it into place. But every time I let go with one hand to reach for the hammer and nail, the board slips down.

'Damn!' I shout, as it falls for the third time and lands on my foot.

I slump to the ground, my arms aching. I'm not going to be able to do it without help. But I have no one to help me; there is only me.

I think for a moment, then reach for my bag and take out my phone.

'Thank you so much for coming, for doing this. I know it's an odd request,' I say to Mr Barriston, an hour later. 'I didn't know who else to call.'

He's standing in Papa's bedroom, his shirtsleeves rolled up. There are beads of sweat along his hairline.

'I've never been asked to do this for a client, I have to say,' he replies with a smile. 'But I have a daughter and if she needed help with a job like this, I'd want someone to give her a hand. It was lucky you called when you did. And it's good for me to get out during lunchtime.'

'Thank you,' I say.

He looks around the room.

'You're . . . decorating?' he asks.

I feel a flush of embarrassment. 'Yes. I feel like I need a change.'

He nods. 'Right.'

I walk behind him down the stairs.

'Well, good luck with everything,' he says.

'Thank you again,' I say gratefully, and he leaves with a wave.

I return to the bedroom and work until dusk, pulling up the threadbare carpet and stripping off the wallpaper. When I've finished, I go to my bedroom, strip the bed, drag the mattress through to Papa's room, and place it in the far corner, against the wall. And then I close the door. With the window boarded up, the room is completely dark. Moving to the mattress, I lie down, pull my blanket over me, and close my eyes. And for the first time in weeks, I sleep.

12

September melts into October. I sit at the green wrought-iron table I bought for the garden, listening to the radio on my phone, my legs stretched out in front of me, my head tilted towards the sun. It's a beautiful autumn day and I feel an unexpected burst of happiness. I try to hang on to it – but as always, memories intrude, always the same memories, of Carolyn, of Justine and Lina. Of Hunter.

I want so much to be at peace with myself, for my mind to be still. But how can it be, when I've seen so much?

The news comes on.

Human remains, thought to be from two bodies, have been found in Epping Forest by a member of the public. The police are releasing no further information at this time and are asking people to stay away from the area.

A strange stillness comes over me. In a trance, I pick up my phone, locate my news app. The breaking news story is a repeat of what I just heard: human remains, thought to be from two bodies, have been found in Epping Forest.

A low, dull thud begins in my chest. I go into the house and hunch on the sofa, switching to different news sources on my phone, checking the story. There is nothing more, just the same bleak headline repeated over and over again. I draw my legs up, wrap my arms around my knees and lay my head down, subconsciously protecting myself from the emotional blow that I'm scared is coming.

It does, the next day, when I click on the BBC News alert banner on my phone. There's just one line: bodies found in Epping Forest confirmed to be female. I wait desperately for the news story to load, read it once, then again. It doesn't say much, just that the police can confirm that, in an effort to identify the bodies, they are investigating all reports of missing women aged between twenty and forty.

There's a part of me, a huge part of me, that wants to phone the police anonymously, and give them the names of Justine and Lina as possible victims. But the bodies might not be those of Justine and Lina. And what if they trace my call? They might ask questions that I won't be able to answer for fear of incriminating, not just myself, but my kidnappers. What if, under the strain of the questioning, I crack?

I think about the relatives of women who have gone missing, who will be in desperate anguish, waiting to hear if their daughter, sister, mother, wife, is one of the victims, and my guilt increases. It haunts me that the police investigation to identify the bodies might drag on for weeks when I could help it along, if only I wasn't frightened of the consequences.

I find myself grieving for Justine and Lina all over again. It comes in huge insurmountable waves. I can't eat, I can't sleep, not even when I lie on the mattress in the room with the boarded-up window, wrapped in my blanket. And then, a few days later, the news I've been dreading, but which also comes as a relief. After an anonymous tip, the bodies found in the forest are confirmed as those of Justine Elland and Lina Mielkutė, former employees of *Exclusives,* the magazine run by Ned Hawthorpe before his suicide six weeks previously. Before the media can start speculating about the involvement of Ned in the murder of two of his staff, the police announce that their deaths have been attributed to Amos Kerrigan, a man with links to the underworld, who was shot at point-blank range sometime in August, in what police say was a gangland killing.

It stuns me, the news that Amos Kerrigan, the man who I'm sure disposed of Justine's and Lina's bodies, is dead, until I realise that he had to be killed, because he was the link between the murders and Ned. In a search for a motive for Lina's and Justine's murders, a theory is put forward – perhaps by someone wanting to steer the investigation even further away from Ned – that Amos Kerrigan was a drug dealer and that the two women had threatened to denounce him to the police. A stab of bitterness at the efforts to protect Ned cuts through the crushing numbness that has invaded my body.

I sift through my emotions, my throat swollen with unshed tears. It's good that Lina and Justine have been found, and can now be laid to rest. But who will organise a funeral for Lina? If she doesn't have a family, who will be there to say goodbye? And Justine? Will her family come from France, or will her funeral be in Bordeaux, where she came from?

I don't know what happened to *Exclusives* after Ned's death; I haven't been in contact with anyone at the magazine since I left for Las Vegas with Ned and came back married to him. What must Vicky and the other staff have thought when they heard the news of our marriage? I hadn't found any messages of congratulations on my phone. Maybe they'd thought me a gold digger, who had tricked Ned into marrying me.

I find the new laptop I bought, log in to Facebook, and bring up the *Exclusives* home page. I don't expect to find anything except a notification that the magazine has been shut down, due to Ned Hawthorpe's death. But to my surprise, it still exists, and is now run by Vicky. My heart goes out to her. She must be feeling terrible, she will know now that the messages she received from Lina, saying she was back in Lithuania, weren't written by her, but by someone else.

I scroll down, reading the posts. There's already an outpouring of grief for Justine and Lina and a colleague has asked about a funeral or memorial service. As the day progresses, there is talk, not just on the *Exclusives* website, but on various platforms around the world, of a vigil, and I'm glad their story has touched people's hearts.

My phone rings. It's Paul Carr.

'How are you, Amelie?'

It's a hard question to answer when I don't know how much he knows.

'I've been better,' I say.

'I'm sure. I imagine you knew Justine Elland and Lina Mielkutė from your time at the magazine.'

'Yes, I did.'

'Can I do anything?'

'No, thank you. It's kind of you to phone, I appreciate it.'

'Well, you know where I am.'

'Yes, I do. Thank you.'

I hang up, wondering if he phoned me on his own initiative, or if he'd been asked to check on me by the kidnappers.

13

I'm standing in Boots, trying to find shampoo, when I realise I'm in the men's section. It's so bright in here, I can feel
a headache coming on. I hoped I'd feel better, now that
there has been closure for Justine and Lina. But I can't
shake the mountain of grief that has built up inside me, or
cope with the guilt I feel over the deaths of Lina and Carolyn.
And then there's Daniel, Carolyn's partner. I should have
called him, but I was too scared to, too scared I'd blurt out
the part I played in Carolyn's death. Because if Carolyn
hadn't come to Ned's house the day of the press interview,
she'd still be alive.

Without thinking, I pick up a shower gel and open the lid,
press the air out of the bottle and breathe in. It smells of
eucalyptus. I close the lid and pick up another bottle; it smells
more orangey. Before I know it, I'm working along the bottles
of shower gels and shampoos, sniffing the contents then
pushing them back onto the shelves, looking for the scent
that keeps haunting me: cut grass and citrus. The smell of my
captor.

The smell of Lukas.

The bottle I'm holding clatters to the floor. Turning, I run
to the door, pushing past a woman holding the hand of a
toddler.

'Hey!' she calls out.

But I don't stop, I can't.

Outside, I turn in desperate circles, trying to find my way out of the mall. I'm on the verge of tears and I can see people looking at me as they pass by.

'Are you all right, dear?' An elderly woman stops in front of me, her hand on her shopping cart.

'Yes, I'm – I'm just a bit lost,' I stammer. 'I can't find the way out of here.'

'You go down there, past the café. There's an exit there.'

'Thank you,' I say, breaking into a run. 'Thank you.'

I run through the exit and keep running until I can't run anymore. I double over, pull in large gulps of air. I don't want it to be true – but it's staring at me in the face. I had imagined Lukas masterminding our kidnapping from his home in Vilnius. But he had been there all the time, in the house in Haven Cliffs. He was my captor.

My mind feels as if it's coming apart as I walk the rest of the way home, my head down, my shoulders hunched up around my ears. It must have been why he never spoke to me, in case I recognised his voice. I reach the house, stand in the hallway a moment, letting the silence wash over me. I move to the kitchen, sit down at the table, and take my phone from my pocket. My hands are shaking as I google Stockholm syndrome:

An emotional reaction victims can have after being held captive: feelings of having bonded with a captor, of missing them when they are separated. People suffering from Stockholm syndrome can experience insomnia, flashbacks, high suspicions of others, nightmares.

Is that what I have?

I go upstairs and crawl onto the mattress without

undressing, wanting to hide my shame. How could I have bonded with the man who had Hunter killed? I screw my eyes shut, craving oblivion. But it doesn't come.

14

A few days later, my phone rings. It's Paul Carr again.

'Amelie, you may have heard that there's to be a memorial service for Justine Elland and Lina Mielkutė next Wednesday.'

I feel a wash of relief. I hadn't checked the *Exclusives* Facebook page for the last few days. 'Thank you for telling me,' I say. 'I would hate to have missed it.'

'Ah.' There's an awkward pause. 'I'm afraid it has been suggested that you don't go.'

My heart thuds. 'Why not?'

'Something to do with media presence, I think. Concern about you being put in the spotlight, perhaps.'

'Who?' I demand. 'Who suggested that I don't go?'

'I hope you understand.'

'No, I don't. Could you please go back to whoever gave you this message and tell them that I need to be there, that I need the closure?'

'I'm afraid I only receive messages.' Paul sounds unhappy. 'But I would have only been asked to pass this message on to you if it was important.' Another pause. 'Can I have your assurance that you'll respect it?'

It's not his fault, he's just the messenger. 'Yes, of course. Goodbye, Paul.'

I hang up politely, but inside I'm seething. I've done every-thing they've asked of me, those men who disrupted my life so brutally. But I will not do this for them. I am going to the memorial service, whether they like it or not.

In the dining room, I open my laptop and bring up the *Exclusives* Facebook page. There are more messages about Justine and Lina, and details about the memorial service, on Wednesday, at St Anne's, near the *Exclusives* building. I make a note of the time – 2 p.m. – and then I do something that I hadn't thought to do before. I look for articles about my marriage to Ned.

I'm surprised at how much space was given to it, mainly in the tabloid press. But with Ned described as one of the most eligible men in England, perhaps it's not surprising. As I read the various articles, I learn things that I already knew – that Ned's fortune was left directly to him by his grandfather, and that his father and grandfather had fallen out, largely because Jethro Hawthorpe disapproved of the way Ned Senior spoiled his grandson – and things that I didn't – Ned, at eighteen years old, assaulting another young man so badly that he ended up in the hospital; a car crash six months later, his red Ferrari wrapped around a tree and a young woman with life-changing injuries.

I don't know why I'm shocked. Ned had told me, when we were in Las Vegas, that he'd been involved in a couple of incidents that had angered his father, because he'd had to put the launch of the foundation on hold. He had never mentioned that he'd caused catastrophic injuries to a young woman, and had put a man in the hospital. No wonder Jethro Hawthorpe was paranoid about any scandal involving Ned.

I continue searching to see what else I can find and I'm about to give up when I come across a news story from 2008, about the death of an ex-girlfriend of Ned Hawthorpe, suffocated in a sex game gone wrong.

I draw in my breath, scared of what I'm going to read. But all the four-line article mentions is that the young woman, Tanya Haughton, was an ex-girlfriend of Ned's. There's no mention of who she was having sex with when she died, just that the police are investigating the circumstances surrounding her death. I search for related articles later that year, and the year after, and all the years up to the present day, hoping to find the results of the police investigation. But there is nothing, nothing at all. Which means that somebody must have made it go away.

Nothing can calm the anger I feel at Ned being able to get away with so much because his father is a powerful man. I tell myself that I don't know for sure that Ned was involved in Tanya Haughton's death. But everything points to it, from the method to the cover-up.

Remembering that I was trying to find out what was reported in the press about my marriage to Ned, I return to those articles. There's little about me personally. Some digging had been done, because there's mention of me being an orphan, and of me being reported missing at seventeen years old, after the death of my father. But the focus is more on how Ned and I met, and our sudden marriage. Interviews with Vicky, and others from *Exclusives*, tell of their surprise at the news, because they hadn't known that Ned and I were in a relationship. No one calls me a gold digger, at least not in writing. But reading their words, I can feel the accusation beneath the surface.

There's a flurry of articles about Ned's suicide, and as I read, I learn about the extensive trolling Ned had been subjected to because of Justine's accusation of sexual assault, and his subsequent persecution by the media. It makes more sense now, the easy acceptance of a suicide verdict. But I hate that he was portrayed as a victim, when he was guilty of so much.

There's something I've wanted to do for a long time, something I haven't been able to do, because I haven't had the courage. But I dig deep inside me and type 'male body found Dorset' into my search engine. There are several articles, and I scan them quickly, my heart thudding, discarding each one until I find the one that I hoped I wouldn't find, Wednesday, August the fourteenth, about a man's body being found along the B222, not far from Haven Cliffs, the seeming victim of a gangland killing.

The room tilts, I grip the table, wait for the dizziness to pass. At the time, the all-consuming murder of Lina just days before had taken precedence over Hunter's; it had seemed wrong to mourn a man I barely knew. But now, waves of grief rack my body, for what might have been, if Lukas hadn't ordered him to be killed.

Lukas. I can hardly bear to think about him now that I know he was my captor. But he is still the only person who will be able to give me the answers I need. My mind goes back to the phone call from Paul, warning me away from the memorial service. It has nothing to do with me being besieged by the press; why would I be? The service isn't about me, it's about Justine and Lina. Even if someone recognised me, they wouldn't ask why I was there, not when everyone knows I worked at the magazine. The warning to keep away is about someone else being there, someone the kidnappers don't want me running into, and that person can only be Lukas. And if Lukas is coming over from Vilnius, or Los Angeles, for the memorial service, the chances are that he'll stay in his home away from home, the house in Haven Cliffs.

15

I step off the train in Bournemouth, exit the station and walk to the taxi stand. The driver rolls down his window.

'Where to, love?'

'Haven Cliffs, please,' I say, climbing into the car.

'Do you have an address?'

'The house is called Albatross, but I've stupidly forgotten which road it's on.'

'No problem.' He fiddles with his GPS. 'Got it.'

'Great, thank you.'

I sit back, look out of the window, trying to calm my nerves. I have no idea how the next hour will play out but I know what I'd like to happen. Lukas is there, he agrees to talk to me, he admits giving the order for Hunter to be killed, admits kidnapping me and Ned, admits killing Ned. He tells me that everything was revenge for Lina's death, because he once loved her, or because he was meant to look out for her, and then I leave, and go straight to the police with the recording I've secretly made on my phone. But I'm not so naïve as to think things would go exactly as we'd like.

'Here you are,' the driver says, some fifteen minutes later.

I look out of the window and see a pair of black double gates with a high white wall stretching on either side of it. I recognise the small black gate a few yards along from the main gates; it's the gate I went through when I pretended to look for Ned on the beach.

I pay the driver, get out of the car and stand for a moment, studying the upper windows of the house where I was held captive for two weeks. When the kidnappers first brought us here, I didn't smell the tang of the sea in the air. But maybe the fear I felt as they dragged Ned and me from the car had blunted my senses. Even if I had smelled the sea, I wouldn't have thought we were at the house where Ned and I had had lunch with Lukas. In my mind, the place we'd been brought to was old and derelict, hidden away in some woods.

I wait until the taxi has left before pressing the intercom button. While I wait for it to be answered, I look up and down the wide road, noting how each house is so far from its neighbour that I could have screamed as much as I liked, and nobody would have heard.

I press the intercom again, but nobody answers, and I feel suddenly furious, because if Lukas is going to the memorial service for Justine and Lina tomorrow, he should be here by now. It's why I waited until today to come, why I didn't come yesterday or the day before, in case he hadn't arrived yet.

I press the intercom again and again, refusing to believe Lukas isn't somewhere behind the high white wall. Unless he decided to stay in London to be nearer to the church. But London is only a couple of hours by train from Bournemouth, and surely this is where he'd come to grieve for a woman who meant so much to him that he resorted to murder and kidnapping to avenge her death?

I move away, hoping to lull Lukas into a false sense of security, in case he's watching me on the camera perched above the gate. I walk along the length of the wall to the right and, tucked away at the end, I find another pair of double gates, not quite as stately as the main gates. There's no camera, and no one around, so I grab hold of the top of the gates and try to pull myself up. The gates are too smooth for me to get a toehold; my shoes scramble uselessly and I drop down to the path. I move to the stone pillar on the right-hand side of the gate and this time, when I grab the top of the gates, I manage to get enough purchase on the pillar's rough surface to haul myself up. I just have time to peer quickly over the top before my foothold slips, and I see that the gates lead to a wooded area at the side of the house. These are the gates that the kidnappers drove through the night they brought me and Ned here.

I return to the main gates, press on the buzzer, keeping my finger on it, enraged that Lukas is refusing to answer, enraged that it hasn't worked out as I'd hoped. Defeated, because I can't stay around forever, I raise my head, look straight into the camera, and slowly mouth a message to Lukas: *See you tomorrow.*

16

I walk into the church. It's already full, but I don't want to stand at the back, I'd feel too conspicuous.

Turning to the right, I walk up the side aisle and slide into a space at the end of a bench, hoping that the young woman who shifts along to give me more room isn't someone from the magazine. I tug on the brim of the blue hat I'm wearing, bringing it down on my forehead, and pull my hair forward, hiding my face, but keeping my eyes clear. Where is he?

During the service, I close my ears to the sounds of gentle weeping around me. I'm scared to cry, scared that I might not be able to stop. I focus on Justine, on the last time I saw her, at dinner at Carolyn's, when she made us laugh with stories about an interview she'd done with a famous jockey, in a stable full of horses. For Lina, it's harder to conjure good memories.

The service ends, and I slide quickly out of the pew, wanting to get out of the church before people start coming down the central aisle. My plan is to stand somewhere to the side and scan the faces of the exiting crowd until I see Lukas. But as I hurry towards the door, I see a man stepping out of the shadows on the other side of the church, also making his way to the door, in as much of a hurry to leave as I am. My breath comes quicker; it isn't Lukas, but I know this man, I'm sure of it. I try to place him: he's of medium height, medium build, but there's nothing else to give me a clue as to his identity.

I tell myself that I must be mistaken, that I don't know him. As he approaches the door, I hang back to get a better look at him and notice that his head is shaved. The pieces lock together – Carl, I'm sure it's Carl.

I force my way through the crowd leaving the church and see him walking across the adjacent gardens, towards the main road. Panic takes hold; if he has a car parked nearby, he'll be gone before I can speak to him.

'Carl!'

He doesn't turn, he keeps on walking. But I saw, I saw him falter when I called his name, it's definitely him. He's moving faster now, there's an exit at each corner of the park, he's heading towards the left-hand one, so I start running towards the one on the right. My hat flies off my head as I exit the park, but I don't stop, I run faster as I double back along the road to the exit Carl is heading towards. I can see him through the railings, his head is down, he has no idea that any second now, he'll be face-to-face with me. I burst through the exit, people scatter, he looks up at the sound of their surprise, and sees me heading straight for him. I see alarm flare in his eyes as he tries to step out of my way. But I follow his movements and block his path so that he's obliged to stop.

'I need to talk to you,' I say breathlessly. 'I know you're Carl, and I think you know who I am.'

His face is impassive as he looks back at me. His eyes are dark, I notice, almost black. Then his brow clears.

'Mrs Hawthorpe. I'm sorry – we never met face-to-face, so I had trouble placing you.' He looks back at the church. 'I thought I'd come and pay my respects.'

'Why?'

'Sorry?'

'I'm asking why you wanted to pay your respects to Justine and Lina when you didn't know them. You worked for Ned for only a few days. You never met either of them.'

'Their story has captured a lot of people's hearts, Mrs Hawthorpe.'

I notice it then, his accent. Australian, South African, I don't know. For a moment, I falter. The man guarding Ned didn't speak with an accent. Instinct kicks in. I'm right, I know I am.

I shake my head. 'No. I know why you're here. Closure.'

'I'm not sure—'

'Don't.' I lower my voice as people come along the path towards us. 'You may be speaking with a different accent, but I know you were one of the men who held me and Ned prisoner.'

He looks around, concern in his eyes. 'Are you with someone? Could I get them for you?'

'Please don't treat me like an idiot.'

He checks the time on his watch. 'I'm sorry, but I need to be going.'

He tries to step around me but again, I block his way. 'No. I need answers, and after all that I've done for you, you owe me. So, tell me – where's Lukas? Why isn't he here?'

He looks so bemused that for a moment, I think I've got it wrong. But the same gut feeling tells me again that I'm right.

'If you refuse to talk to me,' I say, incensed, 'I'll go to the police and tell them that I saw Ned Hawthorpe kill Lina Mielkutė.'

I see it in his eyes, a flash of something. But whatever it was disappears as quickly as it came.

'Yes, that's right,' I hiss. 'I saw Ned kill Lina. I saw him suffocate her with his own hands. I was hiding behind the door in the library, and I saw everything. I also saw Hunter being shot at point-blank range – but of course, you already know that, you said as much in your letter of instructions.' I barely notice his hand on my elbow as he steers me towards a bench, barely notice the tears streaming from my eyes. 'Have you any idea what that was like for me, to witness two murders? You might have closure, but I never will, not until I have the answers I need.'

'I know you won't want to hear this,' he says, as I fumble in my bag for a tissue. 'But, Mrs Hawthorpe, please believe me when I say that I have no idea what you are talking about.'

Anger flares.

'You're right, I don't believe you!' I stand up, swing my bag onto my shoulder. 'And I'm not Mrs Hawthorpe! I know you think that I won't go to the police, but I will. Until I have answers, I'll never be free, I'll be just as much a prisoner as I was before.' I choke back my tears. 'Do you even care that the only way I can sleep is on a mattress in a darkened room with a boarded-up window? That's how messed up I am, that's how much you and Lukas messed me up.'

I start to walk away, then turn back. 'Give Lukas a message from me. Tell him I'm coming for him, wherever he is.'

17

I walk away fast, but not so fast that Carl won't be able to catch up with me, because he will come after me, he has to. As I approach the exit, I hang back, waiting for him to shout out, call me back, tell me what I need to know. But he doesn't, and something inside me dies. I want to crumple to the ground, give up. If Carl won't help me, who will?

The reality of my situation hits. If I walk away now, I'll never get the answers I need. Once Carl is out of sight, he'll be lost to me forever.

I spin around. But there's no sign of him, he's already left. I turn in circles, trying to see which way he went and then I spot him again, on the other side of the railings, walking quickly along the pavement. He must have taken another exit.

I run after him, and when I'm closer, I slow my pace and follow at a safe distance. He's carrying a bag over his shoulder, something I hadn't noticed before. At the end of the road, he stands for a moment, turning his head to the right and left, then checking his watch, and I realise that he's not trying to cross the road, but looking for a taxi. My heart drops; if he jumps in a cab, I'll lose him forever, unless another taxi comes along straight after, and I ask the driver to follow Carl's. *Please don't let there be any taxis,* I pray, and someone answers my prayers, because after a couple more minutes, he quickly crosses the road.

I move from where I'd stopped behind him, and hurry after him. I know where he's heading: to the Tube station ahead. I run down the steps, follow him through the barriers, down the escalator to the Piccadilly Line and onto the platform.

My fear that he might see me following him begins to evaporate. If he had thought that I might, he would have turned around at least once to check. A train comes in; I get into the same carriage as he does but through the door at the other end and sit watching him surreptitiously as he stares blankly ahead, his bag lodged between his feet, lost in thoughts I can only guess at. Carl was Ned's captor, I know it. Why else was he at the memorial service for Justine and Lina, two women that he didn't know? Unless he did know them. I search my mind, but I can't recall Justine or Lina ever mentioning someone named Carl.

The carriage soon fills up but I'm not worried, I can still see Carl. My plan is to follow him all the way to wherever he lives, and once I have his address, harass him day and night until he agrees to speak to me. It's only when he doesn't react to any of the stops, not even to check our whereabouts, that I realise he's not concerned about missing his station because he's going all the way to the end of the line. My eyes dart to the map on the wall; the terminus is Heathrow Airport, Terminal 5.

My heart thuds. How can I follow him onto a flight? He could be going anywhere. I remember his accent and my heart thuds again. What if he's going to South Africa or Australia? How could I ever find him there?

The train pulls into Terminal 5. He moves to the door, and seconds later, I follow him out. I wait as he heads towards the escalators, making sure he doesn't check behind. He moves to the left and begins walking up, past the people standing on the right. He seems in a hurry so I walk up too. He arrives at the top, leaps off and starts running through the concourse, and for a panicky moment, I think that he's seen me. But as he runs, he's fumbling in his pocket and I see him take out his phone. He approaches the security area with the individual security gates, slams his phone onto the reader and hurries through the barrier. I arrive seconds later, and stand watching him until he disappears out of sight.

18

It hits me during the night as I lie curled up on the mattress. What if Carl worked for the same security firm as Hunter had? I saw the name on the front pocket of Hunter's black jacket often enough to remember it. If I call them and ask to speak to Carl, I might be able to find out something. It's a long shot – Ned might have called another security firm for a replacement after Hunter was murdered. But it's worth a try. I've been watching the time since 3 a.m. At 9 a.m., I call them.

'Hello, I'm trying to trace a security guard we employed last year and who was sent to us by your company. His name was Carl – I'm sorry, I can't remember his surname.'

'Can I have the name of your company, please?' a woman asks.

'Yes, it's *Exclusives*.'

'Hold on a minute, let me check . . . I can't find a contract in the name of *Exclusives*, I'm afraid.'

'Oh. He must have been sent by another company, then. Do you have any Carls at all on your books?'

'No, the only Carl we had was our director, Mr Hunter, and he no longer works here.'

My phone slips from my grasp, clatters to the floor. Blood drains from my face. Dizzy, I push through to the kitchen, then out to the garden, gulping fresh air into my lungs. Carl

Hunter? What does it mean? Is it just a coincidence: two people with the same name, one a surname, one a Christian name? Or was Hunter the surname of the man I knew as Hunter? If it was, does it mean that Carl and Hunter were related? And if they were, is that what the kidnapping was about, revenge not just for Lina's murder, but also for Hunter's?

My head feels as if it's about to explode. I massage my temples, telling myself that it will be all right, I'll get to the bottom of it, somehow. But how? Each time I think I've made a slight step forward, there's always something to knock me back.

I go to the kitchen, retrieve my phone from the floor, stand for a moment, thinking. When I have a plan, I call the security company again, ready to disguise my voice so that the woman won't know it's me calling back. But this time a man picks up.

'Could you put me through to Carl Hunter, please?' I ask.

'I'm sorry, but he no longer works here.'

'Ah. That could explain why he hasn't picked up his suits from us. He put them in to be dry-cleaned over a month ago. Do you have a phone number for him?'

'No, I'm afraid not.'

'Or an address? They're good suits, it seems a shame for him not to have them. Maybe I could arrange for them to be couriered to him.'

The man laughs. 'You could, but it might turn out to be a bit expensive. He's gone back to New Zealand.'

My heart leaps – bingo. 'Is that where he's from? I detected an accent when he came in but I couldn't quite place it.'

'Yes, he's a Kiwi.'

'What about his brother? Maybe he would have Mr Hunter's contact details.'

'His brother? I don't know anything about Mr Hunter having a brother.'

'Oh – I was sure he said that his brother worked with him. Or maybe it was a cousin.'

'Not here, that's for sure.'

'It might have been a few months ago now,' I persist. 'I think Mr Hunter said his brother used his surname as a Christian name, so he would have been known as Hunter. Mr Hunter said he employed him as a security guard.'

'Really? I suppose I could check our records.'

'Could you? As I said, they're expensive suits.'

'Give me a moment.' I wait, my mind still spinning at the confirmation that Carl's surname is Hunter. 'No, I can't see anything, I'm afraid.'

'Well, I suppose I'll take his suits to the charity shop. Thank you, you've been very helpful.'

I hang up and stand for a moment, puzzling it out. Why are there no records of Hunter having worked at the security firm when he wore a jacket with their name emblazoned on it?

And how am I ever going to find Carl in New Zealand? I can't, I realise dully. It would be like looking for a needle in a haystack. I fetch my laptop anyway, google 'Carl Hunter New Zealand,' but there are over 12,800,000 results. I try 'Carl Hunter security New Zealand' but there are still 8,810,000 results. I type in his name, 'New Zealand,' then the name of the security firm, and try images, but I find nothing.

Deflated, I wander into the kitchen, press my nose to the window. If I can't find Carl, I can't find Lukas. And if I can't get to the truth, I'll never be free.

I walk into the building where Paul Carr has his offices and head straight to the reception desk.

'I'd like to speak to Mr Carr, please.'

A young man a few years older than me looks up.

'Do you have an appointment?'

'No.'

'Can I suggest you make one?'

'No. I need to see him now.'

'I'm afraid that's not going to be possible.'

'Can you tell him that Amelie Lamont is here to see him, please? I think he'll want to speak to me.'

He sighs under his breath, picks up the phone and presses a button.

I move away from the desk, trying to calm myself. I could have – should have – called first. But I was afraid that Paul would suggest speaking over the phone and I want to see him face-to-face so that I can gauge how much he knows. He's the only person left who can help me.

'Amelie, how lovely to see you.' Paul is standing in front of me. 'Would you like to come through?'

I follow him into his office, already apologising. 'I should have called first,' I say.

He smiles. 'It's not a problem.' He indicates two leather armchairs set in front of a low table. 'I've arranged for Ben to bring coffee. How are you?'

I'm saved from answering by the coffee arriving. Paul serves us both, then sits back in his chair.

'How can I help?' he asks.

'I don't even know if you can,' I say.

'Why don't you tell me what's troubling you?'

I realise then that he can't know what happened to me, because if he did, he wouldn't ask such a question. And if he doesn't know what happened to me, how can he help?

I can't stop the tears of hopelessness that spring to my eyes. 'When we met again after Ned died, something had happened to me, something bad, and I can't move on. I've been trying to block it out, tell myself I'm fine. But I'm not, and I'm scared that I never will be. There are things I need to know but there's no one to give me the answers and it's really hard. I'm twenty, and I feel so old. I've seen things that keep me awake at night, done things that keep me awake at night. I feel as if I've been used as a pawn in some game . . .' I stop, worried that I've said too much, and wipe my eyes on the sleeve of my sweater. 'I went to the memorial service for Justine and Lina, and I saw someone there who I thought might be able to help me. But he pretended that he didn't know what I was talking about, he preferred to make me think I was crazy.' I look at him and see the tail end of something on his face, something I recognise as anger. 'You knew, didn't you?' I say, resigned. 'You knew that I went to the memorial service.'

I expect him to reprimand me, ask me why I disobeyed his orders. But he gets to his feet and walks to the window and stands with his back to me, looking out. My heart sinks even further. This is going to be harder than I thought.

'May I ask if you have any plans?' he asks, and I feel a small spark of triumph, that I spooked Carl when I told him I was coming for Lukas.

'I'm actually thinking of taking a holiday,' I say, because if Paul is going to relay this conversation back to Carl, I might as well see how much I can push him.

Paul turns from the window. 'Really?'

'Yes. I have the time and the money, and I'm at a loose end.'

'Where are you thinking of going?'

'I really need to get as far away from here as possible, so I'm thinking New Zealand.'

His expression doesn't change but a stillness comes over him and I wait for him to tell me that I can't go to New Zealand, and steer me to a more exotic location on the pretext that I need a proper rest.

'I think that's a very good idea,' he says.

I stare at him. 'You do?'

'Yes. Do you have any specific place in mind?'

'I'm not sure.' I hazard a guess. 'I thought I'd fly to Wellington and take it from there.'

He nods. 'Although I've heard that Christchurch, on the South Island, might be a better place to start.'

My heart starts beating faster. 'Christchurch?'

'Yes, in particular, a place called Akaroa, on the Banks Peninsula. It's supposed to be beautiful.'

I keep my voice calm and even. 'Maybe I should start there, then. Would it be a good idea to go now, do you think? It's almost winter here, so it would be approaching their summer.'

'I think it would be the perfect time to go.'

'And ... I don't suppose you know somewhere I could stay in Akaroa?'

He shakes his head. 'I'm afraid not. But I'm sure you'll be able to find something along the waterfront.' He pauses. 'You should take a trip to Purple Peak while you're there. I hear there are some beautiful houses being built in the hills. Now,' he says, 'I'm afraid I have another appointment.'

'Of course,' I say hastily. 'Thank you for seeing me. You've been very helpful.'

'I hope you get the answers you need.'

'Thank you.' I look at him hopefully. 'I don't suppose you want to come with me, do you? To New Zealand.'

He smiles. 'I think, Amelie, that's a journey you need to make on your own.'

20

I take a taxi to the airport, wheeling the same suitcase I took to Las Vegas four months ago. Around me other people are hugging their friends and family goodbye.

'Have a wonderful time, let us know when you arrive,' I hear a mother say to her daughter, and as she hugs her, I have to look away.

I've already checked in online, so I head straight to the Air New Zealand bag drop. My thoughts turn to Paul Carr and the text I received this morning: *Safe flight, safe trip, Paul*. It felt reassuring that at least someone knew where I was going, and that if I disappeared, he would know.

I've worked out that the fleeting look of anger I saw on his face when I told him I'd been to the memorial service wasn't directed at me, but at Carl, for refusing to speak to me, for making me think that I'd imagined everything. Because why would he help me otherwise, by directing me to Akaroa?

It's a long journey. Approximately thirteen hours to Singapore, a five-hour stopover, then a ten-hour flight to Christchurch. On the first flight, I don't allow myself to think. I read, eat, sleep, watch films. By the time I'm on the flight to Christchurch, anxiety is cramping my stomach. Even with the information I've got, I'm not certain I'll be able to find Carl. And I'll need to be careful. I've researched Akaroa, it's a small place. If I ask about a man called Carl Hunter who's having a house built in the hills, it might get back to him. And I want to surprise him.

The plane finally touches down. I disembark and follow the other passengers through Immigration, then to the baggage claim area. While I'm waiting for my luggage, I reply to Paul, just a simple message: *I've landed in Christchurch. Thank you.*

My suitcase arrives, I pull it onto the floor, open it, put my blanket, which I had with me on the plane, inside, and make my way to the exit. I've ordered a car to take me to Akaroa, where I've booked a one-bedroom suite in a guesthouse on the waterfront. I see a man on the concourse, holding a sign with my name, and make my way over.

'Welcome to Christchurch,' he says, smiling broadly and taking my suitcase from me. 'Is it your first time here?'

'Yes,' I say, smiling back.

'Well, let's hope it's not your last.'

He introduces himself as Bill, and on the one-hour drive to Akaroa, he tells me he has a cousin who lives there. For a moment, I almost ask him if he's heard of a Carl Hunter but decide against it. Instead, I let him tell me what I already know from the guidebook I bought, that Akaroa was New Zealand's first and only French settlement. He tells me about the beach at French Bay, the harbour and the wharf, and when he asks me about myself, I make up a life I'd like to have, a life where I'm taking a year off before starting my master's, a life where I have parents waiting for me back in the UK, and friends in Australia whom I'm going to meet up with at some point.

By the time we get to Akaroa, jet lag has caught up with me and I can't wait to get to bed. We pull up in front of a small building; Bill wheels my suitcase inside and leaves me to check in. The lady at the reception desk, who introduces herself as Glenda, is warm and friendly, and as we climb the stairs to my apartment, I give her the same story as I gave Bill.

The apartment is lovely. As well as the bedroom and bathroom, there's a large room with sofas, a table, chairs, and a kitchen area. There's also a balcony overlooking the sea.

'There's milk and butter in the fridge, tea, coffee, and bread in the cupboards, along with a few other bits and pieces,' Glenda says.

'Thank you,' I say, looking gratefully at a bowl piled with kiwis, mandarins, apples and avocados. 'That's so kind.'

'You're welcome. If you need anything, just shout.'

I shower, get into bed, because it's the middle of the night in England, and fall asleep wondering why Carl made the long and exhausting journey from New Zealand to go to a memorial service for two young women he didn't know.

21

I give myself two days to get over my jet lag and use them to get my bearings, walking around Akaroa or along the beach at French Bay, taking in the beautiful scenery, breathing in the fresh sea air but always, always, watching for Carl. I still don't have a plan and I need to make one. But if I see him, I'll do what I did last time, and follow him.

I wait for Glenda to have one of her quiet moments, after guests have checked out and before new ones check in, then head to the reception area.

'How are you today?' she asks, as I approach the desk.

'I'm fine, thank you. It's so beautiful here, so relaxing.'

'It sure is. And the weather's pretty good for this time of the year.' She leans on the counter, ready for a chat. 'Got anything nice planned for today?'

'Well, I'm supposed to be trying to find some people my parents used to know back in England. Apparently, they emigrated to Akaroa, and my parents lost touch with them. They made me promise to try and find them while I was here.' I give a theatrical sigh. 'I'm not sure how I'm meant to do that without an address.'

'Do you have a name?'

'Yes, Hunter.'

She nods. 'There's a guy having a house built up in the hills back there,' she says, indicating somewhere behind the building. 'I think his name's Hunter. But I'm not sure he's of your parents' generation, I heard mid-thirties. And he lived in the UK until a few months ago, so he's probably not who you're looking for.'

I take a step back, certain she can hear my heart crashing in my chest. He sounds like exactly who I'm looking for.

'No, that doesn't fit,' I say. 'My parents are in their fifties and this couple emigrated years ago.' I'm so shocked that I barely know what I'm saying.

'He could be a son or something.'

I shake my head. 'I don't think they had children, my parents didn't say they had.' My mind fast-forwards, thinking what I can ask without it looking suspicious. 'A house in the hills, that must be nice. Quite a hike from here, though, I imagine.'

'Not that far. If it's where I'm thinking it is, somewhere on the way to the peak, you could get up there on foot in about an hour.'

'Really? Gosh, it sounds like the perfect place.'

'You could go up there, try and speak to him. He's a bit of a loner, by all accounts.'

'No, I won't bother, it can't be the same family. At least I can tell my parents I tried. In fact, I'll call them now, they'll still be up, they go to bed late.' I move away before she can ask any more questions.

I'm shaking so much I drop my key card on the floor, then fumble to open the door. In the apartment, I cross the room to the balcony and stand, my hand clutching the rail, looking out to the sea. It has to be Carl, everything fits, from his age, to his recent return from the UK, to a house in the hills.

I only realise now that I should be afraid of confronting him. But I don't think Paul would have let me come if he thought that Carl might harm me. And I've left a letter at the house in Reading in case I don't return from New Zealand, in case my body is found washed up on the shore, or not found at all. It's addressed to Anthony Barriston, and details everything, from the murders of Justine and Lina by Ned, to the suspected murder of Carolyn by Ned or a third person, and the murder of Hunter by Lukas, or by someone he knew. I've named Carl and Lukas as the men who kidnapped me, and detailed what they asked me to do in return for my life. And there's the rub: if I'd known that my life would be filled with guilt and uncertainty, maybe I wouldn't have valued it quite as much.

Glenda said that it was an hour's walk to where she thinks the house might be, so I grab a bottle of water from the fridge, stick it in my bag, squash a baseball cap on my head, check I've got my sunglasses and run downstairs.

'I got it wrong,' I say to Glenda, shrugging my shoulders. 'The name of my parents' friends was Humber, not Hunter. And they were older than my parents, so they'd be in their seventies.' I force a laugh. 'They might not even live here anymore.'

'You could ask at the post office,' Glenda says. 'They might be able to help.'

'Good idea, I'll do that. But not today. Today, I'm going for another walk along the beach at French Bay.'

'Have fun!'

Outside, I turn left, walk along a bit, and turn left again, checking the map on my phone. The road climbs gradually, then gets steeper. Fifteen minutes later, the road divides; I take the left-hand turn and follow the road up. Despite everything, despite what I'm here to do, I stop now and then to admire the vibrant bursts of colour from the indigenous trees and shrubs, and to take in the spectacular view of sea. There's a beautiful stillness in the air and I try to think of the last time I felt so relaxed. When I work out that it was in Las Vegas, the day Ned and I were married, the irony isn't lost on me.

There aren't many houses around and those I pass look as if they've been standing for years. I carry on climbing, looking for one under construction and just as I'm thinking of turning back, because the road has become a track, I catch a glimpse of something through the trees. I push on and see ahead of me, on a plot of land about the size of a football pitch, the walls of a house. There's no roof yet, and there's still scaffolding up, but the ground floor, complete with a wraparound veranda, seems to be finished. I stop. It's lonelier than I thought up here. If this is the place, Carl could be nearby.

I move into the trees, then creep around the edge of the plot and take another look from the safety of my cover. Because the house is in a slight dip, I'm able to look down on it. Apart from the building equipment that litters the plot, there's also a shed to the left of the house. There are no signs of life, but I wait for another twenty minutes or so, then leave. I hurry back along the track, hoping I won't come across Carl, because I don't feel ready to see him. If he's in a car, he would hopefully think I was just another tourist on their way back from a hike. But if he's on foot and we come face-to-face, he would recognise me.

I only relax when I'm back in the town. The thought of going back to such an isolated place makes me jittery. But it's what I came for.

22

I climb the hill to the house, hoping I've got it right this time. It's morning, and the air is much cooler as I walk.

Yesterday, like the previous day, I only made it up to the site in the afternoon, because I'd spent the morning swimming in the sea. Once again, the place had been empty. But the building equipment had been moved around and there were fresh car tracks, and I realised that whoever had been there had probably finished for the day. Which is why I'm going up early.

As I approach the house, I hear the sound of voices. My heart pounding, I duck into the trees, then creep nearer, pushing branches out of the way.

The first thing I notice is a large truck-like vehicle parked in front of the house. The second thing I notice is a woman leaning against the hood.

I don't know why I'm shocked that Carl might have a woman in his life, but I am. It shocks me profoundly that someone who has held people prisoner, mistreated and threatened them, can go back to an ordinary life.

The woman, dark-haired, is talking to someone; I can hear the rise and fall of her voice although I'm too far away to make out the words. Her head is turned towards the shed, the nearest building to me, and as I watch, a little black dog comes scooting out. I hear the woman's tinkling laugh as the dog runs towards her, then darts back into the shed. A man's voice rumbles, and I draw in my breath, every fibre of my body on alert. And then he's there, coming out of the shed, carrying the dog in his arms. A wave of disappointment hits; it's not Carl, this man is taller and has longish hair. But I know him, I'm sure of it. I hold my breath; is it Lukas?

He turns then, and I catch sight of his face. I stumble back and everything stops. It can't be – but it is.

Hunter.

23

I sink to my knees, my breath coming in ragged gasps, every fibre of my body in denial. *It can't be Hunter, Hunter is dead, I saw him being shot, I saw the blood seep out of him.*

The pain in my chest is overwhelming. I try to suck air into my lungs but I'm breathing too fast, I know where this is going and panic even more. I scrabble in my backpack for water, tug the top off the bottle, take a sip, but it almost chokes me. I cup my hands around my mouth instead, trying to regulate my breathing, stifle the noise that I'm making. Tears stream from my eyes and by the time I've managed to slow my breathing, my whole body is shaking.

I keel onto my side. How can Hunter be here when I saw him murdered, when I read about his body being found? How is it possible? It isn't – so it must be a dream, a dream or a nightmare. I'll wake in a moment, in the apartment in Akaroa, or in my house in Reading.

I don't know how long I lie in the bracken. It's only when I hear a car coming along the track that I slowly sit up. I listen to which way it's going; it's heading away from the house towards the road. Hunter and the woman have left.

I reach for my water, take a drink. All I want is to get back to the apartment. Nothing makes sense. I can't even begin to think of the reasons for Hunter faking his own murder. But whatever his reasons, I'll never forgive him.

Is this Hunter's house, then, or Carl's? I understood from Paul that it was Carl's, but maybe he directed me here because Hunter will be able to tell me where I can find Carl. I move from the woods, start walking down the track towards the house, hoping I'll find something to tell me who it belongs to. I'm so lost in thought that it takes me a moment to realise that the truck is still there.

I crouch down, my heart thumping. There must have been another car here, a car I couldn't see, parked on the other side of the truck. Does that mean that Hunter is still here? Or the woman? I creep back to the safety of the woods and watch the house from above. A few minutes later, Hunter comes out of the shed, walks to his truck, opens the door and takes something from the dashboard. A flash of sunlight on the screen tells me it's his phone. He stands a moment, looking at it. It's strange to see him wearing jeans and a denim shirt. He's thinner than when I last saw him, his hair longer. As I watch, he puts his phone back on the dashboard, stretches his arms above his head then stands a moment, contemplating his half-finished house with its spectacular views. And the thought that he has been here all this time, living a nice life in New Zealand while I grieved and suffered, makes me shake with anger.

He returns to the shed, leaving the car door open. I slide down the slope, run to the side of the shed, wanting to catch him before he leaves. From the sounds coming from inside, I know he's somewhere towards the back of it. I move slowly forward, quiet on my feet, wanting to see the shock on his face when he sees me standing in the doorway. But as I turn the corner, I see an open padlock hanging from the door. Without giving myself time to think, I move forward, slam the door and snap the padlock shut.

'Hey!' Hunter's voice comes from inside. 'Is that you, Mara? Did you forget something?' His footsteps approach the door. 'Very funny, now let me out.'

My heart is beating so fast I'm afraid it will burst from my chest. I back away, scared he'll somehow break through the door.

'Mara.' He rattles the door. 'All right, you've had your fun.'

I find my voice. 'Is that a dead man talking?'

In the silence that follows, it's as if the whole world is holding its breath.

'Amelie?' The sheer disbelief in his voice gives me strength. He wasn't expecting this. 'Is that you? My God, what are you doing here?'

'What are you doing here?' I shout, not bothering to hide my anger. 'Aren't you buried in some hole in the ground?'

'Look, I can explain.'

'Go on, then. I'm listening.'

'Not like this. If I slide the key to the padlock under the door, will you open it?'

'No. I'll open the door when you've told me why you faked your own murder, why you never helped me when you must have known who Ned was, what he did.' I slam the palm of my hand against the shed door. 'People died, Hunter. People I *loved*, people you knew. They've all gone, Carolyn, Justine, Lina.' I hear my voice break and kick the door hard with my foot. 'How could you?'

'Amelie,' he says. 'Please. Let me explain.'

'Go on, then.' I harden my voice. 'Explain to me why you let me believe you were dead.'

'All right. I'm going to sit down, here by the door. I suggest you do the same.' There's a pause. 'It's going to take a while.'

There's a thud against the door as he sits. I move closer, sit down, facing the door.

'I'm not sure where to start,' he says.

'At the beginning,' I say, my voice harsh. 'I want to know everything. You owe me that, at least.'

24

'Carl and I are brothers,' Hunter begins. 'Our father was a New Zealander, our mum is British. We were born in the UK, but our parents emigrated when we were children and New Zealand became our home. When I finished college here, I left. I felt that New Zealand was too remote and I wanted to explore the rest of the world. I travelled around Europe for a while, ended up in England. Eventually, I joined the police force and—'

'You were in the police?' I can't keep the surprise from my voice.

'Yes, in the crime squad. Our dad was in the police, so it probably runs in the blood. Carl went straight to work in security from college, but eventually, he followed me to London and set up his own security firm there. About a year ago, I left the police. My partner and I had recently split up and it seemed a good time to do what I'd been dreaming of doing, which was to come back here and build myself a house. Carl was happy in England. His business was doing well; over the years he'd managed to secure contracts with some high-profile names, including Ned Hawthorpe.' He pauses. 'He was also in a relationship with Lina Mielkutė.'

I'm so shocked I can hardly speak. 'Carl was in a relationship with Lina?'

'Yes. They first met over the phone when there was a problem with the payment for the contract renewal. They hit it off, and eventually met up. But they kept their relationship a secret, even from Justine. They didn't want it getting back to Ned; they didn't think he'd feel comfortable knowing that the head of his security firm and his accountant were seeing each other. They were so paranoid they didn't even use their real names when messaging each other.'

I remember Justine's teasing about Lina having a secret boyfriend, and I feel the threads of the story beginning to pull together.

'Just before I was due to leave England, Carl was contacted by someone highly influential connected to the Hawthorpe Foundation. This person was becoming increasingly concerned by Ned; there were rumours that he was a predator, sexually harassing the young women who worked for him. This person – let's call him Mr Smith – was worried about the negative effect any scandal involving Ned would have on the Hawthorpe Foundation. Not only was Mr Smith one of its most generous benefactors, he'd also been instrumental in getting other wealthy people to donate. The rumours made him jittery, so he asked Carl to find out what he could.

'Carl already knew that Lina was uncomfortable with a couple of payments she'd had to make, although she had never told him who they were to, or why she'd had to make them. When he'd pressed her for more information, she had clammed up, only saying they weren't ethical. Carl agreed to help Mr Smith. But he didn't want to use any of the security equipment his company had installed, to spy on Ned, as it would have been a breach of rules. He was looking for another way in when Ned contacted Carl's company asking them to provide a security guard. Carl realised it was the perfect solution and persuaded me to put off my return to New Zealand, and take the job.' He pauses. 'I knew of Ned from my years in the police. There were rumours of cover-ups, of his grandfather using his influence with those in command to get Ned out of trouble. There'd been a case where a young girl had died but nobody had been able to make anything stick. When Carl asked me to step in as Ned's live-in security guard, I thought it might be a way to nail him once and for all.'

'Did Lina know all this?' I ask.

'Not all of it, because Carl didn't want to put her in an awkward position. She knew that I was going to work for Ned, but Carl told her he was doing me a favour because I wanted a job for a few months before leaving for New Zealand.' I hear the scuff of him adjusting his position. 'One morning, Ned called me early and told me to have the car ready because he needed to go to Las Vegas urgently. He said that you were going with him, and I was to go and pick you up, then return to Wentworth for him. It was only a few days later, when Lina arrived back from seeing friends in Scotland, that she heard from your friend Carolyn about Ned sexually assaulting Justine. Lina told Carl, and Carl told me.' There's another pause. 'I was immediately worried for you, so I tried to find out which hotel you were staying in. But nobody seemed to know, and Ned wasn't answering his phone to anyone. The following day, Carl called me again. Lina was worried because neither she nor Carolyn had been able to get in touch with Justine. She also said that Carolyn hadn't been able to reach you either.'

'Ned took my phone. He made me think I'd left it on the plane. And my computer wouldn't work; I thought I'd broken it when I dropped my bag. But that was down to him too. He obviously wanted to make sure that I didn't hear about his assault on Justine. I only found out when Carolyn called me at the hotel, the morning we were leaving.'

'And by then you were married to him.'

'It wasn't what you think.'

'I know that now. But I didn't know it then.'

I trace a circle on the ground with my finger. 'How did you find out about our marriage?'

'Ned called me on Thursday evening. He told me the good news, then asked me to collect your belongings from your apartment. I asked him how I could do that without keys, and he told me to use my imagination, that it had to be done by the time I picked you up at the airport the following morning.'

'How did you get into my apartment?'

'I found the landlord, told him of your surprise wedding to Mr Hawthorpe and said that Mr Hawthorpe would appreciate it if he could let me into the apartment so that I could move your things into Mr Hawthorpe's house. Believe me, the Hawthorpe name mentioned three times in one sentence has an amazing effect on people.' His voice becomes serious again. 'But there was still no sign of Justine, and although Ned told everyone that she'd gone back to France, we were suspicious. Then Lina came to the house.'

A silence descends on us.

'Carl told me,' he says, his voice quiet. 'He told me that when he saw you at the memorial service, you said that you saw Ned kill Lina.'

My eyes blur. I want to say something but I'm afraid I might start crying.

'Amelie, if I pass you the key, will you open the door?' he asks, after a moment.

I swallow down my tears. 'No. Carry on.'

I hear him sigh. 'Lina's death changed everything. For Carl especially, but also for me.'

'How did you know that Lina and Justine were dead?' I ask. 'And that Ned had killed them?'

'We didn't, not really, not until their bodies were found. We suspected, but we couldn't prove anything. The day Lina came to Ned's house, I tried to persuade her to leave. I knew that she was going to accuse Ned of lying about Justine being in France and I didn't want Ned to know that anyone suspected him of actually murdering Justine, in case he decided to hide any traces he might have left behind. I wasn't particularly worried for Lina's safety. I never thought Ned would be capable of murdering someone in broad daylight, with people around. I phoned Carl to tell him Lina was at the house, and he asked me to let him know as soon as she'd left. But then Ned asked me to go to London to collect a file from the office, and on my way back – it must have been about two hours later, because the traffic was bad – Carl called to ask if Lina was still at the house, as they'd arranged to meet that evening and she hadn't turned up. He'd tried to call her, but he couldn't get hold of her.

'When I got back to the house with the file Ned had said he needed, I asked him if Lina had stayed long. He seemed surprised that I'd asked him, but told me she'd been upset because he had fired her and that she'd left, telling him that there was nothing left for her in England and that she was going to go back to Lithuania.' He gives a dry laugh. 'I can't tell you how loud those alarm bells started ringing. I phoned Carl, he went to the office and checked the security cameras.

He could see Lina arriving at the house, hurrying through the gates behind Ned's car, but no sign of her walking out through the gates. What he did see though, was a black van driving through them around half an hour after I'd left for London. Carl gave me the registration number. It wasn't hard to trace who it belonged to, despite him using an alias.'

'Amos Kerrigan,' I say quietly. 'I heard Ned on the phone to him.'

'I knew the name from my time in the police, and knew it meant that Lina was probably dead. Amos Kerrigan had a reputation as a hit-man, so I thought Ned had got him to kill her. Then Vicky received a message, supposedly from Lina, saying that she was back in Lithuania. Carl wanted to believe it so much, even if, in his heart, he knew that Lina would never have left without telling him. But we needed to check it out, in case it *was* genuine.'

'I can't imagine what it must have been like for Carl, having that tiny glimmer of hope,' I say.

'Incredibly hard. What helped was that he had a possible contact, someone who might be able to get to the truth. Friends of his had moved to Dubai and he was looking after their house in England for them, renting it out for short stays.'

'The house in Haven Cliffs,' I murmur.

'Yes. One of the regular renters was a Lithuanian named Lukas Andris. Carl had begun to get to know him; he knew that Lukas was a big shot back in his own country, so he asked him if he could find out if Lina had arrived in Lithuania. Lukas made some enquiries and discovered that Lina had passed through Immigration at Vilnius the day after she had gone to see Ned. Carl was elated, so it was hard telling him that Ned might have got someone who looked like Lina to travel on her passport, because I knew that kind of thing happened. I also reminded him that there'd been no sign of her leaving Ned's house that day and, coupled with Amos Kerrigan's presence at the house while I was in London – plus Lina's failure to contact him – well, everything pointed to her being dead.'

He falls silent, and I realise that he would have known Lina well, if she'd been in a relationship with his brother.

'When Carl realised the truth of it, he went crazy with grief,' Hunter says. 'And if Lina's disappearance confirmed one thing, it was that Ned was also responsible for Justine's disappearance. We couldn't have him arrested, because we had no actual proof. And it wasn't our call. The point of me being there, as Ned's security guard, was to report back to Carl, who then reported to Mr Smith. If Ned had been arrested for possible murder, that would have been the end of the Hawthorpe Foundation.

'By that time, I wanted out, so when Carl suggested taking my place as Ned's security guard, I didn't try too hard to dissuade him. All I wanted was to get on a plane and start my new life in New Zealand, and all Carl wanted was to get as close to Ned as he possibly could, so it was a win-win for both of us. Ned didn't know Carl, they'd only ever spoken on the phone, so Carl only had to adopt his Kiwi accent when he presented himself for the job. But I couldn't just leave Ned's employ from one day to the next. First, I had a month's notice to give and if I suddenly didn't turn up for work, Ned might have been suspicious, because I had questioned him about Lina. So Carl persuaded Lukas to contact Ned, posing as someone who could get him interviews with the rich and famous for his magazine, and invite him to lunch. And during that lunch, Ned would be set up to believe that Lukas knew

Lina well, and that Lukas knew that he – Ned – had had something to do with her disappearance. Then I would be "murdered" on the way back to Wentworth, putting the fear of God into Ned, and Carl would take my place as his security guard. What we didn't expect was that Ned would frame me for Lina's disappearance by insinuating that I was the last person to see her alive. But it worked in our favour. Before, my "murder" would have been a warning. Because of Ned pointing the finger at me, it became a retaliation.'

'And it didn't bother you that I'd really think you'd been murdered?' I say bitterly.

'You were only meant to think that for a minute. The plan was for Carl to get you out of the car and let Ned drive off, then we would have taken you somewhere safe. But Ned moved too quickly.'

'Carl was the gunman,' I say, realising.

'Yes.'

I frown, my mind stuck on something Hunter had said.

'So – Lukas only pretended to know Lina?'

'That's right.'

'But – if he didn't know Lina, why did he become involved in our kidnapping?'

'He didn't.'

'But he was there in the house with Carl; he was the other kidnapper.'

Through the door I feel this incredible tension emanating from him. It builds and builds, becomes this suffocating thing. At first, I don't understand. And then, with brutal and startling clarity, everything falls into place. And I wonder how I could have been so blind.

I give myself a minute. 'Can you pass me the key?' I ask.

'Of course.' His voice is low. 'Amelie, I—' He stops,

because he doesn't know how to go on, and because he's waiting for me to open the padlock with the key he's just pushed under the door.

I pick it up, get to my feet. And then I walk away.

25

I sit on the beach at French Bay, oblivious to the cold wind that whips in off the sea. How could I have been so blind, so unaware? But I'd thought he was dead.

I replay his murder in my mind, wondering if I'd missed something, something that would have told me it was only an act. But there's nothing; from the way he was pulled from the car to the sound of gunshots, to the blood pooling from him, everything had seemed genuine.

It's the humiliation that is the hardest, because he would have heard my anguish at the moment he was shot. My anger is deep, searing. If Hunter and Carl had thought about me at all, they might have guessed I'd assume that Lukas was involved both in Hunter's murder, and in the kidnapping. And then they might have guessed that I'd think Lukas was one of the men holding us. But they had never thought about me, about what I might presume, about what I might feel. If Hunter had felt any remorse about what he'd subjected me to in the woods, sometime during the two weeks I was held prisoner, he would have told me who he was. But he hadn't. And neither of them, once, had considered my pain at losing my friends.

I don't feel guilty for walking away from him, for leaving him locked in the shed. It wasn't about him experiencing something of what I went through, although I'm glad there are no windows, and that he won't be rescued until the woman with dark hair, who I presume is his partner, wonders why he hasn't turned up for dinner. What I can't bear is the thought of him hearing my distress when I believed him to be dead. He has seen too much of me.

I call the airline and arrange my return journey for Sunday, two days away. I'd like to leave tomorrow but I will have to see Hunter, because there are still things I need to know. But he can come to me. He'll guess that I'm staying in Akaroa, it won't take him long to find me. And he will come and find me, because we have unfinished business.

But he doesn't come, not that evening nor the next day. Early on Sunday morning – my flight is at eight in the evening, and I still need to pack – I march up the hill to the house, burning with resentment that I'm having to go to him. I'm hoping the woman will be there; I want her to know the truth, that she's living with a man who kidnaps young women.

The truck is there but there doesn't seem to be anyone around, so I sit down to wait. It's a while before it dawns on me that everything is exactly as it was when I left two days before. The truck is parked in exactly the same place, the door is still open and, when I take a closer look, Hunter's phone is there on the dashboard. I feel a flash of fear – is it possible that no one has come, that Hunter is still in the shed? What if the woman wasn't his partner but someone involved in the building project, or a friend, someone who wouldn't worry if they didn't see him for a few days? My fear spirals; it will have been stifling in the shed, what if he didn't have water?

I have the key to the padlock, I've had it with me since Hunter pushed it under the door.

I hurry to the shed, scared to go inside, scared of what I might find.

My fingers tremble as I insert the key into the padlock. I snap it open, push open the door, sending a shaft of light into its dark interior. At first, I can't see anything. But as my eyes begin to adjust to the gloom, I see him lying on the floor under a piece of tarpaulin.

'No,' I whisper. 'No.'

Shaking with dread, I force myself forward, crouch down, pull back the tarpaulin. A wave of relief washes over me. There's nothing there, it's just tarpaulin, it only looked as if there was a body underneath.

'A trick I learned from you.'

I spin around. Hunter is standing in the doorway.

'If I hadn't been able to knock out a panel, I'd be dead.'

'I thought—'

'That you'd leave me to die?'

As he starts to move towards me, I grab a plank of wood from the floor.

'Don't come any closer!'

He stops, raises his hands.

'Start talking,' I say. 'From where you left off. And if you so much as move, I swear I'll kill you.'

26

'When you came back from Las Vegas with Ned,' Hunter begins, 'I believed what everyone else believed, that you'd been in a secret relationship with him for months.'

'But you knew about his attack on Justine at that point; you knew what he was. Why didn't you say anything to me?'

'I thought you'd married Ned because you loved him. I thought you'd been playing with me, and I was annoyed.'

'But you must have seen the way Ned was with me during that press interview. You were standing behind us, you must have seen that I was trying to get away, go to Carolyn. If you had helped me, I might have been able to save Lina, save Carolyn.'

'Their deaths weren't down to you, Amelie. Lina would have gone to the house no matter what. And I'm sorry, but as far as I was concerned, you were Mrs Hawthorpe.'

'Never,' I say through gritted teeth. 'I was never Mrs Hawthorpe. I was going to kill Ned. The night we were kidnapped, I planned to go to his bedroom when he was asleep and use his phone to call the police. If he refused to give it to me, I was going to kill him. I couldn't think of any other way out; I was scared that if I didn't kill him, he would kill me.'

'Which is exactly what he planned to do.'

With the light coming through the open door behind him, it's hard to see his face. 'What? When?'

'That same night. But I need to rewind a bit.' He pauses. 'Wouldn't you rather do this outside, in the sun?'

'I'm fine where I am.'

'Okay. After Lina died, Carl found a file in her apartment with the names of five young women, all ex-employees of *Exclusives*, whom Ned had sexually assaulted, along with details of payments Ned had made to buy their silence. There was also a recording where four of the girls had detailed what had happened to them. Carl passed the file on to Mr Smith. Coupled with the disappearances of Justine and Lina, it was a step too far, and an order came for Ned to be handed over before he could do any more damage to the foundation. Carl knew it meant Ned would be killed, but he didn't care; on the contrary, he thought Ned was getting off lightly. He wanted to make Ned suffer for Lina's murder physically, mentally, and emotionally and told Mr Smith that he wanted to keep Ned for a while before handing him over. Mr Smith agreed. But there was a flaw; if Ned suddenly disappeared, the police would look for him, and if he was eventually found murdered, the police would dig to find out why he'd been murdered, and the foundation would be damaged anyway. Mr Smith asked Carl to find a solution.'

He shifts his weight from one foot to the other. 'The night of my fake murder, I was booked on a flight to New Zealand. All I wanted was to get on that plane and leave everything behind. But when our plan to rescue you failed, everything changed. I couldn't leave until I knew you were safe. I wanted to go and get you that same night, but Carl was worried about me blowing my cover, and possibly his, and asked me to wait a couple more days while he thought of a way to get you out. He said you were safe, keeping to your room, out of Ned's way—'

'Only because Ned had locked me in,' I interrupt. 'And that was after he almost killed me,' I add, not caring about the shock on his face.

'What do you mean?'

'He suffocated me like he suffocated Lina. Except he didn't go all the way to the end, because he still needed me.'

He rubs his hand over his chin. 'Christ, Amelie, I had no idea—'

'Carry on,' I interrupt, my voice hard.

He nods. 'By then, Carl didn't care about spying on Ned. That night, the night we kidnapped you, he had listened in to a call Ned made to Amos Kerrigan. Jethro Hawthorpe had been at the house and Ned was angry; he said you'd made him look a fool and that he wanted to get rid of you. He told Amos to go to the house and kill you, and make it look like a burglary gone wrong. Before I could panic, Carl said that he had a plan. He was going to kidnap Ned, and take you as well, because you were the perfect solution to the problem of how to make Ned's disappearance pass unnoticed. I asked what he meant, and he said that if he kidnapped the two of you, he could make it look as if you and Ned had gone on holiday together and that way, nobody would know that Ned had been kidnapped. He could also make it look as if the reason Ned had gone away was because he was being hounded by the press over the sexual assault allegations, which in turn would lead to him supposedly taking his own life. And rather than tarnish the foundation, his death would be met with sympathy.'

It takes a moment for it to sink in.

'So, if I hadn't been kidnapped along with Ned, if I'd been left behind, I would have been killed by Amos Kerrigan?'

'Yes. Carl said that he would keep you and Ned for two weeks and that when they were up, he would need you to tie up all the ends. After that, you'd be free. He told me to book my flight, saying that he had it all in hand, that there was no reason for me to stay. But I couldn't leave you with Carl. Lina had been the love of his life, they were planning to marry, have children, and her death had affected him to the point where I barely knew him. He was so full of anger, and I was worried that he'd treat you the same as Ned. So, I told him I'd help with the kidnapping, and stay around to see it through. I don't expect you to understand, or forgive what we did—'

'Don't worry, I won't,' I say, cutting him off. 'How do you think I feel, knowing that I was kidnapped so that Mr Smith, whoever he is, could get away with murder?' Once again, I can't keep the bitterness from my voice. 'Was it worth it, everything that was done to protect the foundation?'

'Not from where I'm standing, no.'

'Was it you who delivered Ned to Mr Smith?'

'No, it was Carl. He took Ned to the clifftop and told him that someone would come and collect him.'

'Your murder was in the newspaper. Was that down to Mr Smith too?'

'Yes. We needed to make it seem real, in case anyone checked.'

'You could have told me,' I say. 'Once we were at the house in Haven Cliffs, you could have told me the truth. If you had explained what Carl was doing, let me in on it, I could still have backed up the story about Ned and me going away for a break, and I could have spent those two weeks in one of the bedrooms upstairs instead of in a pitch-black room on a mattress, thinking I might die at any moment.'

'I know, and I'm sorry, sorrier than you can believe.' He tries to walk towards me but I hold the plank of wood up higher and he steps back again. 'But Carl didn't trust you. He said that if you saw our faces, you might go to the police once you were released.'

'But *you* could have trusted me.'

'I was supposed to be dead. And I didn't know how you would feel about what we were doing.'

'You knew I hated Ned.'

'Most people who hate someone don't want them dead. Morally, I think you would have struggled, knowing what was going to happen to him.'

'I saw him kill Lina, that was enough to remove any moral obligation I might have felt.'

'If I'd known that you'd witnessed her murder, I would never have put you through something so brutal,' he says quietly.

'She threatened to expose Ned, she told him she had recordings of the women he'd abused.' I pause. 'Where is Carl? Shouldn't he be here, trying to excuse his behaviour, like you?'

'I'm not trying to excuse my behaviour.' There's an edge to his voice. 'I had a choice, go or stay. I stayed and now I have to live with the consequences of that choice.'

Heat rises to my cheeks. He had stayed because he didn't want to leave me with Carl.

'I don't see Carl,' he goes on. 'I haven't seen him since he came back from the memorial service. Finding out how Lina had died – it was hard for him. He went to stay with our mum for a bit but then he took himself off. I don't know if, or when, I'll see him again. For the moment, I need the distance.' He nods at the piece of wood I'm still holding. 'I don't suppose you'd like to put that down?'

I don't want to give him anything, but I let the piece of wood fall to the floor.

'Is it okay if I sit?'

'Yes – but stay where you are.'

He sits down in the doorway, draws his legs up, rests his elbows on his knees.

'Can I ask you something?' he says.

'Go on.'

'Why did you marry Ned?'

I can't lie, it would make me as bad as him. 'For money. I married him for one hundred thousand pounds.'

'Wow,' he says softly. 'You sold yourself for a hundred thousand.'

The judgment stings. 'Don't you dare,' I retaliate. 'You've done far worse things. What happened to the journalist?'

'What journalist?'

'The one Ned asked you to find out about – you know, the woman who dared ask about the sexual assault charge during the press interview? Sally something? Is she dead?'

'No, why would she be?'

'Do you know that for sure?'

'No, but—'

'Did you do as Ned asked, did you find out who she was, did you give him her name?'

'Yes.'

'Carolyn was killed in a hit-and-run three days after the press interview, three days after she called out to Ned, asking where Justine was.'

'Christ.' He rubs his chin, runs his hand through his hair. I see the doubt in his eyes, the questions he's asking himself.

He gets to his feet and walks out of the shed. I don't know where he's gone, or why he's gone, I don't know if I should go after him. But before I can do anything, he comes back with his phone and stands in the doorway, looking down at the screen, searching for something.

'Thank God.' He closes his eyes, pinches the bridge of his nose with his thumb and forefinger. 'She's okay, she's fine. I found her Instagram, she posted yesterday.'

I hear the shake in his voice and I'm ashamed of what I did. But it's too late to take it back.

'I'm so sorry about Carolyn,' he says quietly. 'I could do with some water – would you like some?'

'Yes, please.'

'Do you want to come into the house? I have a fully functioning kitchen.'

'No, I'll stay here, thanks.'

'Okay.'

He leaves, and I wipe sweaty palms on my jeans. It's getting hotter in the shed but I don't want to leave the semi-darkness. I don't want him to be able to see my face in case he sees how hard it is for me to be near him.

27

He comes back with two bottles of water and throws one to me from the doorway.

'Thanks.' I unscrew the top, take a drink.

I wait for him to sit down but he stays standing.

'I still have questions,' I say.

He nods. 'Go on.'

'After I escaped from the room, why were you so mean? I get it, I'd tried to escape. But not bringing me food, then leaving it just inside the door instead of coming all the way in, what was all that about?'

'It wasn't me,' he says. 'I wasn't there. I had to go away for a couple of days, sort something out, and I was already late because of you locking me in the room. I left as soon as Carl let me out.'

'What was it you had to sort out?'

'Amos Kerrigan.'

'What did you do?'

'I spoke with a couple of ex-colleagues, who spoke to one of their informers about the need for him to disappear.'

It takes a moment for it to sink in that he was at the origin of a man's death. I push it from my mind; I can't think about it now.

'I keep going back to the kidnapping,' I say. 'I know you had to make it believable, but why make us think we were being kept longer than we actually were?'

'As I said, Carl wanted to make Ned suffer for killing Lina. He wanted Ned to believe that his father didn't care that he'd been kidnapped, that he was happy to let weeks pass before paying the supposed ransom. But he only had that two-week window when Ned was supposed to have taken you away for a break, so he decided to make it seem as if you'd been kept for longer than you actually were. It's disorienting, being kept in the dark, time loses all meaning.' He stops, realising maybe that he's telling me something I already know. 'I agreed, because I thought that for you mentally, if the days seemed to be going by quite fast, it wouldn't be such an ordeal. When we looked at dates, we realised that if we brought everything to a close on the thirty-first of August, it would tie in perfectly with the postnup you'd signed. It wouldn't have mattered if it hadn't, essentially it wouldn't have mattered if you'd been married to Ned for forty days, or two months. But the thirty-first of August seemed a good time to stop.'

'How did you know the terms of the postnup? From Paul Carr?'

'Yes. Paul thought it was pure genius and mentioned it to Carl, and Carl thought it would be great to use it on Ned, make him think we knew more about him than he thought.'

'How much does Paul know?'

'Enough. He was also working for Mr Smith, keeping an eye on what Ned was up to.'

'Is Mr Smith an alias for Steve Algerson, by any chance?'

'No comment. Where did it come from, the doubling thing?'

'My dad. When I was young, he asked me if I'd rather have a million pounds immediately or a pound doubled every day for a month. I chose the doubling thing without ever working it out. I regret that now; I regret that I didn't work it out and tell him the exact answer.'

'You worked it out on the back of the bathroom door.'

'Yes. I felt I owed it to my dad to do it.'

'I didn't know that you'd lost your parents until Paul told me. It must have been hard. He said that you ran away to London.'

'I was lucky, I met Carolyn. It could have turned out very differently, though.' I take a breath. 'I need to ask you something. The shooting thing. It was horrible. Why did Carl do it? Did you know he was going to pretend to shoot me?'

'No, not to the point where he would fire the gun. He wanted to frighten Ned, show him that he was prepared to kill one of you if he had to. We never expected Ned to actively encourage Carl to kill you; we thought at any moment he would tell Carl to stop, especially once Carl had cocked the trigger. But he didn't, so Carl fired it into Ned's mattress.' He pauses. 'I couldn't believe he'd actually fired it, I put my hand over your mouth to – I don't know – let you know you were still alive, that you hadn't really been shot, that I was there. It all happened so fast.' Another pause. 'We had an argument about it afterwards, me and Carl. I'd had enough, I hated what we were doing. It haunts me, what we did, not to Ned, but to you.'

'I survived.'

'You were extraordinary. I expected you to be terrified, but you weren't.'

'I was, but I was never afraid of you. And I felt safer in that room than I'd ever felt with Ned.'

'I should have done more, I wanted to but—'

He stops, the guilt visible on his face.

'There's something else that's been puzzling me. The photo of me on Ned's Instagram – it was taken at the house in Haven Cliffs, the day we went for lunch with Lukas. I thought Lukas had taken it. But he hadn't?'

He looks down at the ground. 'No, I did. Carl asked me to. His plan, once he had taken Ned – before he decided to take you as well – had always been to make Ned believe nobody was particularly bothered about him being kidnapped, not his parents, nor his wife. He already had a photo of Mrs Hawthorpe playing tennis, and he wanted to have a photo of you. He was going to taunt Ned with the photo, make out that you were so unconcerned about him that you had accepted an invitation from Lukas to go back to the house in Haven Cliffs. After, when our plans changed and we took you too, that photo came in more useful than we'd imagined, as it gave credence to the story that you and Ned had gone away on a two-week break. All we had to do was upload it to his phone.'

'Does your girlfriend know what you did?'

'I don't have a girlfriend.'

'There was a woman here the other day. When I locked you in, I thought she'd come and let you out when you didn't turn up for dinner.'

He smiles. 'It's good to know that you didn't intend to kill me. That was Mara, our sister. She lives in Dunedin, I live here.' There's a pause. 'I did stay on, you know. In England. I didn't come running back here as soon as it was over. I even went to Reading, hung around for a few days.'

I stare at him. 'You came to Reading?'

'Yes.'

'But – why didn't you—'

'Come and see you? How could I, when you thought I was dead? How could I, after what we did?'

'Then why come?'

354

'Because I wanted to make sure you were all right. And I did want to tell you I was still alive. Paul knew that and he said I should write to you. But you seemed okay. I watched you shopping, and you seemed okay.'

I remember the times I had sensed him close, and my throat burns with unshed tears.

'I was never okay.'

'What you said to Carl, at the memorial service for Lina and Justine, the message you gave him, about sleeping on a mattress in a room with a boarded-up window. Was that true?'

It's too much. Tears begin to leak from my eyes. I wipe them away with my fingers but they keep on coming.

I see him kick the door shut, blocking out the light. And suddenly, I'm back in the house in Haven Cliffs, in the room with the boarded-up window, and my captor is walking towards me in the darkness. I close my eyes, wait to feel his hands on my shoulders – but instead, his arms come around me. And in that moment, a huge weight lifts from my shoulders.

I don't know how long I stand wrapped in his arms, thinking about him coming to Reading, wondering what might have been if he had had the courage to tell me he was alive.

'I'm sorry,' he says softly, after an eternity. 'For everything.'

I breathe in the scent of him. He smells of sun and sea.

'You don't smell the same,' I say.

'What do you mean?'

'You smelled like Lukas. When you were near me, I recognised the same smell that I had smelled on him, like freshly mown grass. It's one of the reasons I thought you were Lukas.'

He gives a low laugh. 'That'll have been the shower gel. Lukas left a whole bottle of it, unopened. He brings his products over from Lithuania and doesn't bother to take them back with him.'

Lukas's shower gel. He had been using Lukas's shower gel.

I step back and his arms fall from around me.

'I need to go. I'm leaving tonight.'

'Won't you stay?'

'I can't.'

He follows me to the door.

'Will I see you again?'

'No.'

I walk into the sunlight, up the slope to the track. When I get to the top, I turn around. He's standing in the doorway, watching me, and I feel this terrible tug inside me. I've lost everyone and despite everything, I don't want to lose him too. He's all I have left, and there's so much about him that I don't know. I don't even know his first name, I realise.

I raise a hand, shading my eyes from the sun. 'Maybe,' I say.

ACKNOWLEDGMENTS

My heartfelt thanks to: (this time, to ring the changes, in alphabetical order)

My fellow **authors**, for their invaluable friendship and support, and for taking the time to read my book when their TBR piles are already stacked high.

The amazing **bloggers,** for giving their time to read and review. My wonderful agent, **Camilla Bolton,** for her advice and enthusiasm, and for always being there for me, and the rest of the team at Darley Anderson, with special thanks to Mary Darby, Kristina Egan, Georgia Fuller, and Rosanna Bellingham, Sheila David and Jade Kavanagh.

My amazing UK editor, **Jo Dickinson,** and the wonderful team at Hodder, with special thanks to Alice Morley and Steven Cooper.

My **editors** overseas, for their continued faith in me.

My **family,** which became one person larger this year, with the arrival of beautiful Nina.

My **friends,** both in France and the UK, with a special shout-out to the LF crowd. Thank you for welcoming me into your community. **Readers** everywhere, for reading and reviewing, and for their lovely comments, which lift me up and give me the motivation to write another.

My amazing US editor, **Catherine Richards,** and the wonderful team at St. Martin's Press, with special thanks to

Jen Enderlin, Lisa Senz, Nettie Finn, Marissa Sangiacomo, Brant Janeway, Katie Bassel, Kiffin Steurer, Jeremy Haiting, and Lizz Blaise, also to copy editor NaNa Stoelzle, and to proofreaders/cold readers Steve Hicks, Susan McGrath, Lani Meyer, and Stephanie Umeda.

To **technology,** in particular Google Earth and Google Maps. In 2020, I planned to go to New Zealand and spend some time in Akaroa, where I wanted to set part of this book. Circumstances meant that I couldn't, so I had to rely on my ability to map-read correctly. Needless to say, any errors with regard to Akaroa, and to New Zealand in general, are entirely my own.

My brilliant **translators,** for bringing *The Prisoner* to life for readers abroad.

I would also like to give special thanks to *Paul Carr*, who made a very generous donation to the Books for Vaccines auction for the right to appear as a character of my choosing in **The Prisoner**. Thank you for bidding, Paul!